THE FAIRY TALE MURDERS

The race is on to stop a twisted killer

IAIN HENN

Published by The Book Folks

London, 2025

ISBN 978-1-80462-333-6

www.thebookfolks.com

*"At his best, man is the noblest of all animals;
separated from law and justice, he is the worst."*

Aristotle

Prologue

Nowhere

She woke to find herself in total darkness. She held her hand up in front of her face but she could not see it. There wasn't even the slightest sliver of light. Fear enveloped her, and her heartbeat hammered in her ears. She had no idea where she was or even how she had got here.

She strained to remember the last thing she'd been aware of, but the memory wouldn't form, her mind was hazy, her thoughts like wisps of smoke that dissipated as soon as she tried to focus on them.

She rose to her feet and listened for a sound, any sound, that might give a clue as to where she was. Nothing. Not even a breath of wind or the creak of a floorboard. That was when she realized that what lay beneath her bare feet was hard and ice-cold.

In darkness, even total darkness, the eyes adjust and it should be possible to make out very close objects, but that wasn't happening.

Am I blind?

She wanted to scream but fear froze her voice and instead, she swallowed hard, her throat heavy, her breathing labored.

She reached out, feeling nothing but empty air, and she eased herself forward, sweeping her arms around. Nothing.

Panic stilled her again, but this time she managed to call out although her voice was weak, not like her voice at all.

"Hello? Is someone there?"

Her tired limbs were like weights, dragging her down, and she knelt first and then lay down again, sleep overcoming her. As she drifted off, a memory came, snatches of the words that were the last thing she remembered from before: "Turn back, turn back…"

Turn back from where?

The next time she woke, her mouth was even drier than the first time, her head still heavy, her mind a jumble of thoughts just out of reach.

Once again, she pushed herself to her feet and reached out as she stepped slowly forward. "Hello?" she called out. "Is anyone there? Where am I?" She thought she heard a sound. Very soft. She couldn't discern what it was; she couldn't even be certain she hadn't imagined it.

The hairs on the nape of her neck stood out in abject terror. "Hello?"

And then, as much as her croaking voice would allow, she cried out for help, a thin sound that didn't even carry an echo in this vast silence.

She groped forward once more, casting an even wider circle, but as before, there was only dark space. She felt as though she no longer existed, as though she was nowhere, at no time, and then she thought she heard a breath, close by. She stood still, listening, and she was certain she heard breathing, coming from what seemed like every direction. Was it real? In the void that surrounded her, it was impossible to know anything for sure.

She focused on the sound and the breaths seemed louder and more frequent. Every nerve end tensed. She was ready to lash out at whatever came near. She held her breath and then – nothing.

"Who are you?"

Dead silence.

Had it been the sound of her own labored, panicked breathing that she'd heard? She was so consumed by fear and helplessness that she was no longer sure.

And then she heard it again. The whisper of a breath. Not hers.

Her heart raced and she imagined something in the dark, reaching for her out of the nothingness, and she recoiled in horror, her scream deafening inside her head, but no more than a whimper on the outside.

PART ONE

Chapter One

The rain had stopped, leaving shimmers of reflected moonlight in tiny pools across the darkened parking lot. The ground here had been uneven for as long as Bec Rowan could remember. She pulled into the lot, cursing herself yet again for having left her phone in her dance studio earlier in the evening. She'd been at home for a few hours before she realized what she'd done and she needed it for the morning. She had some important early calls to make from her home. It was nearing midnight and she didn't like being out late on her own, but it was only a twenty-minute drive. She'd be in and out of the studio in mere minutes, she told herself. No big deal, but now she felt a sense of unease as she switched off the ignition and sat in the darkness, looking through the gap between the buildings to the main thoroughfare.

There was just one overhead light in the lot and it was faulty, its dim light flickering as though it was taking its final breaths. Rowan had never been in the parking lot this late and hadn't counted on just how eerie the silence would be.

She opened the car door and stepped out. As she did, she was overcome by a peculiar sense of dread. A rush of cold air stung her face and she felt as though the darkness was closing in around her.

She pulled her coat tighter against the night air and walked briskly through the gap and onto the main street, the hairs on the back of her neck standing up. Get a grip, Bec, she told herself. Just go in, get the phone, and leave. Easy peasy.

The moment she rounded the corner, Rowan saw the body. A young woman, her limbs splayed at unnatural angles, lying on the sidewalk directly outside the studio door. Rowan ran to her, but as she knelt before the woman, she saw the vacant eyes and the lifeless expression frozen on the woman's face.

Bile rose in Rowan's throat and she turned her head, suppressing the urge to vomit.

She pushed herself to her feet but even as she did, she couldn't stop her eyes from glancing again at the frozen features of that face and there was an unexpected jolt of recognition.

I know that face.

Rowan's blood felt like ice flowing in her veins as she stared at the woman. It was a face she knew, a face she would never forget.

How is this possible?

And then her eyes were drawn to the body's shoeless feet, and with a gasp of horror, she realized that both feet had been mutilated. It was as though someone had sawed part of them off. This time Rowan couldn't help herself from lurching to the side and being sick.

She knew she had to pull herself together and act. She glanced about, seeing no one, but she didn't feel safe. She snapped herself out of her stupor and, hands shaking, she fumbled for her keys and opened the studio door. She dashed in, locking the door behind her, her footsteps echoing across the empty wooden floor as she ran to her office. She grabbed her phone off her desk and dialed 911.

The operator's voice was like a beacon of calm. "911, what's your emergency?"

Rowan's voice wavered as she hurriedly told the operator what she'd found.

"Stay on the line, ma'am," the operator said. "Keep your studio door locked and wait for the officers to arrive."

Rowan did as she was told. Unable to shake the sense of dread, she stood by the window, looking out on the street, her glance drawn now and then to the body, to the remains of those misshapen feet. The rain began again, just a drizzle this time, peppering the windowpane.

She peered further along the street and caught a glint of moonlight on a vehicle parked by the side of the road, on the next block. It was parked away from the streetlights so she could only really see its shape. The car's lights came on and she saw it was an SUV. It pulled out from the curb and drove away.

A floorboard creaked behind her and Rowan whirled around in sheer panic.

There was no one there. It was just the groan of the old building, amplified in the quiet hours.

And then she heard the wail of the police sirens in the distance. As she listened to the sirens drawing closer, she had the strange sense that she'd never be able to stop seeing that body and that she'd never feel quite the same, here in her dance studio, ever again.

Chapter Two

Day One

The voice was Greek-accented and female. Calm and natural sounding, with just the right note of authority in its tone. But it wasn't human. Themis was the predictive AI program around which the FBI's Unsolvable Crimes Unit had been formed, and it had identified the murder of a young woman as one of the cases our team should consider taking on.

"Themis, can you fill us in on the details of the murder?" The question came from Zoe Marshall, the tech guru turned special agent who created the AI program, which she'd named after the Greek Goddess of Justice. I'd been working with Zoe for many months now, across several cases, but the sometimes mischievous, dark-skinned, brown-eyed imp of a girl was still very much an enigma.

"Of course, Zoe," said Themis. "The body found outside a dance studio two nights ago was identified as Emily Yarros, a former student of the studio. She had been reported missing four years earlier. The cause of death was a single gunshot to the head and the police report states that the body was shoeless and that a part of both feet had been hacked off postmortem. The medical examiner established from the position of livor mortis in the body that it was likely that she had been shot at another location and dumped outside the studio. What was particularly unusual were the items found clasped in each of the victim's hands. One hand contained a page torn from a book with the printed text in German and the other hand held a silver button."

I wasn't sure I'd ever get used to the natural human-sounding cadence of the machine's voice. "And why does this murder have a high probability of remaining unsolved?" I asked.

Zoe had programmed Themis to recognize our voices, along with the curious habit of sometimes acknowledging us when it first replied.

"Hello, Ilona Farris," it said. "Aspects of the crime scene can be linked with other murders. Firstly, that of Jack Corris, found outside a bakery six nights ago. Corris was an employee of the bakery. He had been reported missing five years earlier. The cause of death was also a single gunshot to the head and similar items were in his hands. The main difference was that his feet had not been mutilated, however, both hands were severely burned, once again postmortem. Some of those details also match three other bodies found eighteen months earlier, in Tacoma. Rayna Jackson, Mark Foreman, and Wanda Smythe. The first of those, Jackson, had been missing eight years; Foreman for seven years and Smythe for six and a half. All of those cases remain unsolved, with no leads, and these two most recent Seattle murders are now definitive of there being a serial killer at large. There are more than sixty unsolved serial murder cases in the United States, committed since the mid-twentieth century. For example, the Zodiac Killer in the 1960s, the Alphabet murders from the early 1970s, the Edgecombe County murders between–"

"Thank you, Themis," Zoe said, and the AI, just like a human, took the hint that nothing further was required.

Zoe swiveled her chair away from the horseshoe-shaped console, casting her glance over me and the team's supervisory special agent in charge, Will McCord, and our operations coordinator, Marcia Kendall.

"These two recent Seattle murders will have gone on the radar of the Behavioral Analysis Unit," Zoe said, "but unsolved serial killer cases also fits *our* remit."

The FBI had jurisdiction to take on certain serial murder cases and Zoe was right, these new murders, in short succession, would attract the BAU's attention. Zoe was nothing if not ambitious about proving the worth of her AI creation, and this was a case likely to become as high profile as a case could be, so I could understand her wanting the UCU to take it on. It would be as big a challenge as anything we'd faced because apart from solving a case that Themis deemed likely unsolvable, it would also need to be solved quickly before it escalated.

"I'm going to register our intent to investigate, drawing on support from the BAU's profiling," Will said. He shot me a glance. "You agree, Ilona?"

I nodded.

"Was it the same text on each of the pages found on the victims?" Marcia asked. She shifted the spectacles on the bridge of her nose, a common trait, and I briefly wondered if she'd ever considered contact lenses.

Zoe tapped her keyboard and copies of the police reports, with Themis's commentary overlaid and highlighted, graced her PC screen. "A different text in each case. Translators were brought in on the earlier cases, and it seems the text passages were parts of a story, or perhaps from various stories."

"I'd like to translate these two recent pages myself, and take a look at the earlier ones," Marcia said.

Marcia was also an analyst, as well as one of the Bureau's translators. Will and I had met her when we needed a German translator on the UCU's first case and she'd stayed with us part-time, alternating with the Languages division.

"I'll arrange that," said Will.

"Themis, who is the investigator of the Seattle murders?" I asked.

"The investigating officer is Detective Paul Radner of the Seattle Police Department," came the response.

I turned to Will. "Let's go have a chat with our old friend Radner, and with the medical examiner."

Chapter Three

Dr. Marla Liu's hands were soft and warm, her handshake firm. She was new to the Seattle coroner's office, and after being introduced to Will and me by Detective Radner, she donned latex gloves as she led us to the morgue table. She was petite, with slicked-back dark hair and eyes, her dark-blue blouse a stark contrast where it was visible beneath her open, white lab coat.

The room was expansive, and the steel of the table had a harsh gleam under the strong lighting.

"No signs of a struggle premortem," she said, her voice crisp and businesslike. "The headshot was clean, entering the occipital lobe from behind and death was likely instantaneous. A PBI – penetrating brain injury – is one of the most lethal of all firearm injuries, with an eighty percent plus death rate."

I stared at the pale, naked body of Emily Yarros, laid out on the table, as Dr. Liu indicated the neat, round bullet hole. "Minimal damage to the skull at the entry wound but, as expected, a much larger exit hole, indicative of a military-grade sniper rifle fired from a great distance. I expect that the head was the intended target, as it's the body part that a bullet is most likely to exit, in this case leaving no bullet for ballistics."

I exchanged glances with Will and Radner. "A very skilled marksman," I said, my mind conjuring a faceless shooter, sighting Yarros through a high-powered scope.

Dr. Liu moved along the side of the table, stopping and indicating Yarros's feet. "Both feet have suffered part amputation postmortem."

I forced myself to look at the ragged stumps but only for a moment.

Her face impassive, Dr. Liu continued, "The cutting is precise but with ragged ends and shredding, compatible with a manual saw."

I sucked in a deep breath and let it out slowly.

"Is there any significance to the sections removed?" Will asked.

"The sides of the foot and part of the toes. Can't speak to the significance, but it's the same area and amount on each foot, as though they're meant to match, or to fit something."

"Like a trophy cabinet," Radner suggested. He shrugged. "But the previous murders didn't have body parts removed."

Dr. Liu's expression conveyed her understanding. "I saw in your report that certain details about this body, and that of Jack Corris a few days ago, match previous murders, quite some time ago, in Tacoma."

Radner nodded but remained silent, his brow furrowed in deep thought.

"Each of those victims," Dr. Liu continued, "was also found in the same outfits they were wearing when they disappeared. All had been shot in the back of the head while running away and were killed somewhere other than where they were found."

"Correct," said Radner, "which explains why no bullets were ever found. And in each case, the bodies showed no signs of where the killings had taken place."

"Toxicology?" Will asked.

"No alcohol or drugs in her system," the doctor said.

"Also a match with the previous victims," Radner added.

"What about the items that were found in her hands?" I asked Dr. Liu.

She raised her eyebrows. "A page torn from a book, in one hand, and a silver button in the other. These items had to have been placed in the woman's hands, and her fists closed around them, soon after her death, before rigor mortis set in." Her gaze settled on me. "Which is the same situation as with Jack Corris. I take it from the FBI's involvement that this is now a serial killer investigation."

"There isn't any doubt about that," I said. "I take it you also conducted the autopsy on Jack Corris's body?"

"Yes."

"The report stated that the body's hands were burnt."

"Severe burn marks. Once again, an injury delivered postmortem, and obviously before the items were placed in the hands."

"Were you able to determine how the hands were burned?" I asked.

"The signs are consistent with the hands having been placed in an open fire, or perhaps in the flames of a gas oven or a stovetop."

Radner had been standing back, having already observed Yarros's corpse before Will and I arrived. "As we know, she is believed to have been wearing the same dress as when she disappeared. Any observations about the clothing, Marla?"

"We examined her clothing for blood spatter, fluids, damage, dirt, grass, anything that helps shed further light on the death. Once again, as with Corris, there was nothing. Their clothes had been newly washed, either immediately before the death occurred, or, if after, the body was undressed, the clothing freshly cleaned, and then the body redressed. Either way, highly unusual. As for the gunshot, the same as with Yarros, a single shot to the back of the head, with a bullet powerful enough and fast enough to pass rapidly through the target without lodging in it. Hitting the same, vulnerable spot each time requires expert knowledge and precision. Every step of the way, a meticulous mind has been behind this."

A chill touched my spine. Meticulous, very evil, and it seemed, emerging from the dark after a strange and lengthy absence.

Chapter Four

Radner, Will, and I went to Radner's office and I stared at the crime scene photos spread across his desk. Emily Yarros, her blonde hair falling across her forehead, covering the bullet hole in her forehead, marring what would have otherwise been, in life, an attractive face. Alongside Yarros's photos were those of Jack Corris, slumped against a dumpster in a lane alongside the bakery, his baker's attire still as crisp as it would have been in the pre-light early morning when he'd vanished on his way to work. Two murders, four days apart. No obvious connection between the victims except their violent ends and the bizarre fact that both had been reported missing, in Corris's case, five years before, and in Yarros's case, just over four years.

Radner's voice broke through my thoughts. "Yarros was a supermarket worker and she disappeared on her way home from the dance studio, where she took evening classes twice a week. Jack Corris was a baker, married with a young kid. No known association between them." His tone betrayed a sudden weariness and I met his eyes, recognizing the haunted expression I'd seen there on other occasions.

I wondered if every time Radner was confronted with a corpse, it always instantly reminded him of his personal loss. "No leads on Emily Yaros's murder?"

He shook his head. "I've spoken with Missing Persons, but the detective, Caulfield, confirmed he'd never dug up anything remotely useful on either Yarros's or Corris's cases. No activity on their bank accounts or phones and no reported sightings of either of them. Not a thing. I've also been speaking with Detective Pulman in Tacoma about the three similar murders eighteen months back. Same MO – bullet to the head. Bodies posed with silver buttons and torn pages."

"Where was he with his investigation?"

"Pullman did pick up, from the translations he ordered, that the pages contained passages from fairy tales. But with no further murders, no connection between the victims, and no leads from his interviews with family and friends, the trail had gone cold."

My pulse quickened. Pieces of a puzzle were emerging but at this point, there were just as many holes as there were pieces.

Beside me, Will folded his arms. "I'd like to speak further with Caulfield about the missing persons reports. And the dance studio owner – Rowan, was it? She discovered Yarros's body."

Will's pragmatic nature always had him looking a step ahead, with a razor-sharp focus on procedure. One of the many traits we shared, though he was far more practiced at holding his emotions in check than I was ever likely to be.

My eyes caught on the framed photo of Radner's daughter with her smooth hair draped over her shoulders. It sat on the shelf behind his desk, standing out among the journals, magazines, and police report folders. So young when she fell from that rooftop, chasing thrills with a reckless group of urban climbers. I hadn't realized when I'd been in here before how much that photo instilled Sarah's presence and warmth into this office.

With effort, I returned my focus to the case. Three victims in Tacoma, now two here. The torn pages and the postmortem body injuries were significant, but so too, I thought, was the eighteen-month lapse between killings. This was an MO that was escalating and evolving. I couldn't shake the powerful sense that a third murder in Seattle was looming, I could feel it in my bones. If that proved to be the case, then it meant that this shooter was already planning their next strike and we needed to move fast.

"The torn pages... perhaps a calling card of sorts." I was thinking out loud. "But why the eighteen-month gap between the third and fourth killings?"

Radner rubbed his temples and then scratched at his gray-flecked, short-cropped hair. "You'll have seen in my crime scene report that the text on the torn page was in German. From the translation, it seems to be from some old fairy tale. And while media interest petered out after there were no further murders in Tacoma, I expect that's about to change."

"We can safely bet on that," I said.

"Marcia Kendall's organized for your lab to send her photos of the pages," Will said, "so we'll take care of looking further into the story content. And she's obtaining the Tacoma pages as well, for comparison." He began pacing, something which was practically Will's signature move when he was doing a deep mental dive into the details of a case. "The Tacoma killer used the same kill method for three victims but very specifically differed with each of them in the interference with the bodies. The killer takes a break for a year and a half, then resumes in Seattle with the same core MO."

Radner's eyes narrowed. "You think the passages on the pages are sending some kind of message?"

"Either that," Will said, "or it holds some special relevance to the killer."

Radner cleared his throat. "There's one other thing. Added to my initial report after I interviewed Bec Rowan. She saw a dark-colored SUV further along the street, which drove off shortly after she'd phoned 911. She now wonders if the body had been dumped from that vehicle."

My chest tightened. "Could she give much of a description?"

He shook his head grimly. "No, just that it was an SUV and a dark color. And there are thousands of them on the roads."

"CCTV?" Will said.

"None in that street. It's a quiet spot."

Will had stopped pacing and he glanced at me. "So we need to speak with Caulfield, Pulman, and Rowan, for starters. And see what Marcia makes of the translation of these latest pages."

"I gather your unit will be taking these cases on, which is a big help, given the caseload we've got here at the moment," Radner admitted, "but keep me updated. And you know you can call on me and my team for backup." He flashed me a grin. "Anytime."

Will nodded and I gave a tip of my head in Radner's direction. I'd had a good working rapport with the detective, ever since I'd assisted him in his crackdown on urban climbers in the Seattle region. Recently, the UCU had played a part in apprehending the reckless young climbers who'd been responsible for encouraging Radner's daughter to climb with them.

I glanced back at the photo on Radner's desk as we headed for the door. His daughter Sarah smiled back at me, frozen in happier times. I could empathize with the grief I knew must always sit on Radner's shoulder, and I compared it with the long, lonely months of grief I'd suffered after the death of my father, a former assistant director at the FBI, who in his final years had been retired and estranged from the Bureau that he loved so much.

* * *

Will and I were out on the street, headed for his car, when I said, "The killer's MO. I think it's two-pronged. The buttons and the pages mean something personal to the killer, but they're *also* sending a message."

I didn't state it out loud, but I was thinking back on Themis's reference to the Zodiac Killer, and the Alphabet Murders. Just two examples of a killer announcing themselves to investigators, and leaving clues sprinkled like breadcrumbs at the crime scenes.

The gap between the murders nagged at me. Why continue the ritual now? What changed?

"I agree," Will said. "The killer's communicating with us."

My eyes locked on his. I didn't need to state the obvious, that we needed to decode what these messages meant.

Chapter Five

Will and I arrived back at the UCU to find that Marcia and Zoe were a step ahead of us when it came to decoding the killer's messages. Entering our main ops room, I saw we had a familiar visitor. The lanky, wiry-haired Professor Zach Silverstein in his regular attire of turtleneck and long coat, was seated at the console alongside Marcia and Zoe. A university lecturer across the diverse subjects of criminology, science, and history, the professor didn't do anything by halves and had an encyclopedic knowledge of myths and legends from all over the world. He had consulted with us on several cases.

Shifting the spectacles on her face, Marcia shot us a glance. "I gathered from my translation of these latest victims' pages, that like the others, they seemed to be from folk-type stories, so I got in touch with Zach."

"All of the pages have narratives from the Brothers Grimm folktales," Zach said, "although you wouldn't necessarily pick up on that from some of the passages, as they're from tales that aren't generally well known." He spread his hands and I couldn't suppress my smile; there was a certain charm to Zach's overly zealous manner when it came to his passions. "After all, there are over two hundred tales that were collected and published throughout the nineteenth century, across several editions, by the Grimms. And there are some in which the details differ from the most famous versions."

Will pulled up a seat but rather than sit, he took hold of its backrest and leaned against it. "And why is that?"

"The stories in the original early nineteenth-century German editions of the Brothers Grimm collection, are very different from the later, sanitized versions that modern readers are familiar with," Zach said.

"In what way?" I asked.

"They're much darker. Gruesome, not at all what a modern-day parent wants their children exposed to."

"The modern versions are pretty grisly," Marcia remarked.

"And those are the watered-down interpretations. What is not generally known is that Jacob and Wilhelm Grimm didn't originally publish the stories as fairy tales for children. It was an academic exercise by two scholars, done to record and preserve legends and folktales from a wide variety of sources – many of them from the oral tradition, told from one generation to the next. But from the commentary of their peers in the academic world and the interest of the wider public, the brothers were persuaded to produce a vastly changed, shorter, more family-friendly edition, and with each successive edition, the popularity of the tales became more widespread. These were the versions translated into English and dozens more languages."

"But the passages on these torn pages are from the earlier, German-language editions," Will said.

"German, yes, but not necessarily the original versions. What the passages have in common is that they're drawn from the most bloodthirsty parts of the stories, in some cases that's the earlier versions, but not always. The most macabre bits weren't always edited out of some of the later editions."

"But this killer knew which editions to use for the darkest versions."

"Yes, and it was only in recent times that an English translation of the original texts was even published." Zach had the habit of speaking faster as he became more embroiled in a subject dear to his heart. "To give you some examples, one of the original tales, *How Some Children Played at Slaughtering*, is so horrific it was cut from most of the later editions. A boy cuts his brother's throat as part of a game in which the two of them are playing at being a butcher and a pig. Consumed by grief and rage, the boy's mother stabs the boy in the heart, leaving her remaining child in a bath where the child drowns. Realizing what she has done, the woman hangs herself."

"That was a so-called Brothers Grimm folktale?" Marcia said in horror.

Zach nodded. "*Was*, yes. And in their original telling of *Cinderella*, the evil stepsisters hacked off part of their feet so they'd be able to fit into the golden slipper and marry the prince. In the end, the sisters are set upon by pigeons that peck out their eyes. Neither of those incidents are in the later, child-friendly versions."

This gave me a jolt. "They hacked off part of their feet? That mirrors the condition of Emily Yarros's body."

"The page found on the previous victim, Jack Corris, contains that very passage from the original Cinderella story," Zach said. "I've taken a look back through the pages found on all of the previous victims. Wanda Smythe's body, even though it was found eighteen months before Corris's, has a narrative from *Hansel and Gretel*, in which Gretel pushes an old witch into an oven. The witch had intended to cook Hansel in the oven but became the victim of her own evil intentions. The passage could be referring to the burns on Jack Corris's hands and, of course, he was found outside the bakery where he once worked. And what does the work in a bakery revolve around? Ovens."

Will's jaw jutted out as it usually did when he was leaning heavily, mind and body, into a vital piece of information. "And the others?" he prodded.

"The page in the first Tacoma victim, Rayna Jackson's hand contained a passage from *King Thrushbeard*, another Grimm tale. In that story, a king secretly smashes the pots belonging to a woman, as a punishment for the woman having ridiculed him. The next victim of a bullet to the head, Mark Foreman, was found three days later in Tacoma outside a garden and earthenware market, and the corpse had broken porcelain fragments from pots sprinkled all over it. The words on the page in this second body's hand were taken from *Saint Joseph in the Forest*, in which disobedient children, walking through the forest, are killed by stings and bites from snakes and lizards. The body of the third and final Tacoma victim, Wanda Smythe, was found with snake bites on her arms, outside a reptile sanctuary."

"And that was the victim that had the page from *Hansel and Gretel*," I noted. "So, it appears that the narratives found on each victim are a clue to where the *next* body will be found and how it is presented or mutilated."

"Yes," said Zach. "What's more, in each case the fairy tale also has a tie-in to where each of these victims either worked or lived."

I mulled this over for a moment. "Rayna Jackson's body wasn't mutilated or presented with any theatrics."

"Probably because she was the first," Zach said. "There's no preceding victim's body to carry clues."

On her screen, Zoe was scanning the police reports for each of the cases and she clarified Zach's point. "Mark Foreman worked at that earthenware market and Wanda Smythe was an attendant at the reptile sanctuary."

"With those Tacoma victims," Zach said, "the stories those passages are from aren't very well known so the connection to the Brothers Grimm wasn't made. Only that they were what seemed to be fairy tales."

"And what was the passage found on Emily Yarros's body?" I asked Zach.

"This one's clearly from *Snow White*. In the version most of us know, the queen orders the huntsman to take Snow White into the woods, kill her, and bring the queen the heart of the young girl. Still bloodthirsty, but in this gory original, the queen orders the huntsman to bring back the heart, lungs, and liver of Snow White."

Marcia shook her head. "I don't like the sound of that. At. All."

Will cast his gaze over all of us. "Okay, so I think we can ascertain that the heart, lungs, and liver are the clues to where another body will turn up." His brow knitted. "So, we're talking about a killer with a fascination for the fairy tales of the Brothers Grimm. It seems strange, then, that the method employed for the murders is a sniper's bullet. No connection to the tales."

"Actually, there is," Zach said. "In *The Two Brothers*, a king is turned to stone by an old witch. The brother of the king fires a gun that fails to kill or wound the witch. But when the brother fires silver buttons instead of lead bullets, this weakens the witch, who is then forced to restore the king to life."

As Zach retold the story, Zoe brought up the Yarros crime scene photo and enlarged the section showing the button clenched in the dead woman's hand. "Which is reflected by the silver button found on each victim," she said.

I could hardly believe what I was seeing and hearing, and by the looks on the faces of the others, neither could they.

"Heart, lungs, and liver seem to indicate something medical," I suggested.

"Maybe a transplant unit," said Marcia.

"Zoe, let's get Themis to run a search of all people on the missing persons list, for anyone with a connection – work-related or otherwise – to medical establishments," I said.

Once prompted, Themis's search facility could access law enforcement and government-held data and zero in on specifics, often within minutes, and it was no longer than that when Themis's voice sounded over the speakers. "Ryan Moreton, a registered male nurse at the Specialist Transplant Center in Seattle. He was reported missing after leaving work late one evening, four years ago."

"The messages are cryptic but decipherable," Zach said. "I'd say this killer *wants* them to be decoded. It's like a game is being played."

Will grimaced. "I'll organize for special cams to be set up outside the center and its surrounds. But unfortunately, we haven't the resources to get it staked out 24/7, and we don't know when a body might appear there, whether it's days, weeks, or even another eighteen months."

I moved closer to Zoe's desktop screen, my eyes roaming over the reports. "Another point of similarity, Will, is that the bodies were all discovered in the early morning. It seems they were dumped at the various locations sometime during the night." I turned to him. "We could call in some backup to do surveillance from late night through to dawn, for at least the next seven days. No guarantee, but the three Tacoma victims were killed and dumped over eight days. Maybe the same frequency is in play here, and we're already four days into it."

"Worth a try," Will said. He turned to Zoe. "Let's compile a list of any people or groups that have an association with anything Brothers Grimm-related. Maybe an appreciation society, a readers' club, something along those lines." He glanced at me and Marcia. "Between the friends and families of those bodies that have turned up and the investigators on those cases, we've got some ground to cover." Returning his attention to Zoe, he said, "The precise long-range nature of the shots indicates we're looking for a skilled sniper. Let's look at the possibility of anyone with military or law enforcement experience who has a record or a background that might fit the profile."

"Themis can fast-track that for us with ex-military, but current armed forces personnel will be trickier," Zoe replied.

"Marcia, can you start talking with the friends and families of the victims," I said. "See if there's anyone they know who fits those descriptions. And follow up with forensics. They're working to determine the age of those buttons and torn pages. See if you can track down where those items are from."

Marcia nodded, her fingers already flying over her keyboard. "On it," she said, her voice quieter than usual but as determined as always.

Chapter Six

Speaking with Bec Rowan on the phone, I learned that through her association with local educators, she visited schools in the area, in the mornings, to give dance lessons to children. In the late afternoon and early evening, she gave after-work lessons to adult students at her studio.

Rowan had a brief window of time in which she could see us, before prepping for her afternoon classes.

On the drive over to her studio on the city's outer rim, Will was – as he had been for over a month now – overly quiet. His face was stern, eyes on the road, not even speculating on aspects of the case as he normally would. Toward the end of our personal relationship, over two years earlier, Will had accused me of rarely opening up, of being mentally closed-in, deeply focused on my caseload, and afterward, reluctantly, I had to conclude that he'd been right. I'd needed to loosen up. But during these past weeks Will had himself turned 'not opening up' into something of an art form. He'd kept, not just me, but the whole team at arm's length, bottling up the grief I knew he was suffering after the death of a close friend.

This past week I'd wanted to gently lead him into a conversation, about how he was feeling, what he was thinking, just to get him to release some of that pent-up emotion. He needed to do that. I'd almost prompted such a conversation a couple of times, the words on the tip of my tongue, but on those occasions, I'd hesitated. Held back; thinking, give it a few more days.

Maybe this brief drive was just the moment to touch on how he'd been coping. "You're quiet, even for you," I said.

"I've got a lot on my mind. You know that."

I tried to keep the tone light. "You know what the counselors say, it's good to open up and share how you're feeling."

"We've arrived," he said, pulling the car into the parking lot behind the studio.

Not an answer, I thought, but I said nothing. Another time.

Bec Rowan greeted us warmly and led us across the spacious hall to a side annex that functioned as a small office. The walls of the dance hall were adorned with a series of photographs of dance recitals. I noticed there was a simple artistry to the photos that captured the emotion in the performances and I asked who had taken them.

"I'm the guilty party," she said with a laugh. "Some were taken of recitals at the studio here, and quite a few are from school performances or other studios. I've found they serve as inspiration for the students."

She had a desk against the wall in the annex and she sat, turning her chair around to face us. "You want to know about Emily Yarros?"

Will and I pulled up visitor chairs. "Anything you remember about her could prove useful," Will said.

"She hadn't been here very long," Rowan said. "About a month, if I recall. Didn't say much but she did let on to me that she hadn't danced for a while. She was rusty but wanted to get back into it, dancing was like a tonic to her. I got the impression she seemed troubled and when I asked her if everything was okay, she said she'd been through some trauma and that she was getting her life back on track."

"She didn't elaborate any further on that?" I asked.

Rowan shook her head. "No. The only other thing that comes to mind is that she commented on one of my photos, a shot that I'd taken at a studio recital in Olympia.

She said it reminded her of her early dancing days. I asked if she was from Olympia but she didn't answer. But I got the impression she was."

"When you heard she'd gone missing, did you think it might have anything to do with the trauma she said she'd been through?"

"It was in the back of my mind." Rowan shifted uncomfortably in her chair as though unsettled by her memories of the young woman. "I did phone the Missing Persons people at one stage, introduced myself, and asked to speak with the detective handling her case. I was told he would be in touch and would drop by to see me but I never heard from him and, well, I suppose I let it go. Now, after seeing her body like that, I can't shake the feeling… If I'd pestered the police…"

"You did what you could," I assured her.

"Were any of the other students here at the time, friendly with Emily?" Will asked.

"Not that I was aware of. But it was four years ago…"

"Of course," Will said. "It's been a long time."

I handed her my card. "If there's anything else you remember about Emily, anything at all, you can reach me on this number."

She stared at the card for a moment, her eyes tearing up. "That poor young woman…"

Outside, I said to Will, "It seems unusual that the Missing Persons detective didn't want to interview Emily Yarros's dance instructor."

"Senior Detective Rob Caufield," Will said. "I phoned him earlier before we left. He'll be in his office all afternoon, and he's next on our call list. Let's see what he can tell us, not just about Emily, but about all of these missing people whose bodies have turned up."

Chapter Seven

It was just over an hour's drive along the I-5 S to Olympia, where the Washington State Patrol was headquartered. It was in a modern, five-story, 225,000-square-foot building, with an atrium that delivered shafts of natural daylight to every level. Not that there was much of that today, with the cloud cover and rain that had blown in during our drive. As Will and I entered the foyer, it took a moment for my eyes to adjust to the interior lights that seemed harsh against the gloom outside.

Rob Caulfield was one of the senior detectives with the WSP's Missing and Unidentified Persons Unit, or MUPU. A cadet led Will and me through an open-plan office space, busy with conversations, phone calls, and the low hum of dozens of desktop PCs. A steady patter of rain beat against the long windows that ran along the exterior wall. We reached one of several glass-walled offices at the far end and from behind his desk, Caulfield looked up, his eyes heavy with circles that seemed darker than I'd expect of someone who otherwise appeared to be a mid to late thirtysomething. The cadet left us and Caulfield stood.

"So, what is it that we can do for the Feds today?" he said in a lazy drawl that had an air of sarcasm about it.

Will and I pulled up chairs and introduced ourselves while Caulfield glanced at his wristwatch.

"As I mentioned on the phone," Will said, "we're looking into a series of murders in which each of the victims has previously been listed as missing."

Caulfield's expression was bland. "That so?"

"Five murder victims," Will said. "All reported as missing to MUPU. I sent over the details."

"Haven't had a chance to take a look." Caulfield shifted his attention to his computer screen and reached for the mouse. We waited while he took a cursory glance at the information. "You think there's a killer out there targeting missing people?"

"That, or the killer had a hand in their disappearances."

Caulfield leaned back in his chair. "Our unit here, with all our resources, couldn't trace these people and there were no signs pointing to kidnap." He scratched the back of his head. "Doesn't make a whole heap of sense."

"No, it doesn't," Will agreed, "which is why anything and everything we can learn about those victims will be crucial to the investigation."

Caulfield crossed his arms over his broad chest. "Everything you need to know is in the MUPU reports." His tone was oddly dismissive and I was beginning to wonder what this guy's deal was. "I see that the first of the five murder victims had been reported missing eight years ago. Putting it in perspective, Agent McCord, we have over six hundred people reported missing every year in this state. That's around 4,800 over those eight years. Five of those people being murdered, you'd have to agree, is an infinitesimal percentage of that, not necessarily indicative of a serial killer. Keep in mind, that while some of those who vanish have been abducted or murdered, there's a reasonable percentage who don't want to be found. They've simply walked away, for whatever reason, from everyone and everything they've known, and started afresh, under an assumed name. There's no crime in not wanting to be found."

The muscles in my jaw tensed as I watched Will's reaction to Caulfield's indifference.

"You're not suggesting it's mere coincidence that these five missing people all turned up dead with their bodies exhibiting the same signature details?" he said.

"I'm not suggesting anything. Just taking the statistics into account."

Will's eyes flashed but he kept his voice even. "There is likely some link between these people, some detail, however small, that takes on new meaning in light of these murders."

"We're not here to step on any toes," I said, keeping my voice soft enough to be non-combative without losing authority. "But as the lead investigator on those cases, you're best placed to cast your mind back to the interviews you conducted with families, friends, and colleagues of those five, and maybe there's something that comes to mind, something you'd regard differently given these new developments."

It was rare but I'd come across unhelpful officers like Caulfield before. They had a chip on their shoulder when it came to any interaction with federal authorities. Playing to their ego didn't always work but I hoped, on this occasion, it would get this man onside.

After a tense beat, Caulfield shrugged and his eyes turned again to his computer. "Let me take a look through my old reports and think back on them, keeping in mind that in all of these cases, it's been at least several years."

"Thank you, Detective," I said, offering a small smile that I didn't feel inside. If there's one thing that could raise my hackles, it was uncooperative law enforcement officials. We were all on the same side. As we waited, I glanced at Will, his impatience evident in the rigid set of his shoulders.

Looking at Caulfield again, I noticed a shift in his eyes as he was reading. "The first person on your list," he said presently, "Rayna Jackson. I recall a close friend of hers saying that Jackson wasn't happy in her marriage and that her husband could be abusive. We found no evidence to support that. Jackson's neighbors had never heard any arguments. Her husband said there were no problems in their relationship. But as I said, some people simply decide to disappear and to make certain they aren't located. Quite possibly, Jackson was one of those. Maybe she came into contact with the killer later."

This seemed more like Caulfield giving credence to his own theories. "People separate all the time," I commented, "they don't normally feel it's necessary to cut ties completely with their former life."

"Rayna was a single child, her parents had died, so who knows?" He squinted at the reports on his screen. "Another one of the victims. Mark Foreman. He worked at an earthenware market at the time of his disappearance, but it was the latest in a string of jobs. This guy was known to the local cops as a small-time drug dealer and user though they'd not had enough evidence to make a charge stick. He was getting his supplies from some pretty dodgy characters. At the time, I figured it quite possible there'd been a drug deal gone bad, Foreman got popped, and his killer got rid of the remains. But maybe what happened is Foreman took off to get away from those dudes." He turned to face us. "You said these people died from a bullet to the head. Close range?"

"Fired from a distance," I said.

"Like a sniper's bullet?" His eyes narrowed in confusion. "That seems to indicate someone was watching them, maybe stalking them."

"We haven't ruled that out," Will said.

I leaned forward. "Was there anything in your investigations into those people, that related to shooters, such as military personnel, or fairy tales? Specifically, Brothers Grimm fairy tales?"

"Shooters? No. As for Fairy tales" – he shifted in his chair – "no. Why...?"

"It ties in with the killer's MO," I said. "We've spoken with Emily Yarros's dance instructor, Bec Rowan, and she told us she tried to pass on some thoughts about Yarros being troubled but none of the detectives here got back to her. Do you know why that would be?"

"We have limited resources and, as I've pointed out, a massive caseload, but any information passed on will have been taken into account. We have to prioritize, and I'm guessing that setting up a meeting with Ms. Rowan wasn't deemed essential to progressing the investigation."

I had the sense there was nothing more to be gained, at the moment, from this man. Will clearly felt the same and he rose from his chair.

"Thank you for your time, Detective," Will said but he offered no tight-lipped smile, no handshake.

"I know the FBI takes on some serial killer cases," Caulfield said, "but this one doesn't cross state lines, so I'm wondering why you wouldn't think the WSP and SPD's criminal investigation branches wouldn't be able to handle it?"

"Agent Farris and I are part of a new unit, tasked with taking on specially selected cases," Will said.

"Special cases," the detective repeated with a casual air. "Sounds like another layer of bureaucracy, if you ask me."

Will's jaw flexed but he remained silent.

I took one of my cards from my pocket and, reaching across, pressed it into Caulfield's fleshy palm. "If you remember anything from your investigations that now strikes you as a little unusual, no matter how small a detail you might think it is, you can reach me on this number. Anytime."

Caulfield nodded. "Of course."

* * *

"That felt like a waste of time," Will muttered as we stepped out of the building into the damp Olympia air.

I took a deep breath. The fresh rain-scented breeze felt like a tonic after the stifling atmosphere in Caulfield's office.

"Not necessarily. We've got Caulfield thinking about those cases. Hopefully, he'll recall something that seemed insignificant at the time."

"You'd think from that guy's manner that we were trying to discredit or take over his precious missing persons unit."

"Last thing we'd want."

"Last thing anyone would want. Anyway, you handled him well."

I punched Will playfully in the chest. "Good cop, bad cop."

For just a moment, I thought maybe he was letting himself relax a little, and our old camaraderie was kicking into place. But just as quickly, Will's attention had wandered, his jaw set in a firm line again. He strode forward to where he'd parked the car.

Chapter Eight

Marcia motioned to Will and me as we arrived back at the UCU. "Zoe has Themis compiling a background on the five victims," she said. "A more comprehensive check now that they are murder victims and not missing persons. We hit a bit of a wall where Emily Yarros was concerned. She'd taken up a rental in Seattle just two months before she vanished. But before that, nothing. No trail leading back to where she lived previously, where she worked, or where she went to school. And, we've now uncovered, there's good reason for that." She turned to Zoe.

"She'd legally changed her name," Zoe said. "Her birth name is Emily Warner and I can confirm she was from Olympia."

"The Missing Persons reports didn't pick up on that?" I asked.

"As you know," Zoe said, "the Missing Persons investigators prioritize missing children, and adults believed to be in immediate personal danger, whether from potential accidents, being lost, or criminal threat. None of which was the case with Emily, so the report focused on the usual: who last saw Emily, where she was in the time leading up to her disappearance, what she was wearing."

"Does she have family who knew she'd changed her name?"

"No," Marcia said. "Emily Warner was raised by her aunt. I've just phoned and spoken with her and she told me she and her niece hadn't been in regular contact; there was something of a rift. She said Emily was a troubled young woman and she thought her niece had simply taken off for a while without telling anyone. She said Emily could be inconsiderate like that. I didn't press her any further over the phone, I'd just had to break the news to her that Emily had died, and she was understandably in a state of shock."

Troubled? The same comment had come from Bec Rowan.

"We'll need to speak with the aunt," Will said to me. He turned to Marcia and Zoe. "And in the meantime, we'll need to find out everything we can about Emily Yarros when she was Emily Warner."

The UCU's landline phone rang and Marcia reached across to the main console and answered it. "It's the front desk, for you," she said, handing me the phone.

I raised the phone to my ear. "Ilona Farris."

"Agent Farris, I have a Ms. Jill Reiberger on the line for you," the receptionist said.

I felt a jolt. Jill Reiberger? There was a name I hadn't expected to ever hear again. A real blast from the past. "Put her through to the landline in my office," I said.

I excused myself and strode along the connecting corridor to my office. Jill and I had been friends in college, back in DC. Friends, that is, until my boyfriend at the time dumped me to take up with Jill, and the chasm that opened up between us couldn't have been deeper or wider. Despite that, several months later, Jill and I were at the same college party. When I left the party, I was unaware that Jill had left just before me, and by chance, on the quiet, leafy street that ran alongside part of the campus, I saw Jill, ahead of me, grabbed and dragged into the brush of the adjoining reserve. I'd been learning self-defense skills and I leaped forward, following them into the reserve. I grabbed her attacker by the shoulders, pried him away from her, and then felled him with a series of kicks to the lower torso and groin. I'd then phoned 911 and the attacker, one of the male students at the college, was arrested.

Jill and I had been on better terms after that, never friends as such, never close, but there was a mutual regard for one another. It was many years since I'd seen or heard of her although I knew she'd gone into law after university and she'd long since split up with that loser boyfriend. In hindsight, she'd probably done my younger self a favor.

"Jill, this is a surprise."

"I can imagine. Thanks for taking my call." This didn't sound like a social call. Her voice was tense.

"Is everything okay, Jill?"

"I'm in Seattle and I'm calling because of my younger sister, Sam. I know I don't have any right to call you up out of the blue and ask for anything, but… it's just…"

"Jill?"

She sounded on the verge of tears, her voice a croak. "I could really use your help, Ilona."

* * *

The dampness of the air seeped into my bones as I approached the waterfront café where I'd arranged to meet Jill. The café had a nautical design, its exterior ringed by old-style lanterns that glowed like the lights of a ship in the darkening twilight. The rain had stopped and out on Puget Sound, harbor lights cut through the mist that had settled over the water.

The familiar aroma of dark roast coffee enveloped me as I stepped into the warmth of the bustling café. The deep naval blue of the walls was offset by the sharp white of the chairs and tables, and the wooden, deck-like flooring completed the seafaring theme. I spotted Jill sitting at a window table, nursing a latte, her posture rigid, and her face drawn tight in worry. It must have been seven or eight years since I'd last seen her, and although her face was now that of a professional and serious woman, she was still recognizable as the once carefree student I'd been friends with. When she saw me, a look both of recognition and relief crossed her features, and she motioned me to join her.

I slipped into the chair across from her.

"Thanks for coming, Ilona." Her voice wavered. "I feel like I've hit a wall. So frustrated. I knew you were in Seattle, and you've had such an incredibly successful career with the Bureau, which I knew you would. I didn't know who else to turn to."

"That's okay," I replied. A waitress ambled by and I ordered a cappuccino. "You said you were calling about Sam?" I'd only met her once but I remembered Jill's charismatic younger sister who always seemed to attract trouble.

"She went missing six months ago," Jill whispered, her voice stronger now, the determination I recalled she'd always had creeping back into her eyes. "She'd been living here in Seattle, trying to get her life back together, and then... just gone."

"Trying to get her life back together from what?"

"I don't know if you remember, but back in DC, she used to hang with a bad crowd. She got into drugs and was involved in a store robbery." She took a breath, running her hand through her willowy mane of blonde hair. "She was arrested and charged but got off on a year's probation. But she was still hanging with that mob for a few years, and she had a reputation with the cops."

"And you were in law school," I observed.

"I'd graduated by then and was working with public defense. Anyway, Sam finally decided to break ties with those guys, she didn't want to face prison, and she decided to head here to Seattle for a fresh start."

"Why Seattle?"

"A guy, although I gather he's no longer in the picture. She got a job but then, well, I don't know if it's because trouble is my sister's middle name, but she started hanging out in a local bar that attracted the wrong types, got involved in drugs again, and struck up a friendship with a guy who was a druggie. He died and Sam was arrested on suspicion of murder for supplying him with the drug that killed him."

Jill's revelation sent a shiver down my spine. "Murder? They thought it was deliberate?"

Jill clenched her fist, a mix of anger and grief on her face. "Yes. It was dismissed due to lack of evidence. But I know Sam is innocent of anything like that, Ilona. She's made mistakes, but she isn't a killer, she doesn't have a violent side like that, never had. Even with that damn stupid robbery years ago, she was the lookout person and the driver. She told me she'd never given that friend any drugs and I believe her."

The thought of Sam Reiberger as a murderer didn't sit right with me either but then I hadn't really known her and I knew better than to underestimate anyone's capacity for violence.

"When was this?" I asked.

"A year ago. I spoke to her on the phone several times and she sounded upbeat, had a new job, and was kicking herself for ever getting involved with the drug scene again. She sounded like a different person and was determined to stay on the straight and narrow."

"And then she disappeared?"

"Six months ago. I had a phone call from her employer, I was the family contact she'd given them. They told me she hadn't been into work for two days running and hadn't responded to phone calls, and did I know where she was. I tried calling and emailing her, and then I flew here and went to the apartment she was renting. It was locked up, and none of her neighbors had seen her."

The waitress delivered my coffee and I took a sip, savoring the taste. I felt my energy level rise as though I'd been given a shot of adrenaline, and then I refocused on Jill. "Were there any signs of a break-in, or a struggle?"

"No. Nothing. So, I reported Sam missing, and then I had to head back to DC, I was due at a trial."

"What's happened since then?"

Jill vented her frustration. She told me how the Missing Persons Unit at the WSP had done little, in her view, to locate Sam. They hadn't even interviewed any of her work colleagues or friends. Three months had passed with no leads and Jill had made another trip to Seattle to meet with the detectives. Now three more months were gone and she'd returned, increasingly frantic, desperate to find out what had happened to her sister.

"I never thought MUPU was taking Sam's case seriously enough."

"Because of her background?"

"Precisely because of her background."

"Who is the detective responsible for the case?" Even before Jill answered me, I knew what she was going to say.

"Detective Rob Caulfield."

Jill must have seen the note of recognition on my face. "Do you know him?"

"I met with him earlier today over a case I'm working on."

"So, you could have some influence with him about Sam's case?"

I reached across the table and placed my hand over hers. The gesture seemed to bring some calm to her. "I'll touch base with Caulfield, and I'll look into the details of your sister's case myself."

Relief surged in her green eyes. "How can I thank you?"

"I'm just repaying the favor."

"What favor?"

"Taking that loser boyfriend off me all those years ago. I've never looked back since."

Jill relaxed a little more and allowed herself a soft smile. "Well, it shows. You look good and that chestnut shade of hair of yours is to die for." She made a face, correcting herself, her mood lightening a little for the first time. "Oh, given you're in law enforcement, maybe not to *die* for."

I smiled in return. "Maybe not."

Walking back to my car, I glanced up at the city nightscape. The clouds had thinned and shafts of moonlight mingled with the lights of the buildings. I felt the irresistible urge to indulge in the one passion that gave me a soaring sense of exhilaration, always eased my tensions, and sharpened my mental focus. But it was too wet from the earlier rain, making it too dangerous, so I would have to resist it tonight. What's more, I needed to be able to react quickly if we heard from the midnight-to-dawn surveillance team we'd put in place in the alley beside the medical transplant unit.

* * *

Back in my apartment, I opened up my laptop and navigated to the WSP website and the photos listed there under the Missing Persons section. I found the photo of Sam Reiberger. The likeness to Jill was evident, although Sam had darker hair and was fuller in the face. I wouldn't have recognized the face, it had been years since I'd seen her, but I did recognize the cheeky glint in the eye.

I felt compelled to help Jill but at the same time, I also knew I had to restrict the time I spent on it. I couldn't let it interfere with the murder investigation that Will and I had agreed to have the UCU take on.

What I did need to find out more about was what Sam Reiberger had been involved in before her disappearance. I could see that Jill loved and cared about her sister, she was a fiercely loyal person in that respect, but that also meant she wasn't necessarily objective when it came to considering all the angles. If Sam had walked away of her own volition, then what was she walking away from? And if she hadn't, then her connection to criminal elements might very well be the key. What worried me the most was the possibility that Sam was dead and the shattering effect that would have on her sister.

Chapter Nine

Jill's motel room was neat, tidy, and functional. That was the best rap she could give it, but it didn't concern her, she wasn't in Seattle for a vacation.

She and Ilona had ordered a light meal before they left the café so she wasn't hungry. But she was restless. She went out onto the tiny balcony, if you could call it that – it was more like a boil on the side of a building that was crying out for some renovation. She stared down the street and her curiosity was piqued by the sight of a white hatchback, parked further along the quiet, suburban street. It looked identical to a hatchback she'd seen on the street when she'd been walking back to her rental car from the café. The only reason she'd noticed it on that occasion was that a snazzy-looking sports vehicle had been backing into a car space behind it, catching her eye. She hadn't given it another thought; no reason why she would, until now. She leaned against the railing, watching it.

I don't even know for certain it's the same hatchback.

She shrugged it off and went inside. She switched on the TV but she couldn't focus; she wasn't even sure what it was she was watching, or more correctly trying to watch. One of those makeover reality shows where everyone acted as though they were on an adrenaline high.

After a while, she wandered onto the balcony again. The white hatchback was still there; why wouldn't it be? She watched it for a few minutes. It was dark, the hatchback wasn't parked under a streetlight, but she could've sworn she saw the movement of what looked like a person through the windshield. There must have been hundreds of white hatchbacks in Seattle but she felt certain this was the same car and that it had followed her.

Am I being paranoid?

She decided to take charge and find out. She went down onto the street and marched with determination toward the vehicle, her steps echoing on the wet sidewalk. The streetlights cast an eerie yellow glow, leaving the dark spaces between them in shadows that seemed to close in around her as she went. As she got closer, she heard the engine of the hatchback start up, its headlights illuminating her path before it slowly pulled out from the curb.

She watched it disappear into the night, feeling a chill in her bones.

* * *

My cell rang and, having just left her a little more than an hour before, I was surprised to see it was Jill. "Everything okay?"

The edge was back in her voice. "I'm not sure. I noticed a car, a white hatchback, across the road and not far from me when I got back to my car. It seems the same car's been parked down the street, watching the motel."

"Watching? Are you certain it's the same car?" I asked.

"I can't be certain but I think so. I went down to see what was going on but it drove off as I approached."

"Did you see its license plate?"

"No, it was dark, and I didn't get close enough."

"Jill, there are plenty of white hatches on the roads. It could have been a resident of the street, or someone visiting one of the locals."

"You think I'm acting a little crazy?"

"No, of course not, I–"

"It's okay, I'm thinking the same. Maybe I'm just jumping at shadows. I shouldn't have called you."

"Jill, your sister's been missing so it's only natural you'd be on edge. But it's probably nothing."

"You're right, of course."

"I can come over if it would make you feel better. You're in a strange city–"

"I'm a grown woman, for God's sake. And I'm a defense attorney. No, you stay put, I was just having a moment. I'll be fine. And you're right, there are hundreds of white hatchbacks on the roads."

After we'd ended the call, I wondered if Jill's paranoia was a lingering result, even after all these years, of the aborted attack on her after that college party. It made sense, there's a part of a person that's irrevocably changed after an incident like that. I should know. Kidnapped when I was just fourteen, I'd been put in a box at the base of a deep shaft on an abandoned building site, while my kidnappers blackmailed my father, who at that time was an assistant director of the FBI. I'd managed to get out of that shaft, but I wasn't the same girl, there was a steeliness in me that wasn't there before, a heightened awareness of everything that was going on around me, and it was one of the reasons, the main reason, I'd joined the FBI.

I tried to put Jill's sister and the folklore-related murders out of my mind, I needed sleep. Eventually, I began to drift off, conscious of a low boom of thunder in the distance as the rain started up again, heavier this time, beating against the windows as though it was trying to get my attention.

Chapter Ten

Day Two

I woke before my alarm. I knew, from not receiving any calls or texts during the night, that there'd been no activity on the surveillance outside the transplant unit.

I didn't want breakfast this morning. I made coffee, but as I often did, I barely drank half of it in my haste to get ready and get into the office. I only ever applied make-up lightly, and I ran a comb through my shoulder-length hair. It was getting longer than normal but a hairdresser appointment was the furthest thing from my mind and I didn't feel like messing with a ponytail this morning.

Will was one of the earliest risers you would ever meet and, true to form, he was at his desk even though I was in earlier than usual. Zoe was also in, seated at the Themis console like she was one of its permanent fixtures. Sometimes it seemed to me that Zoe and her AI creation were joined at the hip. I'd commented that in our line of work, balance was needed, and she should invest some time in other pursuits like having fun and dating. She'd said that both were high on her agenda but I wasn't certain they were, despite whatever good intentions she may have had.

I was checking in with Will when Zoe called us and we joined her at the console. "We've been running that search of anything statewide that's got even a tenuous connection to the world of the Brothers Grimm. Themis has flagged this guy who doesn't just meet that criterion but a couple of others as well."

I focused on the Themis-created profile that Zoe had cast on one of the large screens positioned above the console, against the adjoining wall. "Thomas Rodwell," I said.

The picture on the screen was of a heavyset, thirtysomething man, bespectacled, with dark, curly, unkempt hair and a bushy, prematurely gray-flecked beard.

"Rodwell runs a small group for enthusiasts who meet once a week to discuss the work of the Grimms," Zoe said. "In addition, he has a small part-time business, touring Washington schools with a one-man children's storytelling performance, orally relating and acting out the well-known tales. That's enough for Themis to list him as part of this prompt, but he's been flagged for special interest on two other points, one specifically that relates to the case. The storytelling doesn't earn him much and is more of a hobby, his main source of income is that he's a part-time worker for the same bakery Jack Corris worked for."

"He's a baker?" Will asked.

"No, a driver. Makes a few runs each morning, delivering the bakery's products to the supermarket transportation hubs and he's been doing it long enough that he could have known Corris."

Marcia arrived and quietly joined us, motioning that we should carry on and silently mouthing to me that she could be filled in later.

"You said there were two points of interest," I said to Zoe.

"The other point is unrelated to any of the case details but is nonetheless out of the ordinary. I'll get Themis to outline the background."

"Two years ago, a death occurred at Thomas Rodwell's residence in Bellevue," Themis informed us. "The casualty was Eva Wyatt, who died when she fell down the steep stairs at the residence, while she was intoxicated. Wyatt was Rodwell's girlfriend. She didn't live with him but she is known to have been spending most of her time there. Rodwell was interviewed as a matter of procedure by the police and their report contains a suspicion that he might have been involved in Wyatt's fall. They based this on an interview with a friend of Wyatt's, who told them that Wyatt was unhappy in the relationship. She'd seen an ugly side of Thomas Rodwell, moments when he'd become verbally abusive over trivial matters, and she intended to break up with him. But there was no physical evidence for the police to establish a prima facie case."

"Zoe," I said, "did you access an online schedule of Rodwell's school appearances?"

"Yes."

"Anything listed for today?"

"Yes. Later this morning, he's at an elementary school in Redmond."

Will and I exchanged a glance. "Perhaps an impromptu visit to see Rodwell at the school," I said. "Maybe catching him off guard with a few questions. See if he acts like he's got anything to hide."

"Couldn't have put it better myself."

Once again, for just a moment, it was as though the spark of that old camaraderie was back, but just as quickly Will's eyes clouded over and he moved off. I noticed that Marcia was observing him just as closely as I was, with the same look of concern on her face.

* * *

The elementary school was a private school with a small auditorium. Toward the front of the hall, there looked to be around one hundred students, aged between eight and ten, seated on an enormous rug.

On the slightly elevated stage, I recognized Thomas Rodwell, dressed in a blue and gold swirl of robes, holding a ceremonial scepter. He was seated in a large wicker chair, everything about his appearance and posture embodying a fairy-tale king.

He had a deep voice and it boomed out, with no need for a mic. "The King told the woman that he had disguised himself as the horseman who had ridden by and smashed her crockery. He had done it to bring humility to her proud spirit, and to punish her for her insolence."

He then stood and swung the scepter out before him, like a wand. There were gasps of delight from the children and, off to the side, one of the teachers, a middle-aged brunette woman, beamed with a smile so wide you would have thought that a real-life king had graced the school with his presence.

"The King then told her that the evil days were past and they would be able to marry and celebrate their happiness with the whole court."

I recognized it as the story of *King Thrushbeard*. Rodwell completed his performance, bowed, waved to the children, left the stage, and entered a door to the side and rear of the hall.

I had a word with the teacher, who escorted Will and me through to the area at the back. Rodwell had removed the crown and robes, sporting underneath a sweatshirt and cargo pants. Will introduced us and asked if he was okay if we asked him a few questions about the culture surrounding the Grimm fairy tales, and that it could prove useful to a case we were working on.

"Of course," Rodwell said, looking a little perplexed. "I must say I'm intrigued as to how the Brothers Grimm tales could be of any use to a federal criminal investigation."

"You may have seen news reports of two murders in Seattle over the past week, the victims found outside a dance studio, and a bakery," Will said, "and while most of the details are being kept under wraps, we believe the person responsible has a deep interest in the Grimm fairy tales."

"Why is that?"

"As I said, details are being kept under wraps. But given you run a group of enthusiasts, we hoped you might be able to shed some light on why someone might have a particular interest in certain tales."

Rodwell tugged at his beard. "I see. Why don't we pull up a few chairs."

He moved across the room to where plastic chairs were stacked and removed three of them from the pile.

"There was also a similar set of murders in Tacoma, a while back," Will said once we were all seated. "The particular stories that were referenced at each crime scene were *Hansel and Gretel, Snow White, Cinderella, The Two Brothers,* and *King Thrushbeard,* which I see you just performed."

"Oh, just one of many, although as you can see" – Rodwell tugged at his beard again – "that one quite suits me." He grinned, and it seemed to me he was more at ease than most people when unexpectedly visited by federal agents, asking questions. I got the sense he was enjoying the attention.

"Is there anything in particular about those stories, and anything comparable between them?" Will asked.

Rodwell gave an expansive gesture. "Well, many of the Grimm tales have kings, queens, witches, or ogres, and many have children who are either lost or threatened or led away, as in *The Pied Piper.* They all act as a kind of morality play, holding up a mirror to society, warning us of its ills."

"Have you come across anyone who seemed overly zealous about those themes, and perhaps those particular stories?" I asked.

"I hope you're not implying that someone in my Grimms appreciation group would be capable of something like murder."

"Not at all," I assured him, "it's just that with so little to go on, we're casting a pretty wide net at the moment, seeking out anyone with knowledge on this subject. How well do you know the people you've met through your appreciation group?"

He shrugged. "Not terribly well, I suppose. We mostly just share thoughts at our get-togethers, and over the years

I've had a few come and go from the group. But like me, they would all be horrified at the idea of someone blackening the legacy of the tales by committing murders." He shuddered.

"To your knowledge, do any of the people you've met through a shared interest in the Grimm tales, have an interest, or background, in shooting?"

We both watched closely for Rodwell's reaction.

"Guns? No, the subject has never come up. To be frank, most of the Grimm fans I've had dealings with are pretty nerdy types. These murder victims, they were shot?"

"Yes," Will said. "And coincidentally, one of the Seattle victims was named Jack Corris. He worked for the bakery that you do delivery runs for. Did you know Mr. Corris, by any chance?"

Rodwell's eyes narrowed in surprise. "Jack? Well, not really. He was one of the bakers. He often helped out some of the other guys loading stock into the truck that I drive for them. He never said much. Quiet type. But Jack Corris went missing, must have been four or so years ago. Where had he been?"

"That's another aspect of the case we're looking into," Will said.

"Could you provide us with a list of your appreciation group members?" I asked. "We'd like to have the same conversation with each of them as we're having with you. With investigations of this type, there's quite often someone who has a piece of information that doesn't seem to be of any import to them, but which makes a difference to the direction a case can take."

"Is that something I'm legally required to do? It's just that… Well, it's a private group, the only one of its kind in the state, as you're no doubt aware."

Will's voice took on a grave tone. "We can get a warrant, but to be honest, Mr. Rodwell, this is urgent. People's lives could be at stake, and people in your group could know something that makes a real difference in how we proceed. Both state and federal investigations rely heavily on information from the public, and people often underestimate how useful their knowledge can be."

Rodwell acknowledged the point with a tilt of his head. "I can get you the list."

When we were back in his car, Will said, "Rodwell certainly didn't tense up or show any evasive signs when we mentioned the murders and Jack Corris and queried those particular tales. Nothing suspicious in his behavior. The fact he knew one of the victims seems likely coincidental."

"You don't believe in coincidence," I reminded him with a gentle nudge. It was a comment that usually elicited a smile but Will's face was as solid as granite.

"Looks like I've stumbled on an exception."

I nodded my agreement. "Even so, I'll have the bakery send us his delivery schedule, so we can rule out any other 'coincidences.'"

We watched as Rodwell came out of the building, lugging a bag with his costume and props, as he headed to his vehicle. It was then, as he reached the end of the parking lot, that my jaw tightened and I threw a questioning glance at Will.

Rodwell's car was a black SUV.

Chapter Eleven

As we drove into Lacey, the suburb of Olympia where Emily Yarros's aunt lived, I was struck by the abundance of parks and open spaces. On a couple of occasions, I glimpsed riders on the bike trails that wound their way through the swathes of natural reserves that were visible from the roadway.

"I raised Emily in this here house," Irene Warner said as she welcomed me and Will into the older-style, 1970s single-level home, its exterior clapboard paneling showing its age. "Emily's mother, my sister Iris, was a single mom who died young. I felt duty-bound to look after young Emily and I loved her like she was my own. I could see a lot of my sister in her."

The living room was small but comfy, although the sofa we sank into had seen better days. Irene hadn't stopped talking since she'd opened the door to me and Will. I had the distinct impression that was her way of coping with the grief of hearing of Emily's death.

"We are both so sorry for your loss," I said to her.

"Well, it's four years since she disappeared, but it's the shock, you know, of learning she's passed and I won't ever be seeing her again." There was a faraway look in her eyes and the deep lines around them deepened and her shoulders slumped. "I thought she'd just gone off somewhere, she was a troubled girl. It was when the people she worked with were looking for her that I knew something wasn't right and I reported her missing. Not that that did anybody any good. Initially, the police didn't even think she was missing, but I gather that's because she was in their system and they had a low regard for her type."

Will looked at me with a veiled expression and my pulse quickened.

"You described your niece as troubled," Will said. "I gather that's due to the drug use and the crime she was suspected of?"

"Oh yes. It all goes back to that dreadful night, six months before Emily disappeared. She and her boyfriend, Mikey, and her best friend, Gabi, were high – on what, I've never been certain; alcohol for sure, and whatever was the party drug of the week, I suppose. They'd gone back to Mikey's place, a second-story single-room apartment, one of the old-style blocks." Irene rolled her eyes. "Mikey and

Gabi started tongue kissing, and Emily went wild, yelling at the two of them and breaking them apart. This is the story as Emily told it to me and the cops. A fight broke out, Emily and Gabi pushing each other around, and Gabi threw her glass at the wall and stormed off in a huff, flew right out the door full throttle but must've forgotten they were on the second floor and she went right over the railing of the block's walkway, hit the ground below and died on the spot." She paused for a moment, reflecting on the tragedy, and then her eyes widened, and she said, "Where are my manners? Can I get you something to drink, maybe tea or coffee?"

"We're fine thanks, Ms. Warner," Will said. "Please go on."

She nodded. "For whatever reason, the police suspected Emily had pushed Gabi. Emily swore to me she didn't and I believed her. She was just a party girl, maybe a little on the wild side, but she wasn't vicious. The cops might've got that idea because Emily had been in trouble in school, suspended a couple of times for getting into fights with other girls, always over some boy, but that was a phase she'd gone through when she was in her teens, she'd long since grown out of it."

"What happened then, with the police?" I asked.

"They had her in for questioning several times, and Mikey, he was no help; he admitted there'd been some fighting but that he'd been too out of it to know why Gabi stormed off right into the railing like that, although he didn't believe Emily had run after her and pushed her."

"But he was vague?" I pressed.

"Oh yes, that kid never had much between his ears," Irene said, "and he and Emily stopped seeing each other after that. For a while there, it looked like the cops were going to charge Emily, but ultimately they didn't have any evidence that would stand up in court. Emily was a changed girl, no going out with friends, no parties, no alcohol, stopped going to the dance classes she'd loved since she was a tiny tot, and she sank into a bit of a depressed state. After a while, one of the detectives, a woman, began turning up at Emily's apartment, and at Emily's place of work, asking questions, like she was trying to goad her into a confession. That's why I thought Emily had taken off, to get away from the cops, to get away from everything."

"She'd been living in Seattle under the surname Yarros for a couple of months and then went missing from there," I said. "Does the name Yarros mean anything to you?"

"It was me and my sister's maiden name," Irene replied. "Something easy for her to remember, I guess."

"Do you remember the name of the policewoman who was showing so much interest in Emily?" I asked.

She thought for a moment. "Tranter. A name I'd rather forget. Who did the damn woman think she was, some sort of female Columbo?"

"You said on the phone you and Emily had been estranged for a while. When did she move out?"

"A couple of months after Gabi's death. I was on her case a lot, telling her that her wild living would only keep on leading to troubles like this. She said she'd had enough of being lectured, threw a few things in a bag, and took off. We spoke a few times on the phone and I tried to keep things light, but it wasn't easy, you know?" Irene cleared her throat and began fidgeting, her voice wavering. "The police told me she was shot. Who on earth would've wanted to kill my poor Emily?" Tears glistened at the corners of her eyes.

"We'll be doing everything we can to find out," I assured her.

* * *

On the drive back to Seattle, Will said, "Irene might have been right in thinking her niece wanted to get away from the suspicion around her and start afresh. We now know that constituted a new name, new job, new city, although she didn't go far."

"Most likely couldn't afford to," I said. "She'd only been in Seattle for a short time, living as Emily Yarros, when she disappeared. So where was she for the past four years and how and why was she gunned down sniper-style when no one knew where she was?"

"While we're here in Olympia, we might as well call into the OPD and have a word with this Detective Tranter."

The Olympia Police Department was housed in a sleek building with a wide, glass-walled entrance. At the front desk, the duty sergeant showed his surprise when we asked for Tranter. "I hope you didn't come all the way from Seattle to see her," he said. "Detective June Tranter moved to the Seattle PD two years ago."

Chapter Twelve

Earlier, on the drive over to Olympia, I had told Will about the visit I'd received from Jill Reiberger. Now, as we headed back to Seattle, I thought about how two missing people, Sam Reiberger and Emily Yarros, had both been under suspicion by police for unrelated but serious crimes.

A criminal record only contains a history of crimes for which a person was found guilty, not if they were found not guilty or if their case was dismissed, so Yarros didn't have a criminal record. Sam did, from her younger days back in DC, but not for the drug overdose death of the guy in Seattle. Like Yarros, none of the other victims of the folkloric killer had criminal records.

I ran through all of this with Will as he drove. "You have a theory?" he asked.

"Not so much a theory, rather something we should check, so that we can rule it out." I phoned Zoe. "Can you get Themis to access all Washington police and court records, and run the names of, not Yarros, but the other four murder victims against the information and notes in those records?"

"Sure. You want to give me a heads-up on what you're looking for?"

"Let's just see what comes back. Might be nothing."

It wasn't nothing.

When Will and I arrived back at the UCU, Zoe brought us up to date on Themis's findings. The other four victims had all been either questioned about, or charged with murder, and in each instance the charge had been dropped or the case dismissed, for various reasons relating to lack of evidence or legal technicalities, with no press coverage.

"Who were the detectives involved in making the charges?" I asked.

Zoe reeled off several names, officers stationed at the time at Seattle, Tacoma, and Olympia precincts. One of them was June Tranter. "We learned from Yarros's aunt that Detective Tranter had been making unscheduled visits to Emily, with questions about the death of Yarros's friend," I told Zoe and Marcia.

Scanning for more detail from the data on June Tranter, Zoe said, "Five years ago, Jack Corris was arrested by Detective Tranter and her partner in Olympia, where he was calling at his ex-wife's home, to pick up his daughter. His ex was found floating in the property's swimming pool, and Corris was charged with drowning her."

"What happened?" asked Will.

"Corris and his ex-wife were still at odds over a protracted, drawn-out custody battle. Friends and neighbors attested to hearing vicious arguments whenever Corris was there to pick up the young girl and they believed he was wearing different clothes when he left that day to those he'd arrived in. The coroner ruled that the time of the woman's death coincided with the established time of Corris's arrival, but ultimately the prosecution ruled they didn't have enough evidence to proceed. With no evidence of foul play, the coroner ruled it as an accident."

"Was Tranter involved in any of the other arrests?"

"No. But she was one of the detectives involved in questioning Sam Reiberger in another murder case."

"And in each of these cases, who determined that the charges would be dismissed?"

"Ultimately, the assistant prosecuting attorney here in Seattle."

I was looking for a pattern, for connections, but instead, I was seeing only fragments that didn't fit together.

"We were on our way to speak with Detective Tranter anyway," Will remarked. "We'll speak as well with the other arresting detectives, and with the deputy PA. Maybe there's an unforeseen link between the victims or the crimes they were suspected of."

Before Will and I headed off, I phoned Paul Radner at the SPD. "How well do you know one of the other detectives over there, June Tranter?" I asked him.

"June? She's partnered with Bill O'Halloran, and I compare notes with them a fair bit. I haven't worked any cases with June myself and she doesn't tend to get involved socially with the department. But she's got a good track record, very no-nonsense, methodical, by-the-book. Why do you ask?"

I told him what we'd found out. "It's just routine, but we'll be having a word with Tranter, maybe she remembers something about Yarros or Corris that could prove useful."

"Anything about that I can help you with?"

I gave this a moment's thought. Even though Radner had been a good ally of the UCU, I didn't want to give too much away at this stage, I certainly didn't want to cast any aspersions on his colleagues in the SPD. "Do you know if Detective Tranter is in at the moment?"

"Let me check?" A minute later, he was back on the line. "Yes. Looks as though she and her partner will be in the office the rest of the day."

* * *

June Tranter had straight black hair and a serious expression that fitted the description of her as methodical and no-nonsense. There were no welcoming words and no smiles when Will and I introduced ourselves and asked if there was a quiet place where we could talk. She led us from the busy criminal investigations area to one of the interview rooms.

"I'm afraid I can only spare a few minutes," she said. "We're incredibly busy. I've never figured out how politicians think budget restraints and cutbacks are in any way positive when it comes to law enforcement anywhere, let alone in a major city like this one."

"We won't need any more than a few minutes, Detective Tranter," Will assured her.

"It's June," she offered but there was no change in her po-faced expression.

"You'd be aware that one of the local murder victims this past week was Jack Corris, who you'd interviewed concerning a suspected murder case several years back, in Olympia."

"That's right. Detective Radner is assigned to Corris's murder but I made the connection when I saw the name on the daily reports."

"Were you aware that one of the other murder victims, Emily Yarros, was actually Emily Warner, a suspect in another case you investigated in Olympia?" I asked.

Tranter barely raised an eyebrow. "Warner? *She* was Emily Yarros?"

"Yes. She was reported missing back then, as you know. We've discovered that she came to Seattle and started using her mother's maiden name. And then vanished a second time, her body only turning up now. Is there anything that comes to mind, looking back on both those cases, that might give us a hint to where they'd both been all these years and what might have led to them being gunned down by a sniper?"

"I've come across some pretty bizarre situations, in this job we all do, but this might just take the cake. I couldn't say, though, that anything comes to mind that would tie in with your investigation."

I leaned in. "Here in Seattle, a year ago, you interviewed Sam Reiberger, in another murder investigation. Were you aware Reiberger was reported missing six months later?"

"I hadn't made that connection, no."

"Does it seem odd to you that three people you've interviewed as suspects in murders were later reported missing, and that two of them have now turned up dead?"

Tranter's voice remained as monotone as her expressionless face. "Not really. I interview, in collab with my colleagues, hundreds of people every year, many of them with criminal connections of some kind or another. So, three of them being the subject of missing person reports is, statistically speaking, neither here nor there."

"A little background on the cases might give us a few pointers on which way to direct our inquiries," Will said. "In the case involving Emily Yarros/Warner, what made the police suspect that Emily had pushed her friend, Gabi, off the second floor of the apartment building?"

"We had a witness. Another resident of the block was standing on the second-floor walkway and told us she saw Emily come rushing out of her boyfriend Mikey's apartment and body-slam Gabi over the railing."

"Why didn't the case proceed?" Will asked.

"We had the go-ahead from the prosecution to lay charges, that it was a winnable case, but mere days later the witness was killed in a car crash. She was a young woman, thirtysomething. It was a terrible tragedy, but for Yarros, a stroke of luck. Without that witness we had no case, and the prosecution said they wouldn't proceed to court without the testimony, and as it was the only evidence we had, the charges were dropped."

"We spoke with Yarros's aunt; she didn't appear to know anything about this witness," I said.

"It had been kept under wraps at that point and we didn't publicize it once the case was dead in the water."

"And why was the charge against Jack Corris dropped?" Will asked.

"When Corris arrived at his ex-wife's home, his five-year-old daughter was inside watching TV. Corris said he went out the back and saw his ex floating face down in the water. First responders confirmed to us that Corris's clothes weren't wet when they arrived, so he couldn't have been in the pool to drown her. But my partner and I suspected he could have held her head over the side of the pool, submerged, until she drowned, and then pushed the rest of her body in. We arrested Corris, based on the neighbor's testimony that they'd heard a scream and that there'd been vicious arguments between the two of them before, and they were certain he'd arrived at the house that morning in a different set of clothes."

"Meaning he could've been in the pool and changed out of the wet clothes," Will remarked.

"Yes. We didn't find any wet clothes on the premises but we hoped we could wear Corris down into a confession, but even after excessive hours of interrogation, we could hardly get him to say a word or to even break a sweat. And then his current wife gave testimony that he'd been wearing the same clothes when he left their home that morning as the ones he was wearing when the emergency crew arrived." Tranter printed off a sheet from the interview records with the neighbors and handed it to me. "This is the kind of threatening language overheard on those other occasions."

I read through the notes. "It doesn't constitute evidence of murder," I pointed out as I put the sheet of paper aside.

"Which is another of the reasons the prosecution decided not to proceed," said Tranter. "But everything we learned in our interviews with friends and neighbors of the deceased formed a profile of Corris as violent and abusive toward his ex, and possessive of their daughter, quite different from the quiet persona he exhibited with his new family, and his work colleagues."

In the case of Sam Reiberger, Tranter then told us the police had found a cache of drugs in Sam's apartment, the same kind her friend had OD'd on, but when those drugs went missing from the police evidence locker, sensitivity surrounding the implications of that led to the charges against Sam being dropped.

"The drugs weren't found," she said. "I believe they were stolen by someone who had access to that locker, which implicates a lot of people. Sending Sam to trial meant that the details around the missing evidence would get a lot of media attention, stir up an even bigger widespread internal investigation, and all for a case that would be hard to prove in court anyway."

I leaned forward. "June, as different and as unrelated as the Warner and Corris cases were, can you think of anyone you came across that could have a link to either of the victims?"

She shook her head. "No. I wish it were otherwise. If there's one thing that makes my blood boil, it's loose ends."

"I can relate to that," I said.

"If anything does come to mind, I'll get in touch. But if there's nothing more…"

"We'll get out of your hair," Will said.

* * *

On our way out, Detective Radner approached us. "How did it go with June?"

"She's one cool customer," I said.

Radner nodded. "Has a good head on her shoulders. Was she able to shed any light on the Yarros and Corris cases?"

"Not at this stage."

"What's become more and more apparent," Will said, "is that the two Seattle victims, and the three in Tacoma, appear to have been targeted by this shooter because they were all suspects in murder cases. But as the charges were dropped or the court cases dismissed, none of the victims had a criminal record, nor had there been any media reports of the police's interest in them."

"Which means," I added, "that either the killer personally knew each of the five well enough to know they'd been questioned by police, or they have access to police and court files enabling them to track down that information."

Radner screwed up his face at the latter point. "I don't like the sound of that."

"It opens up the ugliest possible can of worms," I said.

Chapter Thirteen

Something else was on my mind. As Will and I headed out to the car, I phoned Marcia. "Can you look into the missing male nurse, Ryan Moreton's, background?" I asked. "Make a note if he's ever been interviewed by police as a suspect in a crime, or had charges laid against him and then dropped."

"Leave it with me," Marcia said.

Will made eye contact, nodding his agreement it was a query we needed to pursue.

It was a short drive to the King County Courthouse, the multi-level brick, steel, and concrete historical landmark where the state prosecuting attorney's office was located. PA Melanie Lynskey had the air of a woman with little time to spare, and she leafed quickly through the printouts that contained the details of the five murder victims.

"All had been at one time or another suspects or defendants in murder cases where the charges were dropped," she said, summarizing the contents for her own benefit rather than ours, it seemed. She cast a curious eye over me and Will. "I can see where your minds would be headed with this."

"It implies the killer knew these details and didn't agree with them," Will responded, "and that the killings weren't purely random. I appreciate that these cases go back several years but I wonder, taking a look at the five of them together, whether anything strikes you as unusual, or similar."

"No," she said, "but these decisions are always made in consultation with the deputy prosecuting attorney handling the case. I've asked Deputy PA Martin Elderson to join us. His main jurisdiction is violent crime and he was the handler of the judicial process on these." She glanced toward the doorway. "Ah, speak of the devil."

The man who entered was late thirtyish, tall and fit, impeccably and stylishly dressed as though he was a corporate legal eagle on Wall Street. His eyes were a piercing blue, his dark, slicked-back hair exhibiting just a hint of early graying at the sides, somehow presenting more like a fashion statement than anything else. Accompanying him was a woman of similar age, walking with a slight limp. She had a sinewy build and inquisitive green eyes that complemented her spiky red hair. Lynskey introduced Elderson and his paralegal, Steph Allsworth.

They pulled up seats. "Melanie filled me in on your visit," Elderson told us, "and I put a few things aside to take a walk back through memory lane on these." He and Steph Allsworth were holding folders that I gathered contained the case information. He opened his folder. "These are all charges where evidence problems or other circumstances coming to light, led to a decision not to proceed. Never taken lightly, I might add, but simply put, where evidentiary problems or procedural errors make conviction doubtful, it is sometimes in the best interests of the state to dismiss."

"Not a decision that goes down well with the arresting officers, I expect," I said.

"Nor should it. But in all such instances, the detective who presented the case is advised and may appeal the decision, although that hasn't happened in any of the cases listed here." He shifted his frame in the chair. "You think that these murder victims were targeted by someone in the know because the criminal charges were dropped?"

"It's high on the list of possibilities," Will said.

"Normally I'd agree. But if you weigh it against the fact that, despite the overall percentage of dismissed charges being low, there are still hundreds of violent crime charges every year that don't proceed, then you'd have to ask why all those others haven't also been targeted?"

"Hopefully, that's where you come in," Will said. "There must be something about those five that led to their disappearance and subsequent murders, and perhaps that's got something to do with the legal circumstances surrounding the case dismissals."

Elderson leaned forward, a conspiratorial gleam in his eyes. "My paralegal here has one of the sharpest minds in the building. If there's ever anything hidden in the details, she'll find it. And... well, I'll let Steph take over. Steph?"

Allsworth smiled in acknowledgment of the compliment but there was nothing smug in her response. "As Martin said, there are any number of reasons a case is dismissed." She didn't open her folder. It remained closed in her lap. "And what I noticed with these five cases is that although only a couple of them even made it to court, in each instance the defendants were set for representation by the same state defense attorney."

My gut twisted with unease as I absorbed her words. Where was she going with this? "Who's the attorney?"

"Julian Adler," Allsworth replied. "He took on several murder cases pro bono as a way of raising his profile and building his practice. Which he's done, quite spectacularly. He's particularly strong in getting witnesses discredited so that the cases are abandoned. But that's not the reason I mention him."

"What is?" Will asked.

"What if the killer isn't just targeting murder suspects whose cases were dropped? What if the killer is also sending a message to those responsible either for representing them or having the prosecution dismissed?" She paused for effect, her eyes flicking between us. "There are several assistant PAs here, including Martin" – she gestured toward her boss – "and also the defense attorney, Julian Adler, who are sports shooting hobbyists, and they belong to the same gun club."

"Are you suggesting the killer is trying to get Adler's attention, and the attention of the others, by using the instrument of their hobby as the murder method?" I said.

"It may seem odd, but it struck me as a possibility. In the killer's own twisted mind, they could be sending a message to the judiciary to stop dropping charges against suspects that this killer believes are guilty."

Elderson looked aghast. "Or they will deliver their own brand of justice?"

"Yes."

Elderson took a deep breath. "Good God."

"It's a stretch," Will said, "but we are looking for any ex-military or law enforcement personnel who fit a sniper profile, and we'll include the gun club you mention – we'll include all gun and sports shooting institutions. And it begs the question" – he directed his focus to Elderson – "whether you know if any of the members of your club have a background that would raise suspicion?"

"Outside of Julian Adler and the other assistant PAs here, I'm afraid I've had very little to do with other members of the club."

"Have there been any recent cases presented to your office where a murder charge has been dropped?" I asked, looking at Elderson and Lynskey.

Lynskey's face was grim. "Just a few weeks back," she said. "A man named John Raye."

"And it was another instance," Elderson added, "where the charge was dropped after the only witness, who was found to be a low-level drug dealer, fled the state and hasn't been located."

"And you decided you didn't have enough evidence to proceed and get a conviction?" Will asked.

"Yes."

"Do you have a current address for Raye?" I asked Allsworth. "We'd like to have a word with him."

"I can get that for you," she said.

I didn't have to ask the question that must have been turning in everyone's mind. Would this vigilante killer be targeting John Raye next?

Chapter Fourteen

"I didn't want to give too much credence to Steph Allsworth's theory back there," Will said on the drive back to the UCU, "but she might have a point. We know this killer has access to information about people who have murder charges against them dropped. It could be that the killer is a member of that same gun club and is close enough to these attorneys that they've been able to gain access to case details."

"Perhaps they're even a member of the PA office staff," I said.

Will pursed his lips. "There are over two hundred deputy prosecuting attorneys at King County Court," he pointed out, "and almost as many admin staff."

I shot him a lopsided grin. "That won't keep Themis busy for long."

He smiled back briefly and I caught a glint of the old sparkle in his eye. The scope, urgency, and high stakes of this investigation had his adrenaline flowing and that was the best thing for him at the moment. A case he could sink his teeth into. We were so alike in that regard.

I phoned ahead and briefed Zoe on what we needed from Themis. Zoe had her phone on loudspeaker and Marcia, listening in, came on the line. "That antennae of yours was right to have me check out Ryan Moreton's background," she said. "He was interviewed by police, a suspect in a homicide, but no charges were laid. I've sent the details through to you."

"Thanks, Marcia."

* * *

Will and I arrived back to a bustling ops room. Zach Silverstein having come in and joined Marcia and Zoe in tackling the various avenues of inquiry. The lure of a case with strong links to medieval tales would be far too addictive for him to ignore.

"No lectures today?" I said to Zach.

As a professor across three disciplines, not to mention his wide-ranging knowledge of mythology, he was in constant demand at the university and associated institutions.

"Got some of the others filling in for me," he said. "I wanted to interrogate as much of the data on this case as I can. I can see that everything is pointing to a serial killer who is also a vigilante."

"What's your take on that?" Will asked.

"I think there's more to the vigilante side of this than there is to the serial killer aspect." He swiveled in his chair and stretched out his long legs in front of him. I'd rarely seen Zach maintain any stillness for very long. "And it ties in with this killer's obsession with the Brothers Grimm. The Grimms had a strong belief in criminal justice and its place in society. The tales they collected were allegories for upholding the law and inflicting penance. Referencing those tales with each victim says to me that the killer feels a strong personal connection, both to the Grimms and to the cause of justice."

Before anyone else could say anything, Zach was back on his feet, gesticulating wildly. "Jacob Grimm was himself a jurist who, along with his brother, studied with the founder of the historical school of jurisprudence, Professor Friedrich Carl von Savigny. Savigny believed the spirit of a community's laws grew from that community's customs, traditions, and stories, and that the aim of those tales, at their core, was the same as that of the legal systems that developed: to find the truth, convict the guilty, and deliver punishment. Most people wouldn't think of a fantastical fairy tale as being linked with the process of law but it's there in every tale. The killer references these morality tales to demonstrate they are on the side of right."

"In what way?" Marcia asked.

"The tales present the violence that is meted out as just, while the perpetrator's crimes are viewed as unjust. Think about it: when the wolf devours Red Riding Hood and her grandmother, we see it along the same lines as we see a criminal act, but when the hunter kills the wolf and cuts the little girl and the old woman free, it's an act of justified retribution. Just as the villains in the folktales meet their just desserts, it seems this killer believed these five victims deserved theirs."

"That would tie in with Steph Allsworth's suggestion. The killer perceives that, like the moral code in those tales, they're also sending a message to our judicial system."

Zach nodded enthusiastically, taken by the notion. "Yes, a message to overhaul the system for true justice, and until then, the killer is doing what needs to be done."

"If that's the case," Marcia said, "and if these people were targeted because the killer believed they needed to be punished, and if they were abducted, where have they been since they vanished years ago? If they weren't kidnapped, could it be they knew someone was after them and they went into hiding?"

"It's that very question that leads me to wonder if there is something else, something very odd, going on here," Zach said. "Each of these missing people reappeared wearing the same clothing they were in when they vanished, in roughly the same area from where they are believed to have disappeared."

"You're not suggesting another one of your supernatural theories," Marcia said with half an eye roll.

Zach was well-known for his theory that the supernatural elements in the tales of old were real, that those supernatural aspects were as much a part of the natural universe as everything else and would one day be scientifically explained. They were simply elements that hadn't yet been discovered by the human race.

"Think about it," he continued. "No trace of their whereabouts, no evidence of any activity. There's nothing to indicate where they were when they were shot. It's as though each of these people were nowhere at all in the time between vanishing and being found. And each was found with items linking them to Brothers Grimm fairy tales. What else do we know about the Grimms' tales aside from the strong moral code that evil people meet their just desserts?" Zach was speaking at hyper-speed, his energy spiking as it always did when he was exploring the possibility of something otherworldly. "Most of the tales feature justice being delivered by witches and warlocks. Throughout the medieval lore of old, these are creatures with the unnatural ability to make people disappear by turning them into birds or animals or vanquishing them to strange realms that exist outside of time and space."

"Or another possibility, grounded in reality," I said, "is that they were simply in hiding, as Marcia suggested."

"That makes sense if they knew this killer was after them," Zach conceded, "but how did this killer find out where they were? It still doesn't explain how these people managed to evade any form of detection for so long."

There was an uneasy silence in the room as everyone pondered Zach's words. I let out a breath I didn't realize I had been holding.

"Right now, there's something else we need to focus on." I told Marcia, Zoe, and Zach about the murder charges recently dropped against John Raye, and I looked at Will. "Next stop, John Raye. Let's see if we can get anything useful from him. But if he is likely to be on the killer's hit list, then we need to find a way to make certain he isn't the next one to go missing and then end up with a bullet in the head."

Will shrugged. "Short of putting him into protective custody, there's no easy way to do that. We can't mount a 24/7 watch on him."

I mulled it over in my mind. "But there is at least one way he could signal us immediately if he sensed a threat," I said.

* * *

The run-down apartment building had rotting wood and peeling paint, a stark contrast to the gleaming skyscrapers in the distance. Will and I walked down the dingy hallway to apartment 3C and Will rapped on the chipped wood of the door. Moments later, we heard shuffling footsteps and the door opened a sliver to reveal a sallow face.

"John Raye?" Will asked, holding up his FBI credentials. "I'm Special Agent in Charge Will McCord and this is Special Agent Ilona Farris–"

"I already told the cops everything and the charge was dropped." Raye's grip tightened on the door and he glared at us through eyes underlined by dark circles.

"We're not here to talk to you specifically about the murder charge," Will said, his voice level and authoritative, "but instead, about the possibility that you may be under threat and we'd like to help."

"What kind of threat?"

"This isn't a conversation for the hallway, Mr. Raye," I said. "It would be best if we could come in, and we'll take up only a moment of your time." I kept my voice gentle but firm.

Raye's eyes narrowed and his agitation was palpable.

"You are not under any investigation by us," I added, meeting his gaze.

Raye hesitated, staring from me to Will and then back. Finally, with a sigh, he opened the door wider and stepped back, allowing us entry. "Okay, but I haven't got all day."

We moved inside to a small room cluttered with mismatched furniture and piles of old newspapers. The air was thick with stale smoke. It occurred to me that this man probably had plenty of free time – all day and then some.

"Mr. Raye," Will began, "we've been investigating a pattern recently. Several people who've had their murder charges or court cases dropped have later disappeared and turned up dead."

Raye eyed us warily, his hands fidgeting in the pockets of his worn-out jeans.

"John," I said, "we're concerned that you might be under the same threat."

He scoffed, though I could hear the tremor in his voice. "I suppose I shouldn't be surprised. Sounds exactly like the sort of thing the Warburtons would get up to."

"Who are the Warburtons?" Will asked.

"Monty Warburton and his son Oliver. They run a network of convenience stores and laundromats across the state. It's a cover for money laundering. They make their real profits by offering their services to drug runners. I used to run errands for them."

"Used to?" I pressed, watching him gaze nervously around the room as though he expected these Warburtons to suddenly appear.

"I reckon they framed me for that murder so I'm hardly going to go back to work for them. I was just one of their scapegoats."

"Why would they frame you?" Will asked.

"I've heard rumors that the Warburtons make sure that anyone who double-crosses them or poses a threat to their territory, gets taken out. And that whenever they get rid of someone, they make certain to set up someone else for the crime, so that it doesn't come back to whoever their real hit man is. I'm just one of their easily-framed nobodies."

"But you don't know any of that for certain."

"I know I didn't kill the person I was suspected of knifing. And although there weren't any obvious links between that victim and the Warburtons, not that the coppers could find, I know the victim had dealings with them on the sly."

"Have Monty or Oliver Warburton made any threats to you personally?" Will asked.

"Not their style. They lead you into a false sense of security and then do everything behind your back. Bastards."

"The murders I spoke of, were the result of a sniper's bullet," Will said. "Does anything about that strike a chord with what you know about the Warburton family or their employees?"

"They're criminals so they've got plenty of guns stashed away. I wouldn't put anything past them."

"Are you aware of any shootings they might have been involved in?"

"I don't know anything. I was just their errand boy, got it? But Monty's kid, Oliver, he's a real smart-ass. Liked to boast to me and the others that he had a whole set of rifles and he was a crack shot, and he knew no one would ever give him trouble 'cause he'd blast 'em away if they did."

"You might be under threat, John," I said, "and we'd like to help. We can offer you a panic button. It's small and can be worn around your wrist or attached to a lanyard around your neck."

"You want to keep track of me?" His voice rose, his agitated state heightened. "Why the hell would I trust the Feds with a tracking device? What have your lot ever done for the likes of me?"

"It would be entirely up to you if you had it on you at any given time, John," I said. "But if and when you did wear it, and if you sensed something amiss or felt in danger, or that you were being followed, just pressing that button would send a signal and, yes, we'd know where you were, and be able to rush to your aid, but once again, that would be entirely under your control."

I held out the small black device. He stared at it, indecision on his face, weighing up the safety being offered with his distrust of authority.

"How does that help me if I get a bullet to the head?" he said, coughing, his voice raspy.

"It doesn't," Will admitted.

Finally, Raye took the device into the palm of his hand, studying it as though it held an answer. "Fine," he said.

Chapter Fifteen

Back in the office, I tapped Jill Reiberger's number into my cell, my fingers tapping on my desk as I waited for her to answer.

"Hello?" Jill's voice sounded strained.

"Hey, it's Ilona. Just checking in after last night. How are you holding up?"

"Well, I slept in fits and starts, if you could call it sleeping, and I was up at the crack of dawn." She sighed. "Anyway, I went for a drive in the morning to clear my head but then I saw that damn hatchback again."

"Where?"

"It was following me, and yes, I know there are lots of them on the road…"

"Were you able to see the license plate?"

"No. Once again, it was never close enough. And I don't see it parked out on the street now, either, but even so…" Her voice trailed away.

"You should've called me if you were worried."

"I was going to, and then I thought I was just being paranoid. Right now, I'm just on edge."

"I'm finishing up here, I can drop by and take a look around."

"That would be good. Actually, I have something I need to share with you."

"What is it?"

"It's something I need to speak to you about in person."

I didn't press the point. I said okay, ended the call, and headed out the door.

* * *

The motel was an older-style, middle-of-the-road type of accommodation that looked like hundreds of others. It was twilight and the neon vacancy sign came on but flickered erratically. I scanned up and down the street, and then walked across the asphalt and up the exterior stairs to the room number she'd given me.

Jill opened on the first knock, her face pale. "Thanks for coming."

I followed her inside, my gaze sweeping the room. Rumpled bed, clothes draped over a chair, a takeout container, and a coffee cup on the table. Jill perched on the edge of the bed. She was like a coiled spring, her eyes shadowed with exhaustion.

"I've scanned the area and there's no sign of a white hatchback," I said. I sat across from her in the room's lone armchair, positioned so that I could see out the window, with a glimpse of just part of the road. "I'll keep an eye on the cars that pass by out there."

"Thanks."

"What did you need to tell me?" I asked gently.

Jill took a deep breath. "Before I left DC and caught the flight here, I hired a private investigator here in Seattle. Stan Avery. I asked him to look into Sam's disappearance, and I also wanted to know if he could find out anything about Sam's claim that she'd been framed by the police."

I stiffened in surprise. "Why didn't you tell me this before?"

"I'm sorry, Ilona, I realize now I should have." She stared at a point on the floor, ashamed. "At first, my feeling was that I wanted you to look into Sam's disappearance without knowing Avery was doing the same. I didn't want any inquiries you made to be compromised by what the PI was doing. I wanted to see if working independently, you and Avery came up with the same, or similar, information or theories. But after last night, and thinking about it today, I felt I was misleading you and that's not something I want to do."

I forced myself not to overreact. Getting defensive wasn't going to achieve anything. "Jill," I said, keeping my voice soft but firm, "keeping secrets doesn't help either of us, not if we want to make big strides into finding out what's happened to Sam."

"I know. I'm sorry."

"Did Avery have any information for you when you arrived in Seattle?"

"He said he'd been keeping tabs on the detective that arrested Sam. Given that Sam told me she thought she'd been framed, Avery was interested in seeing what Detective Tranter did after work hours."

"And?"

"He observed Tranter having a meeting in a hotel with Rob Caufield, the missing persons detective from Olympia."

"There's nothing particularly strange about that, Jill," I said. "A missing persons officer and a criminal investigations cop would have reason to cross paths in the line of duty."

"I know that, so did Avery. But he wondered why it was after hours and in a bar. Obviously, Caulfield had driven in from Olympia. And he said, from their mode of conversation and their body language, that they were very familiar with one another."

"Familiar? As in romantically?"

"No, more like they'd known each other for some time and were friends. Given Tranter's pursuit of Sam, and my brief to Avery that I'd found Detective Caulfield unhelpful when it came to Sam's disappearance, Avery said it raised his suspicions."

"Okay."

"But there's something more. I had a call from Avery a short while ago, just before you phoned me."

"Go on."

"I'd also told him about that white hatchback and he was pretty sure he'd noticed the same thing on a couple of occasions over the past twenty-four hours. He said he had some new information for me but he wanted to give it to me in person. He had an uneasy sense his phone might've been hacked as he'd heard a disturbance on some of his calls – he said it wasn't necessarily related to Sam's case; it could possibly be due to another case he was working on, but he couldn't be sure and wasn't taking any chances."

My blood ran cold at the thought of either Jill or the PI she'd hired being monitored. "What did he suggest?"

"He'll text me a meeting place tomorrow morning using a different phone."

"Okay." My mind was racing. "Call me as soon as you get that text and I'll go with you."

She breathed a sigh of relief. "I can't tell you how much this means to me, having your help. I may be a defense attorney but this is all way out of my comfort zone."

I nodded, reaching out and squeezing her hand, a silent promise that I would be by her side.

A short while after, I headed for home. The evening air was damp and heavy with impending rain, matching my mood as I walked across the motel parking lot to my car. What I couldn't promise Jill was that we'd find her sister, or that, if we did, she would be alive. I was becoming increasingly alarmed that Sam could be involved in the folktale case. Like those murder victims, Sam had murder charges dropped against her. Was she out there somewhere, one of the intended targets of this vigilante? Where? Zach's crazy suggestion that we could be dealing with something unnatural, beyond our understanding, was an unwelcome intrusion into my thoughts. I forced it aside as I got into my car.

* * *

I switched on the evening news, curious to see what the media had made of the Emily Yarros murder. It was no surprise to see Brooke Goodman presenting the lead bulletin.

I'd crossed paths with Brooke on several of our cases. She'd suffered a deep personal loss and we'd developed something of an uneasy bond that would stand the test of time. Brooke could be both a help and a hindrance and I'd had to warn her off reporting sensitive case details on several occasions when media intrusion threatened to inhibit our investigations. That wasn't the case here; at least, not yet. Technically, Brooke wasn't crossing any lines but as a gung-ho reporter for the TV channel, and its affiliated newspaper, and with her appearances on a popular true crime podcast, Brooke was, quite literally, everywhere.

Brooke's long, dark hair didn't distract from her intense brown eyes that, I had to admit, had a magnetic pull when staring out at you from the screen.

The camera pulled back to reveal Rowan seated alongside the reporter. "It's not something I would wish on anyone," Rowan said.

Rowan told of how she'd thought Yarros seemed troubled, and how she was out of practice with her dance studies, though keen to get back on track.

I switched off and thought about what would happen if Brooke Goodman was able to link these deaths to the Tacoma victims. Reporting of that could blow up into sensationalized coverage of a bizarre killer stalking the streets. Part of the UCU's remit was to tackle cases and resolve them before that media storm happened, something that had been rendered close to impossible in a 24/7 news world. Once there was widespread coverage and panic, we were less likely to have genuine people come forward with information that might be of use. A killer could be impassioned to step up their murder spree, or at the other end of the spectrum, to go deep underground, making them even more difficult to apprehend.

I crawled into bed, my head awash with fragmented thoughts: Marcia's speculation that the missing people had gone into hiding; Dr. Marla Lui's report that the victims had been killed by a sniper's bullet, fired from a distance as the victims fled; Zach's words about folkloric witches and otherworldly realms. I listed them in my mind as I began to drift.

Chapter Sixteen

Nowhere

When she thought back, she had no perception of how much time had passed. No awareness of day turning into night and then into day again. It was always night; the deepest, darkest night imaginable, without sky, without stars, without moonlight. Just the cold, hard ground beneath her feet. None of the glorious colors of the world. No sound. None of the noises of existence that she'd taken so much for granted. No sense of being part of anything. She did not know whether she'd been here for days or weeks or longer. Time did not seem to exist here, if there even was a *here*. She had no food, no water. She was starving. If it had been more than a week, then without water surely she'd be dead.

Am I dead?

She was naked, and cold, and her head pounded. Sometimes she walked back and forth, hoping to build up some body warmth; sometimes she sat or curled up into a fetal position, her arms wrapped around her body. She slept from sheer nervous exhaustion but she never knew for how long.

There was only one constant. In her dreams, she heard more of those same words she was certain she'd heard at some point before this began. "Turn back, turn back, thou pretty bride…"

She recalled that as she'd struggled up from the depths of sleep, it was as though those words came from a disembodied voice, emanating from every direction. It seemed close and yet at the same time it had the hollow, softly distorted echo of distance. The moment she was fully awake, the voice was gone, left behind in the mists of her dreams, as though the ghosts of this infinite nothingness had faded the moment she'd awakened.

Chapter Seventeen

The harsh ring of my cell jarred me awake. I fumbled for it, nearly knocking over the lamp on the nightstand before I managed to grab it. I glanced at the caller ID – Will.

"We've got a situation. The surveillance team called. A body was just dumped from an SUV next to the transplant unit. They're tailing the SUV now, discreetly, but they think the driver's onto them, making some seemingly random moves as if testing the waters." His voice was tight. "I'm minutes away from your place. We need to get to their current position asap."

"I'll be ready." I swung my legs out of the bed and pulled on jeans and a jacket, adrenaline wiping away any trace of sleep.

Minutes later, Will's Ford sedan screeched to a halt outside my building. I jumped in and we peeled away, tires squealing. Will passed me his phone, the surveillance car's location pinging across the on-screen map.

"What do we know so far?" I asked.

"Nothing more than what we expected." Will's knuckles whitened as he gripped the steering wheel, his eyes locked on the road. "Black SUV, plates obscured, the surveillance team thinks there's just one person in the SUV but it's too dark and there's too much distance between them to be certain of anything."

I checked the phone. "They're heading out of the city." I gripped the door handle as Will pressed down harder on the accelerator. I leaned back in my seat as we turned off the highway, watching the streetlights grow sparse as we sped into a regional area.

"Turn left at the next juncture," I said, my voice barely above a whisper as I watched the pulsating dot on the screen.

Will barely slowed, taking the corner with ease. His driving skills had always impressed me and I knew he'd excelled at the FBI's TEVOC – the Tactical Emergency Vehicle Center – training program. We both had, but I sometimes thought Will could have been a Formula One Grand Prix racer in another life.

Five minutes later, we rounded a bend in the country road and the surveillance car came into view. In the distance beyond it, I could make out the lights of the SUV, but as my eyes focused, I suddenly became aware that the SUV lights were not moving and the distance between it and the surveillance car was closing. My breath caught in my throat. "Something's wrong."

"What is it?"

"The SUV seems to have stopped."

Will cautiously cut back on his speed. Seconds later, the sound of gunfire erupted and with its front tires blown out, the surveillance car ahead of us began to fishtail all over the road as it braked, skidding off to the side of the road, brushing against the wire fencing of a rural property, and then coming to a halt.

Will braked further as we reached the surveillance guys, who had stepped out of the vehicle and were unhurt. Will signaled to them that we were continuing the pursuit and he sped up, both of us able to see that the SUV was on the move again.

"We keep focused on those taillights," Will said. "If we even think they've stopped or slowed, I'll brake and maneuver to the side to avoid any shots."

The fencing gave way to woodland on both sides of the road, deepening the night beyond our headlights. Tall trees whizzed by in a blur, their dark-green shapes illuminated by the faint moonlight. If anything, the SUV's lights were rapidly growing smaller in the distance. Will increased our speed further but it was then, in the dark beyond our lights that I caught a glint of moonlight on something metallic.

"Will, slow down, something's on the road."

Even as I spoke and Will applied the brakes, whatever debris was littering the road came into sharper relief.

"Speed spikes," I said, bracing myself, my hands clasping the seat belt.

"Damn," yelled Will.

The tires shredded as we ran over the spikes and the Ford rattled violently, the world a blur of motion. Will fought to regain control but despite his efforts, the car spun wildly as we hurtled toward the trees. Will managed to narrowly avoid the first tree that loomed in our path but with a sickening crunch, we slammed into the next one, the impact jarring every bone in my body and my head banging against the passenger window as the airbags inflated, cushioning us.

Blood trickled across my forehead and into my eye. I turned to Will. "You okay?"

"Yeah." He pushed his door open and scrambled out.

My door wouldn't budge so I climbed across and crawled out after him. He grasped my hand, pulling me free.

"You're bleeding," he said, his voice strained with concern.

"I'm okay." We collapsed together on the forest floor, breathing heavily, and the cold earth that pressed against my cheek felt strangely calming.

"Damn," Will repeated.

Around us, the woods were quiet and still.

* * *

Will phoned for backup and we stood on the side of the road, waiting. Pacific silver firs towered over us in the darkness. The night air was cool and I rubbed my hands to keep warm, but the sense of dread that had settled in my chest made it impossible to feel any sense of comfort. I bit down on my lip at the thought of that black SUV streaking away to freedom. And the next victim.

When the police cruiser arrived, the driver-side window rolled down and I saw that Detective Radner had made the trip out here himself, his face weary but determined. "I'm starting to realize that you two have no idea how to keep regular hours."

His comment lightened the mood, albeit briefly, and Will clambered into the back while I took the front passenger seat.

"Have you been to the crime scene?" I asked.

"I was on my way there when your call came through, figured I'd make the detour."

Will filled him in on what had happened.

"Speed spikes?" Radner said, lines spreading out across his forehead as he glanced at me.

"Top-of-the-range product for security and law enforcement work," Will said and his jaw clenched with frustration.

Radner exhaled heavily but said nothing, the implication alone of the sniper having access to such equipment was louder than any spoken words. Moments later, Radner's radiophone crackled into life, the dispatcher reporting that a police chopper that had been sent to scour the area had not been able to sight the SUV.

My eyes met with Will's. It could have been anywhere by now.

Will leaned forward. "Paul, can we get an officer round to Thomas Rodwell's house? Keep an eye out to see if the SUV turns up there, and if not, if Rodwell's there and comes out of his house, as he normally would, in the early morning."

Radner nodded as he made the call. He seemed intent on keeping the mood in the car from getting too heavy. "I'm starting to feel like I'm a division of the Feds."

"We could do worse," Will said.

Radner shook his head, smiling.

* * *

We arrived at the crime scene and Will and I followed Radner under the yellow police tape that marked the perimeter. Cruisers and a forensics van crowded the laneway between the side of the transplant unit and a row of warehouses. A body, male and shirtless, lay on the cold concrete, limbs askew.

The medical examiner, Dr. Marla Liu, approached us and motioned to the body. "The family will need to make the official identification, but I can tell you it's the missing male nurse, Ryan Moreton. Like the others, a single gunshot wound to the head, no sign of the bullet. But that's not all."

She pointed to the carvings on the victim's skin — crude, brutal etchings mirroring a surgical cut where the heart, lungs, and liver should have been. Taped next to each hollow cavity were what appeared to be animal organs, their sickly stench permeating the air.

My stomach churned. "This matches the original *Snow White* tale from the page we found on Emily Yarros."

The chill of the night air crept up my spine and I couldn't shake the feeling this was more than just a message being sent by a twisted mind. This was a gruesome cat-and-mouse game and the killer had just upped the ante, big time.

I pulled on a pair of latex gloves and a coroner's mask and knelt beside Liu as she completed her preliminary on-scene examination of the corpse.

"Just like the others," she said over her shoulder, "he's holding a printed page." She gently pried open the corpse's stiff fingers, extracting a wrinkled page from a storybook.

I glanced at the German script. "Like clockwork. Another fairy tale." I swallowed hard against the bile rising from my stomach. Even through the mask, the scent of decay filled my nostrils, clinging to the back of my throat. "And there's a silver button in the other hand," I added, spotting the glint of metal.

I stood slowly and stepped back, watching, along with Will and Radner, as the forensics team began to transfer the body to their van. That was when I saw Brooke Goodman marching toward us.

"Don't tell me you've got sources or police scanners that alert you to something like this in the middle of the night," I said as she reached us.

"Okay, I won't tell you." She grinned broadly but her expression then morphed immediately back into deadly serious mode. "A third murder and my inquiries have indicated that all three of these deaths can be linked to details surrounding three murder victims in Tacoma. Are you investigating all six as the work of one killer?"

"We're taking each of those murders into account, yes," I said.

"So, we're talking about a serial killer, with an eighteen-month break between these groupings of murders?"

"That's one of our lines of inquiry, Brooke," Will said, his voice steely, "but we're not making any assumptions or jumping to conclusions this early on."

"Is it equally as possible these three recent murders could be the work of a copycat?"

"As Agent McCord said, we're not making any assumptions at this stage," I replied. "Every possibility is on the table and as you'd appreciate, we can't comment in any further detail about an ongoing investigation."

I was seething on the inside, not uncommon when I was confronted by reporters as zealous as my old friend, Brooke. But whether it was Brooke or another newshound, I knew damn well that the escalation of these murders meant there was no way to prevent the news from breaking big, with all of the unwanted attention that brought.

Chapter Eighteen

"We won't be getting much sleep tonight," Will said, glancing at his watch – it was 4 a.m. – as he killed the engine on the police vehicle he'd borrowed just for tonight. Once the new day was underway, he'd be organizing with the Bureau for a replacement to the Ford sedan, which we both knew would be a write-off. He'd pulled up outside my apartment building and the city lights cast a hazy blue tint over the street.

My muscles ached from the car smash but adrenaline still pumped through my veins, leaving me wired. "I'm not sure I'll be getting any sleep at all." I leaned back against the headrest, turning to look at him. His blue eyes were bloodshot with fatigue.

"I put your life in danger tonight." His voice was laden with guilt.

"You couldn't have known that maniac would litter the road with spikes." I waved toward him. "And Mr. Precision Driver here if anything, is responsible for *saving* my life."

He let out a long sigh, dragging a hand down his unshaven face. "Tonight's given me a real jolt, Ilona. Made me look back at this past month and realize how I've been keeping you and the team at arm's length, since…"

He didn't have to finish. We all knew how much he felt the absence of his good friend.

"We all have our own ways of coping with grief," I said, "and you needed time." I tried to sound reassuring without revealing just how thrilled I was that he was finally opening up.

"Maybe too much time," he admitted. "When we're on the job, a team deserves more than a leader who's put up a wall around himself."

"Strength isn't always about being stoic. Sometimes it's about letting others in." The words felt strange coming from my mouth, considering how guarded I tended to be myself, especially given the deep secret that I kept not just from Will and the team, but from everyone I'd ever known, a secret pursuit that had been like a drug to me ever since the time of my teenage kidnap.

"Words of wisdom," Will said. "I remember the night I opened up to you about how I'd been impacted, back in my teens, by my uncle's murder. I kind of lost it that night and you were there for me."

"And after, you felt stronger for letting out all that pent-up grief."

"It made a hell of a difference in here." He tapped his chest, his voice steady but filled with emotion.

The vulnerability in his gaze reminded me of the man I'd fallen in love with years ago. A vulnerability he showed rarely, and one I certainly hadn't seen in the two and a half years since our breakup. I felt a familiar warmth spread through me, a touch of the spark that had once burned between us. It was different now, of course. *We* were different, a little older, tempered by time and trials, but even so, once again I felt the stirring of that side to things. I tamped it down quickly, conscious this wasn't the moment for anything even remotely along those lines.

When I first joined Will at the UCU, he subtly indicated being open to rekindling the relationship we'd once had. I made it clear I wasn't interested. We'd both moved on and I knew our focus had to be on the new unit. As the unit's SSAC, Will didn't disagree with that point. He'd kept things professional, as I expected he would. That was Will McCord, always the by-the-book, never-let-emotion-get-in-the-way, consummate pro.

I was a little surprised, I guess, as we worked together, at how quickly the old camaraderie fell into place. As agents, we'd always worked well together, our differing approaches the perfect foil for one another. For one thing, I tended to be more impulsive which, granted, had seen me reprimanded more than once. But our instincts and our teamwork had been like slipping into an old glove.

It was getting harder to ignore the spark that was still there. I'd resisted it as being anything more than just that. A spark. But this past month or so, I hadn't been as sure about that. Times change. People grow. Seeing Will injured in a recent case, and the grief he was suffering over his friend, had me looking at things through a different lens.

"Holding things in would have brought back some bad memories, as well," I said.

He nodded. "I was very sullen after my uncle died, retreated into myself, and for a while there I became a whole different person. I remember I was sent to the school counselor, a guy named Dr. Jeremy Briskin. Young guy, very cool, the kids all liked him and called him Dr. J. He asked me what my earliest memories were of my uncle and I told him as a toddler I had trouble pronouncing 'uncle' and I used to call him 'uncoo,' I guess because it rolled more easily off my tongue, and I went on always calling him that. Dr. J. asked me what kind of man he was and the thing that jumped into my head was that my uncle had such a happy, sunny disposition, Dr. J. pounced on that, told me to always look around for the natural light in the world, to think of it as uncoo's sunny smile, and it would help me through the dark."

"Wow. That's a beautiful story, and a really good way to deal with grief."

"Ever since then, I don't know if I've ever said this out loud, but… well, you know I take a pretty optimistic view, and that's partly because, quietly, on the inside" – he tapped his temple – "I'm always looking for the light."

"But you'd stopped doing that, since…" I didn't finish the thought. I let my eyes search Will's, sensing he had something to add.

"I sank back into that dark place again, but then something triggered a memory of Dr. J. Those sessions with him came flooding back."

I smiled gently. "Sounds like we owe a vote of thanks to Dr. J."

"And speaking of good memories, you remember when we first became an item, we had a weekend away?"

"Of course, I remember. A little cottage by the ocean. Typical of us, hopeless workaholics, that we only went for a weekend instead of taking a whole week's vacation."

He rolled his eyes in agreement. "Yeah. Well, you remember that first night, we were up late, I think it was 3 a.m. and you said we should get some sleep?"

"Yep, and you said you wanted to stay up and watch the sun come up…" I stopped mid-sentence, a light bulb moment going off in my head. "That was this thing of yours."

"I didn't reveal it at the time, but yeah, ever since those teenage sessions with Dr. J. I've been an early riser, always starting the days by looking for the light."

"You're not going to suggest–"

He laughed. "No. With what's left of the night, we both really do need to get some sleep."

I stepped out of the car, noticing as I did a look of remembrance cross Will's eyes. "You're meeting with your friend Jill in the morning."

I nodded. "I might be a tad late getting in but I'll keep you updated."

"Okay." His eyes lingered on my face for a moment longer before he turned the ignition and with a wave, he pulled the car out from the curb.

Once inside, I felt all the energy drain from me the moment I sat on my bed. I lay back, still fully clothed, and the next thing I knew, it was a couple of hours later, and I was jolted awake by that damn phone. It was Jill, calling much earlier than I expected.

Chapter Nineteen

Day Three

The chill in the air stung my cheeks as I scanned the open rooftop of the parking garage. The city skyline loomed in the distance, a jagged silhouette against the early morning sky. Jill stepped out of my car and she paced beside me, arms folded tight against her chest. I had picked her up and driven here, making certain that there was no car, neither a white hatchback nor any other, following. Mine was the only car up here. Stan Avery had texted Jill this address, the top level of a parking garage on the east side of the city, where he parked his car every morning, so he believed his driving up here would not be viewed as out-of-routine by anyone watching. A place he considered safe from prying eyes. The reason for his heightened suspicions wasn't totally clear and I wanted to question him about that.

We had only been on the rooftop a few minutes when I heard an engine and Avery's vehicle, a tan-colored Toyota, drove up the ramp and pulled into a parking space.

Jill breathed a sigh of relief. "Good, he's here."

The driver's side door opened and Stan Avery appeared, his eyes locking onto us immediately. He began to walk toward us but just as he reached us and before he could utter a single word, a deafening crack split the air. Avery crumpled to the ground, a crimson stain spreading across his chest.

"Get down," I yelled, pushing Jill behind my car.

Panic clawed at my insides, but keeping low I scrambled to where Avery lay. He gasped for breath, blood seeping through his fingers as he clutched at his wound. His eyes, awash with shock, fear, and pain, met mine.

"Listen…" he rasped, struggling to speak.

Jill had crawled out from behind the car and she was beside me, clasping Avery's other hand, her face close to his. "Stan…"

He turned his gaze to her, and raising his head a fraction, he whispered something in her ear before his body went limp and his eyes dulled, staring at nothing.

Jill sobbed, saying, "No…" and I felt the anger surge up inside me. I rose on trembling legs, drawing my pistol, and I scanned the rooftop for any sign of the shooter. There, across the car park, on the far railing, a shadowy figure, watching, and now quickly climbing back over the edge, retreating down the outside of the building to the level below from which they'd climbed up, unseen.

"Stay here," I ordered Jill. "Call 911."

My heart pounded as I sprinted down the ramp to the level below, to where I expected the killer had climbed. As I rounded the corner, I spotted the shooter dressed generically in a construction worker's dungarees, jacket, and visored hard hat, stepping onto this level from the outside ledge. From this angle, I could see that the northern aspect of the parking garage was rigged with scaffolding, something that had made little impression on me as we'd driven up through several levels, but it gave this assassin the perfect method of attack, appearing as nothing out of the ordinary, a construction worker on a building's scaffolding.

"FBI," I shouted. "Freeze, and put your weapon down, and hands in the air." I got the only response I expected, with the killer disappearing back over the edge, climbing further down. I raced down the ramp, determined to get ahead of the killer and head them off, but as I reached the next level, I saw the sniper make an impossible leap across the divide to another sector of the multi-tiered garage. I bolted across the concrete to the far side of the level. The space between this tower of the building and the next was narrow, roughly three body lengths, the drop of several floors to the ground a fatal one. A greater leap than I would normally consider in my other, secret life but I instinctively believed I could cream this and if I didn't, the killer would be long gone. I had no doubt the killer had a vehicle somewhere out on the surrounding streets.

I holstered my pistol, gave myself some runway, and then ran, swinging onto the scaffolding and jettisoning myself across the gap, drawing on my secret climbing skills.

I was a little off in the speed and swing I needed, falling just short and grabbing the edge of the opposite railing with my hands, my body crashing against the building's wall and knocking the breath out of me. Lungs burning, breathing hard, I pulled myself up and over with a spurt of adrenaline, glimpsing as I did the figure in the distance, rifle raised.

I tucked into a ball and rolled to the side as bullets ricocheted off the concrete. With my pistol back in my hand, positioning myself behind one of the parked cars, I squeezed off a shot of my own. I wasn't expecting a hit – I was unable to get a focus on precisely where the killer had moved to – but hoped to force them to stop their fire and run. That, I could deal with.

Silence.

I peered out and saw just a flash as the sniper disappeared over the ledge of this level. Following over the side and climbing down to the next level wasn't an option, it would leave me too exposed to further gunfire, so I ran down the ramp, pistol at the ready, scanning the area ahead, this one littered with several cars. I moved stealthily from one of the cars to the next, wary the sniper could be behind any one of them.

Nothing.

I looked down over the edge for any sign of the killer climbing down to lower levels.

Nothing.

I took the ramp and made my way across the next level; more cars here, meaning more blind spots, but once again nothing to see.

The sniper was gone.

I caught my breath and cast my mind back over the past five minutes. And that was all it had been. Five minutes. Another thought gnawed at me: had the killer already been here because they knew Avery's routine, and had targeted him for death anyway, without knowing he was meeting with Jill and me? Was it because of what he'd learned on this case, or because of another case altogether, something unrelated to Jill's sister?

I raced back to the open top level. Jill was sitting, legs stretched out before her, and her back resting against the passenger side of my car. She was staring vacantly straight ahead, avoiding the body that lay just a few feet away.

I knelt beside her, my hand resting reassuringly on her shoulder. "Are you okay?"

She looked at me, in shock, as though she was looking at a stranger. "I caused this." Her voice wavered. "If I hadn't contacted him…"

"Jill, you couldn't have known anything like this would happen, and we don't know this is connected to your sister's case." I gave her shoulder a gentle squeeze. "Okay?"

She didn't respond.

"What did Avery say to you?" I asked.

She swallowed hard, tears shimmering behind her eyes. "He said, 'Safe.' Why would he say that? He knew he was dying. Did he think I'd be safe if he was dead? Oh, my dear God…"

I looked at the phone clutched in her hand. "You called 911?"

"Yes."

I heard the faint sound of a siren, growing louder. I steadied my breathing, my mind awash with thoughts, and the thought that was loudest in my head was that Stan Avery had been killed by a *sniper*-style shot. There was no doubt in my mind that Avery's investigation into Sam's disappearance, and his death on this rooftop, were both connected to the same crack shooter responsible for the six folklore murder victims. And in the split second when the shot rang out, Jill and I lost the chance to know what it was Avery wanted to tell us.

Chapter Twenty

I told Radner about Jill's hire of Avery as we watched the SPD forensics team examine the scene. This time we had a bullet for ballistics. I'd phoned Will minutes before, filled him in, but insisted he didn't need to come over. I was concerned that Jill was still in a state of shock, and I was having her escorted to the hospital for routine checks. After which, I was heading into the UCU.

Radner updated me on his officers' surveillance of Rodwell's house the past few hours. There had been no activity until Rodwell's garage opened and he drove out, in his SUV, heading to the bakery for his early morning delivery run.

It had taken around forty minutes in the middle of the night to get the police officer around to Rodwell's house, so there was a chance Rodwell — if he'd been the shooter on that country road — could have made it back to his home before the officer arrived there. The timing was tight but it couldn't be ruled out. But it meant we had no conclusive evidence pointing to Rodwell.

* * *

When I walked into Will's office, I brought him up to speed on Radner's report. Will expressed how relieved he was that neither Jill nor I had been hurt but his expression was granite-like, his eyes pools of worry.

"Marcia's with Zoe, they've got an update for us," he said.

In the operations room, Will and I pulled up chairs.

"I've checked with every antique silver dealer in the country," Marcia said, "and there are records of silver buttons from the Grimm Brothers era but not every buyer can be traced. Some of the buyers are known antique collectors, and I'm checking with those that I can, but nothing that seems suspicious, and nothing local."

"You think the buttons found on those victims were bought in Europe?"

"Most likely Germany, where they originated, and most likely several years ago."

"Good work, Marcia," Will said. "Keep digging back for anything on the buttons that link to our killer."

Zoe preceded what she had to say with a tilt of her head in my direction. "Your scuffle this morning may cast a whole new light on things," she said, "as does the discovery of the body last night. All of the folklore victims had their bodies interfered with but this most recent one, with three organs hacked out, is by far the most gruesome and indicates that the killer's savagery is escalating." She took a moment, allowing that point some space of its own, and then she continued. "With the discovery of the latest victim, Themis has run an analysis on the combined data thus far and highlighted that the murders of these people are following the same sequence as when they disappeared. Rayna Jackson, missing eight years, was the first victim found. Mark Foreman, missing seven years, was the next victim found. Wanda Smythe, missing six and half years, was next. Eighteen months later, Jack Corris, who disappeared five years ago, is found, followed by Emily Yarros, who was missing for four years."

"And it was the page held by each victim that provided the clue to where the next body would be dumped," I noted.

Zoe nodded. "Yes. So Jack Corris was the next in the sequence after Wanda Smythe, even though his murder didn't happen until eighteen months after hers. What this shows us is that the killer isn't deviating from this sequential order, even if it means a long gap between the killings. But why such a gap if the killer had abducted them in the first place? But if they weren't kidnapped and were evading this killer all that time, I'm wondering if it's because it took the killer that long to find the missing Corris."

"It also occurred to me," said Will, "that if these victims had gone into hiding because they knew there was a killer after them, as we speculated earlier, then it's also possible they had help. Otherwise, how did they all manage to disappear so effectively?"

I told the others about Avery observing the after-hours meeting between Detectives Tranter and Caulfield. "Given their separate involvement in all of these cases, I'm left wondering if they know more than they revealed when Will and I spoke with them."

"You think they could be involved in helping these people disappear?" Marcia asked.

"Well, it would tie in with Will's theory."

"Why would they do that? Wasn't Tranter the one who arrested them on the murder charges that were dropped?"

I shrugged. "I know it doesn't seem to add up, Marcia. But several of the victim's relatives didn't think Caulfield took the search for those missing people seriously enough. Now I'm wondering if he was holding back because he knew they didn't want to be found and knew that they would be in danger if they were. As for June Tranter, she was still investigating these people before they vanished. What if, in the course of her investigations, she became aware a killer was pursuing them?"

"But hold on," Marcia said. "Tranter and Caulfield are police officers, if they thought there was a killer after these people, why wouldn't they report that and instigate police protection for them? We know that didn't happen because I've established that none of the victims were in a protective custody scheme."

"Either way, the killer found those victims, wherever they were." Will turned his attention to me. "And it sounds like you're fearful that Jill's missing sister is now also a potential target of this killer, after what happened this morning."

"Sam fits the profile. Charged with murder, the charge dropped, and then she disappeared. What's different here, is that her sister, Jill, among other things, hires a PI to look into her disappearance, and that PI is gunned down, sniper-style, as were these others."

"But there are some big points of difference with that," Zoe pointed out. "Stan Avery wasn't a missing person who'd once been charged or suspected of murder, and he was shot, not through the head, but in the chest."

"That could have been deliberate," I suggested, "so that Avery's murder wouldn't be connected with the folklore killings. Or the killer was forced to deviate from their usual pattern to stop Avery revealing something he'd discovered."

Will was looking at me, his stare intense, ever since it had been after I'd told him, earlier, about the incident at the parking garage. I *hadn't* told him that I'd gone after the killer on my own, or about the leap I'd made across the six-story-deep gap between sections of the complex. Will, like everybody else, knew nothing of my other life.

"What concerns me now is that Jill Reiberger may not be safe," he said.

"I'm equally as worried about Jill," I said. "I'm going to suggest that she leaves town, goes home to DC, and leaves the follow-through on this to me. As a precaution. At this stage, we can't know for certain that Avery's murder was because of what he was investigating for Jill. He indicated to her last night that if he was being monitored, it could have been concerning another case he was working on."

"But you don't think it was?"

"No."

"Did he tell Jill what that other case was?" asked Marcia.

"He didn't." I took a moment, letting my thoughts settle. I refocused on the most recent victim. "The transplant unit's missing nurse, Ryan Moreton," I said, "ties in, as we expected, with the heart, lungs, and liver component of the *Snow White* tale, and the details Marcia dug up show he was under suspicion for a homicide. I glanced over that document, Marcia, but remind me, what were the finer details?"

Marcia pushed her seat closer to the console and brought up the appropriate portal on her monitor. "Okay, what the police report tells us is that Ryan Moreton was held on suspicion, without an arrest, for poisoning his husband, a man named Dorian King. King was a chef, who had, at the time, recently opened a restaurant, and he'd been the beneficiary of a hefty inheritance." Marcia took her time, scanning the report as she spoke. "As we might have expected, Moreton was the sole beneficiary of King's estate. The murder charge didn't proceed as it was established that King had prepared the meal that ultimately killed him, and Moreton didn't join him in that meal as he'd retired early with a migraine. The police reports show that neighbors confirmed the two of them had been having loud arguments for several weeks although Moreton denied this. The poison mixed in the meal was something that Moreton had purchased a week earlier, but it's a common household pesticide and Moreton told police he believed King had grabbed it accidentally, thinking it to be a spice that was in a similar-colored bottle. Moreton said that he didn't know how that bottle had been placed in the pantry, that either he or King could have done that accidentally."

"And the police bought into that flimsy excuse?" Marcia asked.

"There's not enough in any of that for the state prosecutor to be confident about a conviction," Will said. "I expect they were biding their time, looking for something more substantial with which to lay a charge."

"Who was the prosecutor?" I asked.

"Martin Elderson," said Zoe.

"And was one of the detectives that held and questioned Moreton, June Tranter?"

"Yes." Zoe tapped away at her keyboard. "And Rob Caulfield was the senior detective handling the missing person report."

"Have you been able to translate the passage found on Moreton's body?" Will asked Marcia.

"Yes. I can print you off copies," Marcia said, "and speak of the devil" – she motioned to the entryway through which Zach came striding – "I sent it on to Zach for his analysis."

"Looks like a serious poker face competition going on in here," Zach quipped, pulling up a chair and sliding it into position alongside the console, adjacent to Zoe. His quip didn't alter any of the others' facial expressions but I tilted my head in mock sufferance. He tapped his eyebrow and grinned at me. "I see you're still doing that *thing*."

Zach had some frivolous notion that I always raised my eyebrow as a mode of expression.

"What have you got for us, Zach?" I asked.

He held up a printout of the page. "This latest passage is from the final paragraphs in a Brothers Grimm tale, called *Brother and Sister*. It's a lesser-known tale than some of the others so you may not know it." He read aloud from the page, making a theatrical gesture as he did. "The Queen told the King how the evil witch and her daughter had committed great cruelty against her. So the King had them led before his court, and they were given their sentences. The witch's daughter was taken into the deep woods and left there, where she was torn to pieces by wild animals, while the witch was thrown into a fire and burned to death."

"Which is the clue," Marcia asked, "the witch's death or the daughter's?"

Zoe snapped her fingers. "The sequence in which the victims' bodies have been turning up should give us an answer." She turned her attention to her PC, tapping in commands. "Themis, who was the next person, released from a murder charge, reported missing after Ryan Moreton?"

Within seconds, Themis replied. "Maria Corvici. Reported missing two years and two months ago, in Seattle. Corvici was a cleaner, employed by the Wildlife Haven Zoo, in King County's east. She was questioned but never charged over the deaths of her housemates in a house fire in Maple Leaf."

"Could be either," Will said, clenching his jaw. "The zoo's a perfect analogy for the daughter's death by the wild animals, but the housefire points to the witch's fate."

"The killer isn't just escalating the savagery inflicted on the victims' bodies," Zach said. "I'd say the killer figured that investigators will have worked out how to unravel the clues by now, so is making it harder with the passages."

I exchanged a glance with Will, and I knew he was having the same thought as me. There had been an eighteen-month gap after the third Tacoma victim had been found. "Ryan Moreton is the third murder victim this week," I said. "But does that mean the next victim won't appear for eighteen months?"

"I don't think there's any way to be certain of that," Will said. "And these Seattle killings have less time between each of them than the Tacoma ones did."

I felt a stab of apprehension. "Themis, who is the next person in the sequence after Maria Corvici?" I held my breath, a vein throbbing in my temple.

"Sam Reiberger. Reported missing six months ago," Themis said.

I barely had a moment to ponder this when Zoe said, "Themis is highlighting some newly compiled intel."

"What's it about?" asked Will.

Zoe turned from the screen and glanced at us. "Not what, but who," she said. "Thomas Rodwell."

Chapter Twenty-One

"Themis has accessed school schedules of Rodwell's storytelling act," Zoe explained. A map appeared on the large screen above the monitors, and Zoe shaded an area. "Eighteen months ago, Rodwell did a two-week run of shows in the region shown. Tacoma. It coincides exactly with the time when the first three victims were discovered in the same area."

"Go on," Will prompted.

"Themis expanded the search parameters for anything on file statewide about Rodwell and homed in on this, archived at a suburban precinct. Fifteen years ago, in his early twenties, Thomas Rodwell was questioned about a series of creepy house break-ins."

"Theft?" I queried.

"No. The crime was breaking into the homes of unrelated families, taking photos of them sleeping, and then later leaving prints of those photos in those families' mailboxes with a message telling one of the adults living there to leave the area. Turns out the targeted adult was someone who'd recently been acquitted of a crime."

My chest tightened as I processed that piece of information. "Why did the police suspect Rodwell?"

"A neighbor up late with insomnia claims to have seen someone lurking who looked like Rodwell, and Rodwell, at the time, was a junior clerk in the courthouse where all those crimes had been prosecuted. But Rodwell's mother gave him an alibi and no photographic evidence was found on him. No charges were laid, and there were no further incidents of the type."

"What sort of crimes had these people been accused of?" Will asked.

Zoe took a moment, enlarging the archived report on her screen and zeroing in on the details. "All sorts. Car theft, domestic violence, house robberies."

Zach spoke up, his voice tinged with excitement. "It puts a whole different perspective on Rodwell. What if his actions way back then were just the beginning – an early attempt to act as a vigilante before he later graduated to murder, going after killers he believed had beaten the system." His voice sped up as he delved deeper into his thoughts. "Rodwell's a disciple it seems of the Brothers Grimm, obsessed with the morality in their tales, and he would know everything there is to know about them."

Zoe's PC pinged and Themis's voice sounded. "Additional intel being processed, Zoe."

Zoe navigated to another data stream. "Our search for any gun club names corresponding to the case details has highlighted Rodwell's name." She paused, eyes glued to the information. "He's a member of the same club that Elderson mentioned to Will and Ilona."

"We asked Rodwell if any of the members of his folklore group had an interest in guns," I said. "He didn't mention that he was a gun club member."

"Looks like we've now got more than enough to raise a search warrant for Rodwell's home," Will said.

Marcia picked up her phone. "I'm on it."

* * *

A judge granted our request for a warrant within the hour. Another fifty minutes after that Will and I stepped from an FBI vehicle in front of Rodwell's home address.

The sky darkened overhead, a forewarning of a storm coming in, and a steady spit of rain stung my face as Will and I approached the house across an expanse of unkempt grass.

Positioned at the end of an outer suburban street, backing onto woodlands, the house was a two-story, early twentieth-century Queen Anne, with a steeply pitched roof. Tall, narrow windows were set in a wooden exterior textured with clapboards and shingles, all showing signs of decay. Zoe had told us before we left that according to real estate records, the house had been in Rodwell's family for generations.

There was a multi-level stairway up to the front porch, and rows of gnome statues lined either side, leering from the overgrown lawn.

"Rodwell lives and breathes his fairy-tale world," I commented as Will rapped on the door, his knuckles producing a hollow sound that echoed on the other side.

No answer.

He gave it a moment and then knocked again, louder this time, and called out, "FBI."

More silence. Will allowed another moment and then as he was about to rap a third time, we heard a sound emanating from within the house, but not a sound we would have anticipated. An eerie wail, low and human-like, drifted from within, pierced for just a second by a high-pitched screech which caused the hairs on the back of my neck to stand on end. The wail faded away but it was as though the sound lingered in the air. I shot a glance at Will.

"No choice," he said and I nodded.

We both turned and sprinted to the car. Using force was a last resort but that was where we were at. In a matter of seconds, we'd retrieved a sledgehammer and a pry bar from the trunk. We returned to the front door, unsure what to make of the primal shriek we'd heard. With a determined series of swings, Will smashed the lock with the sledgehammer, while I used the steel bar to pry the weakened hinges. The door gave way and, guns at the ready, Will leading, we entered cautiously, eyes sweeping over the surrounds for any sign of movement.

My eyes quickly adjusted to the darkened interior. The living room was lined with bookcases and shelving, cluttered with books on folklore, with medieval-style figurines and statuettes littering every available space. It was as though every nook and cranny told a story. Heavy drapes covered the narrow windows, the air was heavy and oppressive, and there was a faint hint of incense.

We paused, taking in the layout of the first floor, a small kitchen adjoining the spacious living room to our right, a darkened hallway leading off on the far side of the room, alongside the wooden railing of a staircase. I had the unsettling sense of the walls closing in, and despite the wail from just minutes before, the house seemed enveloped now in suffocating silence.

"Watch the stairs while I check the rooms down here," Will said, but before he made a move, there was the sound of something being knocked over upstairs. "Change of plan. I'll check that out, you cover the entry and exits down here."

Will knew how to look after himself, but even so, my hands tightened on my Glock and my pulse raced as he ascended the stairs, which creaked despite the lightness of his steps.

I moved to the hallway, checking the small bedroom on the right, and a bathroom on the left, both small, both empty. Rising damp blackened parts of the walls. And then the haunting wail broke the silence again. It seemed to come from the far end of the hallway. I crept toward it, senses heightened. At the end of the hall was a door locked from the outside, the cry coming from behind it. I unlatched the lock and pulled open the door, revealing a dimly lit staircase. Once again, the wail faded to nothing.

Holding my gun out in front of me, I descended the staircase slowly, and a large basement room came into full view. It was musty, lit only by a lamp on a corner table, shadows stretching across a largely vacant space, an old sofa pushed against another wall, and an open door that led into another, darker area.

And then, without warning, I felt a sudden, crushing blow to the side of my skull as something heavy connected. The force sent me reeling, down onto the floor of the basement and darkness briefly engulfed me.

I came to with a groan, my head throbbing, each beat sending waves of pain through my skull. I blinked away the fog, the cold concrete of the basement floor pressing against my cheek.

"Will," I croaked, my voice barely a whisper.

Blinking against the dim light, my vision slowly coming into focus, I looked up. I caught sight of Will coming down the short stairwell, his pistol at the ready, his eyes widening as they met mine. I felt a surge of relief but it was short-lived. A hazy figure lurked in the gap between the stairwell and the wall behind it, and before I could warn Will, the figure swung something metallic – a saucepan, I realized –and smashed it against the side of his head. He dropped from the lower step, crumpling to the floor, and lay motionless, his gun clattering across the concrete.

I pushed myself to my knees, ignoring the fiery pain in my head. The figure that emerged from behind the staircase was an elderly woman in a simple, flowing smock, with skinny, ropey arms, frizzy gray hair across her face in scattered trails, her eyes blazing with hysteria as she glared back at me.

Her voice was like a hiss. "Wicked… wicked children…"

She'd dropped the saucepan from her left hand and as she raised her right arm, a sliver of light glinted off the long, serrated knife that she held.

I rose to my feet, holding out my upturned palm as a sign for her to stay where she was. "I'm Special Agent Farris. I'm not here to cause you any harm, ma'am, I'm only here to speak to Thomas Rodwell."

She bristled, her voice becoming shrill. "Wicked Thomas."

Who the hell was this crazed woman, and what was she doing down here?

"Ma'am, I need you to put down the knife and sit down. Can you do that for me?" I kept my voice firm and gentle but my words only seemed to agitate her further.

She rolled her head from side to side and stamped her foot as though she was in a world of pain. "You've been told, but you never, *ever* listen."

Her movements were erratic and unpredictable and then, the wail erupting from her, she lunged at me. I flung myself backward, barely avoiding the knife's arc. She charged again and this time I sidestepped, swiftly moving behind her, disarming her of the knife, and securing her arms behind her back with the set of cuffs I was carrying. She hissed, her body writhing in my grip, unnaturally strong for an elderly person of such frail appearance.

Will stirred, groaning as he raised a hand to his head.

"Will, are you okay?" I asked quickly.

He nodded, wincing as he probed the lump on his head. "I'll survive." He grabbed his gun and pushed himself to his feet as my eyes averted to the stairwell.

"It's okay," he said, seeing my concerned gaze, and he motioned to the floors above. "It was just a cat upstairs, knocking things over in fright."

The woman had gone still in my grip, muttering softly, and then, in a small voice, she said, "Who are you? Have you come to ask me about Thomas again?"

Another sound came from above. A car's engine coming to a stop outside.

I glanced at Will. "We've got company."

Chapter Twenty-Two

We moved up to the first floor and I sat the old woman on the lounge in the living room. She was quiet now, timid-like, her eyes darting about like a frightened bird.

Rodwell peered in through the open front door, his face registering his surprise as he saw us, his eyes narrowing. "Agents Farris and McCord? What the hell are you doing in my house?"

Will held up the warrant. "We have a warrant to search the premises."

"Search? Why? And why have you wrecked my door?"

The pounding in my head had subsided but my anger was at fever pitch. "You might want to tell us who this lady is and what she was doing locked in your basement."

The old woman glanced at Rodwell. "Tommy, you've come home."

Rodwell's tone was like ice. "This is my mother. She has dementia and I'm her carer."

"Carer?" I said. "You keep her in a locked basement?"

"My mother can become unhinged at times, and she can wander off outside and present a danger to others. I gather, seeing as she's in cuffs, you've seen what I'm referring to. When I'm out of the house, I need to keep her locked in, for her own protection."

"In your basement?" Will said through clenched teeth.

"It's not safe for me to leave her alone up here, or on the second floor. The basement is spacious, and there's a small bedroom as an annex." His voice rose. "But why are you here? Why do you need to search my home?"

Will ignored his question and asked him if he had been out in his SUV during the middle of the previous night.

Rodwell told us he'd been at home. Will then queried him on why he hadn't mentioned that he was a rifle owner and a member of a gun club.

"Gun club?" Rodwell's voice was on edge. "I don't own a rifle and I don't belong to any club." His eye twitched and he looked off as though there was something in his line of vision that he didn't want us to see.

"Can you explain why your mother was able to arm herself with a knife while she was in that basement?" I asked.

Rodwell sighed. "I've caught her before taking items down there and hiding them away. Do you know anything about this horrific disease? She can be sweet and unthreatening one moment, as she is now, and hysterical the next."

Will told him he needed to wait with his mother while he and I conducted a comprehensive search of the premises. Given she was now quiet and calm, I removed the cuffs from the woman. Rodwell sat beside her, clearly seething with irritation.

In one of the upstairs rooms, which seemed to operate as a study, with a desk, chair, PC, and lone calendar hanging lopsided on the wall, we found a folder in the drawer of the desk. It was bulging with printouts of the Brothers Grimm stories, with red ink highlighting the most gruesome passages.

Will blew out a breath in exasperation. "Everything we've found here, Ilona, is, at best, purely circumstantial. And there's no rifle. Nothing definitive that links Rodwell to the murders or serves as a motive."

I wrinkled my nose at the mustiness which pervaded the whole house. "One step at a time," I said. "We take this material, we get a statement from Rodwell on his whereabouts last night and the other nights the bodies were dumped, and we build the case. And right now, we get social services in here to assess the situation with Rodwell's mother and the conditions in that basement."

Seeing anyone in an advanced stage of dementia was distressing enough, seeing the cavalier attitude Rodwell displayed toward his mother only amplified that.

I would have to leave it to social services to deal with that but I had no doubt the woman would be removed from Rodwell's so-called 'care.'

We returned to the living room where Will probed Rodwell once again about a firearm.

"I've already said, I don't own a weapon of any kind," Rodwell said. "What is this all about?"

Will told Rodwell our belief that the killer was operating as some kind of vigilante. "You were questioned by police when you were in your early twenties," Will said, "about house break-ins and leaving warnings to people who'd been acquitted of crimes."

Rodwell sneered. "I was innocent and I was never charged."

Will ignored this and pressed ahead. "You were a county law clerk at the time, with first-hand knowledge of the court proceedings. Do you have a personal problem with people whom you believe are guilty, who beat the system?"

"It's not for me to say whether a person is guilty or not. I stand by the court's decisions."

"You didn't continue as a law clerk," I stated.

"I decided it wasn't for me."

"Eighteen months ago, you staged your Grimm performance at three schools in the Tacoma area," Will said. "It's only a forty-minute or less drive to Tacoma but we have records to show you stayed over at a motel for several nights."

Rodwell bristled. "I had a school in that area booked for each of four days in a row. It made sense to stay there as I had a week off from the delivery job and I had some friends there I wanted to catch up with."

"What about your mother?" I asked. "Who looked after her?"

"My mother's dementia wasn't as advanced at that point."

"You locked her in that basement for a week, didn't you?"

"No. And why does it matter if I stayed over in Tacoma, anyway? You can't think I'd have anything to do with these murders."

"We'll need the names of the friends you visited," Will said.

Rodwell complained of harassment as we left, glaring at me and Will as he was told that social services would arrive soon and that we would have further questions for him about his movements over the past couple of weeks and about the timing of his stay in Tacoma.

Even if Rodwell had visited friends during that stay, it didn't preclude him from having executed the kills and dumping the bodies during the nights.

* * *

Our next stop was the nearby Washington Handgun and Rifle Club, near Lake Washington. It was a sprawling single-level compound, with a member's club, bar, and eatery, with both indoor and outdoor shooting ranges. We were able to view the membership application signed by Rodwell twelve months earlier. Will took a photo and we would have a handwriting analysis done but I guessed that would likely be inconclusive. There had been no club sign-ins by Rodwell in the time since.

"No weapon in Rodwell's home and no apparent visits to the club," Will said as we walked back to the car. "So why join this club and why insist he didn't? And if he didn't, who did?" As he unlocked the car, he added, "I'll check whether Rodwell's early morning deliveries took him anywhere near the parking station where you and Jill encountered the shooter."

"Nothing about Rodwell adds up." I got into the passenger seat and my mind flashed back to the rooftop incident that morning. Stan Avery's dying words to Jill.

"I'll go and check in on Jill after this," I said.

Will nodded. "In the meantime, we need to find out a lot more about the cases Avery was working on and establish for certain, one way or another, which one was the reason for his murder, and whether it links to our folklore killer investigation."

"Avery chose the parking station rooftop because it's where he parked each morning," I said, "and his office is in the building adjacent. He suspected he was being watched but figured early morning at his regular parking spot was a safe time and place to meet with Jill."

Will was watching me closely as I furrowed my brow in concentration. "Go on."

"He had something to tell us, or maybe show us, but he didn't get the chance."

Will didn't start the engine; he kept his eyes on mine.

"He told Jill she was safe," I continued, "and she wondered why he said that, given there was a shooter on the rooftop." I took a breath, my thoughts crystallizing. "But his office was only minutes away. What if he intended to show us something in his office?" My gaze on Will intensified. "What if he wasn't telling Jill she was safe? What if he wanted to show us something in the building across the lane, locked in his office safe?"

Chapter Twenty-Three

Back in the office, I asked Marcia to get in touch with the superintendent of the building where Avery's office was located and arrange access to the office, and for an FBI safecracker to be made available.

I booted up my PC and checked the morning's news broadcasts. Brooke Goodman's broadcast topped all the search pages.

As I'd anticipated, this whole thing was already blowing up across the internet.

I navigated away from the news and I was about to phone Jill with my thoughts about the possibility of a safe in Avery's office when Will stuck his head around the corner.

"Initial ballistics report came back," he said. "A .38 caliber, consistent with the wounds on the other murder victims but compatible with a range of weapons, including a compact, lightweight sniper rifle with special ops-style precision."

I nodded slowly.

As Will headed back to his office, the Bureau receptionist called me to say I had a visitor.

A rookie agent escorted Steph Allsworth to my office and then left.

She still had the serious expression she'd worn in Martin Elderson's office but something in her manner was more relaxed, almost informal, although I was certain this wasn't a social visit.

"What can I do for you, Ms. Allsworth?" I asked, gesturing to the visitor chairs.

"It's Steph." A smile broke out briefly as she took a seat.

"Steph."

"There's something I thought would be of interest but I didn't want to mention it at the meeting yesterday as it concerns a member of the judiciary. Judge Malcolm Conrad."

"Go on," I said, intrigued.

"Judge Conrad is one of the judicial members who belongs to the Washington Handgun and Rifle Club. He's also a vet. Served for fifteen years from his late teens, after which he studied law and joined the DA's office. He was involved in an incident a few years back when he shot an intruder at his home. A burglar."

"What happened to the intruder?"

"They died. But because Conrad said the burglar aimed a gun at him, it was declared self-defense."

"No charges laid?"

"No. But Judge Conrad hasn't been in court for over six months now. Most people simply believe he's on extended leave. However, I have a friend, a lawyer involved with a judicial inquiry commission, who let it slip that Conrad is on suspension and undergoing counseling but it's all been kept very hush-hush."

"Why?"

"Six months ago, the judge brought a semi-automatic weapon into the building and kept it in his chambers."

"The judge wasn't screened electronically or manually for weapons when entering the premises?"

"It's not clear how he managed it, but senior judiciary aren't suspected of sneaking in concealed weapons. My friend says there's an inquiry into the US Marshalls Service staff responsible for the security breach but I don't know the outcome – as I said, I'm not supposed to know about any of this."

"What happened with the weapon?"

"Staff reported him after they saw him armed with it while he was watching the grounds from his window."

"Watching for what?"

"It seems the judge is suffering a recurring form of severe PTSD, and that he'd become paranoid that the criminals on trial in the courts were targeting him. All nonsense, of course. He was ordered to take stress leave and to undergo counseling, I gather with any charges deferred, while his mental health was further assessed. But

as serious as all of that is, it's not the sole reason I came to
see you today."

"Okay. What else?" I leaned forward.

"My legal friend said the judicial commission was
concerned about this history of PTSD but their own
inquiry into the judge was of a different issue – the fact
that the intruder to his home was known by police to be
associated with the Warburtons, a family who have been
under suspicion of criminal activities for years."

I steeled myself not to give anything away at the
mention of the Warburton name. "So, what are you saying,
Steph? That the commission suspects there was more to
the break-in of Conrad's home than a simple burglary?"

She nodded. Her hands were folded in her lap and I
noticed a slight tremor in them.

"You're nervous about telling me this," I said.

She acknowledged this with a sigh.

"Why didn't you want to bring this up in Elderson's
office?" I asked.

"Elderson and Conrad are, or rather *were*, golf buddies,
despite their age difference. And the monitoring of Conrad
isn't something I'm supposed to be aware of. Like I said,
my friend let it slip."

"Okay."

"To be honest, I've been mulling over in my mind all
night whether to come and speak to you about it. I'm
breaking all sorts of protocols and confidences. It's just
that with those murders and the victims all having been
crime suspects at some point or other... and with Judge
Conrad known to be an outspoken critic about court
leniency... There's probably nothing in it..."

"Leniency? He doesn't think the system is harsh
enough?"

"No. And he'd made a point of letting his thoughts be
known."

"You did the right thing coming to share those points, I appreciate it," I said. "And I appreciate as well that it puts you in a precarious position."

"You'll keep it just between us?"

"I'll have to discuss that with Agent McCord but you can rely on the two of us to be discreet."

The tension left her shoulders and her voice lightened. "Thank you. It's just that… hearing about those murders kind of got to me and I couldn't live with myself if I didn't tell you what I know. But I really do hope like hell the judge's PTSD and paranoia doesn't have anything to do with those killings." She took a deep breath. "I lost a friend of mine to a random crime of violence when I was young and I guess it's the reason I got involved with the law, and why I felt I couldn't stay silent."

"I can relate to that," I said.

She regarded me for a moment. "Your father was FBI. You're the girl who was kidnapped when you were in your teens. I can see how that might've led you into law enforcement."

"You know about that?"

"I thought I recognized your name when you came to Elderson's office, and after that I googled you and found some of the old news reports, and then of course, I remembered it. I'd followed the story at the time."

"It was a long time ago," I said.

"After my friend was killed, I went through a dark time," Allsworth said, "and then I took up kickboxing. I was always a sporty type and the kickboxing really helped, released a lot of tension, gave me something else to focus on."

"I can understand that," I said. "I'll make inquiries into Judge Conrad and if anything else comes to mind, you can be assured of my confidence."

Allsworth ran her fingers through her short, spiky crop of ginger hair. "Maybe, after this is all done and dusted, we could catch up for a coffee? Or something stronger?"

Her magnetic green eyes were set on mine and I had an inkling there was more to the invitation. "Maybe, but with this new unit, I won't have any time for socializing in the near future," I said in a noncommittal manner, not wanting to give her any ideas. I walked with her down to the front lobby and then I headed back up to the second floor and into Will's office.

"I've just had an interesting visit from Steph Allsworth," I said and related what she had told me.

Will tapped some numbers into his phone. "I know a guy at Vet Affairs, Hugh Sawyer, although it's a while since I've had any contact with him. Let's see what he can tell us about Judge Conrad."

I listened to Will's side of his exchange with the Vet Affairs man and although I didn't know what the other man was saying, I could tell from Will's expression that it wasn't good.

Ending the call, Will said, "The judge didn't attend his counseling session yesterday, he hasn't been answering his phone, and he isn't at his city apartment. Sawyer's concerned about his wellbeing and he's on his way to check on him at the judge's country property in Snohomish County, where he spends some of his time." Rising from his chair, Will grabbed his jacket. "We're meeting Sawyer out there."

Chapter Twenty-Four

The gravel crunched beneath our tires as we pulled up to the wrought-iron front gates of Judge Conrad's country estate. Will parked the car, and I couldn't help but take a moment to appreciate the breathtaking view of the surrounding forest, the towering trees stretching toward the sky as though they were the judge's own private line of sentries.

"Quite a place he's got here," Will remarked, his eyes scanning the imposing house nestled amongst the greenery.

"How the other half lives." I stepped out of the car with a sense of unease settling in my gut. How did Judge Malcolm Conrad figure into what was going on, if he even figured at all?

We were greeted by Hugh Sawyer, who approached us from where he'd parked his car further along the perimeter of the property. He was a tall, well-built man with a stern expression that mirrored my growing concern. There was an unlocked side gate and we went through, approaching the house. I tried to keep my disquiet in check, but for some reason my spidey sense was making its presence felt. Ever since my teenage kidnap all those years ago, I'd had something of a sixth sense, acutely aware of anything and everything in my periphery. Will had always been aware of this and, sensing the build-up of tension, he gave me a reassuring nod.

A shout broke the silence.

"Stay back," a gruff voice bellowed.

The front door opened and the judge stepped onto the wide porch, his grizzled, unshaven face set in a scowl. He raised his rifle and aimed it squarely at the three of us. Will, Sawyer, and I all knew that a vet struggling with PTSD, even many years after their service, could turn volatile very quickly, and we were now seeing that play out.

"Judge Conrad," Will called out, his voice steady despite the threat, "I'm Special Agent in Charge McCord, and this is Special Agent Farris, and you know Hugh Sawyer here. We're simply here to check that you're okay."

"Get off my land." The judge's finger twitched on the trigger. I could see the paranoia in his eyes. "I've told you people to leave me be."

I noticed that Hugh Sawyer had taken a step back, beads of sweat glistening on his forehead.

"Will, let me try to calm him down," I whispered.

Inhaling deeply, I stepped forward before Will could protest, raising my hands to signal to Conrad that I presented no threat.

"Judge Conrad," I called out, "I'm Ilona Farris. Agent McCord and I could use your help on a case we're working on." As I spoke, I withdrew my Glock from its holster, calling out to him that I was disarming myself. I raised the gun in the air before placing it on the ground in front of me. "I'm unarmed and I simply want to talk. Can I come in?"

The judge hesitated, his rifle aimed at me. His eyes darted between Will, Sawyer, and myself, as though trying to gauge our intentions. For a moment, I held my breath, praying that he would see the sincerity in my gaze. And then, just as I was starting to lose hope, Conrad motioned for me to come closer, now aiming his rifle squarely at Will and Sawyer.

"You two stay right where you are," he said. He turned to me. "Okay, just you," he said, his voice softening just slightly, "and no sudden moves, missy. But know that I don't trust you. You're law enforcement, so as far as I know, you're probably part of the plot to silence me – to make me disappear."

"Judge, I assure you that's not the case." I kept my tone calm as I stepped over the threshold, taking in the dimly lit living room. The room was cluttered but tidy, with a long, wide mantelpiece lined with framed photos from Conrad's military days. His sharpshooting medals were prominently displayed.

I turned to face the judge. His eyes were hard, his posture rigid. If paranoia had an expression then it was the one I now saw spread across his face.

"Okay, missy, say your piece."

"There have been six murder victims, all shot from long range; three in Tacoma eighteen months ago, and three just this past week in Seattle," I said. "All the victims were criminal suspects who either hadn't been charged or who had charges against them dropped. The shots were expertly placed, quick, and efficient, and the bodies were removed and dumped elsewhere. The skills fit the profile of someone with military-style sniper training."

Conrad's jaw tightened. "And you think it's me? Are you out of your goddamn mind?"

I lifted my palms placatingly. "I'm not accusing you. But I hoped you might have insights into who could be behind this. Maybe someone you served with shares your views on the justice system?"

"My views?" His voice was a growl. "You mean how our broken system lets monsters walk free every damn day because of outdated processes, errors, and woke, leftist leniency?" He lowered his rifle, his left hand clenched into a fist in frustration. "I speak out about it and the next thing I know, I'm being targeted. They've tried to blacken my name, saying I'm involved with a crime family, who sent someone to kill me because I'd had a falling out with them. All BS. I've never had anything to do with those lowlifes."

"I know about that," I said. "That was the burglar you shot."

"Self-defense, plain and simple. And pure coincidence that the burglar had an association with this family, the Warburtons. I've had phone calls from others, who've kept their mouths shut but who are working under the radar to get the message out about the rot in the system. They've warned me about the conspiracy against me, just as they warned me about you people coming out here today."

"Who's been calling you?" I asked.

Conrad didn't seem to hear my question, he kept talking, swept up by his anger. "I'm not your vigilante shooter and I've never known anyone who would go out on a murder spree. But I can understand what the shooter's trying to achieve. Trying to deliver the justice our courts have failed to provide."

My earpiece crackled to life, Will's voice coming through. "Ilona, Sawyer has reported the incident. Police vehicles are en route. I'll try and keep them at bay but you need to keep Conrad calm and assure him it's routine procedure and that he's under no threat."

"Judge," I interrupted the voice in my ear, my eyes on Conrad. "You have my word I'm not here to cause you any grief, but I don't believe for a moment that your colleagues are part of any conspiracy to silence you. Our legal system may not be perfect, but we live in a democracy, we can instigate change. Surely, though, you'd agree that neither you going off the grid, nor that vigilante shooter out there, is the way to achieve your goal of improving the system."

Conrad's expression shifted from anger and frustration to something resembling contemplation, his eyes narrowing as he considered my words. I could sense the gears turning in his mind. Deep within, behind the paranoia, was a practical, logical brain, battered down by the sheer weight of his post-traumatic stress disorder. Was he the folklore killer? He matched the profile... but something wasn't right. We needed a thorough search of his property for any evidence that would incriminate him. Either way, I had to get him safely into custody.

A distant wail of sirens echoed through the air, sooner than I'd hoped, and I saw a wave of change flit across Conrad's face, turning his expression to one of panic. Raising his rifle again, he moved quickly to the front window. We both looked out, catching sight of the approaching police vehicles.

He shot me an angry glance. "And to think I was beginning to trust you."

"Judge, this is purely a standard police response, you know that. You aimed a rifle at federal agents and your Vet Affairs rep. You know the law. But we can sort this out calmly and peacefully."

"I was warned they were coming for me." He took up a position, opened the window, and aimed his rifle through it.

I stepped toward him, placing my hand gently on his left arm. "Judge, please, take a moment. Think about what you're doing."

His reaction startled me. He lowered his rifle, half-turned, and with a sudden, swift motion, he lashed out with his left arm, knocking me off my feet. I crashed backward onto the wooden floor and Conrad aimed his rifle point-blank at my chest.

"I've had it with being fooled by the so-called good guys," he said and the vacant look in his eyes chilled me to the core.

My mind raced, searching for something that would reach him. My gaze took in the photos on his mantelpiece. "Your buddies from your army days wouldn't approve of you shooting an unarmed FBI agent. This isn't you, Judge. Look into my eyes, for God's sake. I'm simply here to get your help with a case. We're on the same side." I could barely hear myself speak over my heartbeat pounding in my ears.

His finger rested on the trigger but I forced myself to maintain direct eye contact with him, hoping to reinstall the communication we'd had just minutes before. Slowly, his grip loosened, and he lowered his rifle, his eyes filled with a mix of fear and confusion.

"Put aside the weapon, put your hand in mine, and we go out that door together. Safe," I said, my voice firmer now.

Neither of us moved and Conrad simply stared back at me, barely even blinking. It seemed like an age passed before Conrad nodded reluctantly.

I got to my feet slowly, eased the rifle from Conrad's hand, and took his hand in mine. "Trust me, please," I said softly. "My partner and I have got this under control."

There was no response but the anger had drained out of his face.

I maneuvered him to the front door and we stepped out onto the porch, his grip tightening in mine. The late afternoon sun momentarily blinded us which was probably a good thing because it took away the immediate view of the police officers, beside their vehicles, their weapons raised. I squinted and glimpsed Will directing them to hold their fire.

They knew I was FBI but even so, to reinforce the point, more as a show of strength to the man beside me than for any other reason, I raised my credentials into the air, the sun glinting off my badge.

"Lower your weapons," I called out. "We're coming out and we're unarmed."

Conrad's breathing grew rapid. I could feel panic swelling in him, threatening to boil over again as the paranoia fought its way back to the surface.

"All good, Judge," I whispered to him. Turning my attention to the officers again, I yelled, "Stand down. I have this under control and there is no threat here; I repeat, there is no threat here."

Keeping a slow and even pace, I led the judge down off the porch and across the wide frontage of the property, keeping to the gravel driveway that ran from the gates. As we reached the spot where Will and Sawyer waited, Sawyer, with police officers bringing up his rear, came forward and spoke with Conrad. Letting go of my hand, Conrad shifted into a different persona.

"What is this all about, Hugh?" he said indignantly, as though his memory of the past few minutes had been erased.

I remained close as he was persuaded to join Sawyer and one of the officers in getting into Sawyer's car and heading into the city with the other police vehicles following.

Will gave me a brief embrace. "Despite all the time we've worked together," he said, "you still never cease to amaze me."

"Part of my charm. But I'm not Superwoman, my nerves are a little frayed. I could use a stiff drink."

Will grinned and we both took a moment to catch our respective breaths and steady ourselves.

"I think we deserve a stiff drink," he said.

* * *

One of the new, upmarket hotels in the city was exactly the right place. From its trendy cocktail bar, we had the perfect vantage point to take in the sights of Seattle harbor. The scent of freshly muddled herbs and citrus wafted through the air as we settled onto the balcony, our glasses glinting in the fading sunlight. From this height, we could see the bustling city streets below and the sparkling water stretching out into the distance. The sound of clinking glasses and laughter filled the air. Will relaxed even further and surprised me by showing his sentimental side. He told me about his recent visit to his retired parents in Florida. He'd been pleasantly surprised that his father had shared more than a few memories of his younger years with Will's now-deceased uncle. That uncle, a storeowner, had died when a robbery at his store had ended badly and over the years Will had been frustrated that his father bottled his grief up, never speaking about Will's uncle. But the years pass, and our behaviors change and evolve, and during this visit, Will's father finally opened up.

We were on our second beer, thinking about ordering a meal, when my phone rang. It was Marcia. "I've got the superintendent at Stan Avery's building, and our safecracker, organized to meet you there tomorrow morning."

"Thanks, Marcia." I wondered whether I was on the right track about Stan Avery's safe and I said as much to Will. And if I was right, what was in there – what had Avery wanted to show us?

Chapter Twenty-Five

It was a very different kind of bar that John Raye stepped into, a couple of hours later, in a suburb on the outer rim of the city; a run-down, older-style establishment that seemed to be in a standoff with the newer buildings in the area. It was the kind of place that had long ago given up on attracting an upmarket crowd, if, in fact, it ever had. The neon sign, half burnt out, cast its glow over the cracked sidewalk. Inside, the air was thick with the scent of stale beer and the low hum of tired conversations.

Raye slid onto a stool at the counter, the vinyl creaking under his weight. The bartender, a man whose age was as indeterminate as his faded tattoos, gave him a wave.

"Evening," Raye muttered, his voice rough around the edges, "a beer, please, Grizz."

"Coming right up," Grizz replied – it was the name by which Max Griswold had long been known – and he pulled a glass from beneath the counter.

As he waited for his drink, Raye took in the familiar surroundings. The walls were covered in faded pictures and posters, most of them depicting local bands or events long gone. The furniture was worn and stained. There was a small group of rowdy blue-collar workers in one corner, a couple engrossed in a heated conversation in another, and an older man sitting alone at the far end of the bar, nursing a glass of whiskey like a character from a Billy Joel song. This was more like home to Raye than his own low-rent apartment.

Grizz set the drink in front of Raye, the foam kissing the rim but not spilling over. "You look like you've been through the wringer, Johnny."

Raye took a long pull of the beer, feeling it wash down the grit of the day. "Had a recent visit from the Feds," he said, keeping his tone even.

"Ah, the Feds," the bartender snorted, polishing a glass with a cloth that had seen cleaner days. "Wouldn't trust them as far as I could throw them. And what was all that about?"

"They think I could be in some sort of danger." Raye's fingers tightened around the glass, the cold sweat on its surface mingling with his own. There was a weight in his pocket, a small shape that pressed against his thigh – the panic button, courtesy of federal paranoia. He made a conscious decision to keep that detail to himself.

Grizz set the polished glass aside, his furrowed brow showing his concern. "What kind of danger are we talking about here?"

"Recent killings," Raye said, taking another sip of his beer, "and they've got an inkling that I might be next on the list." His gaze didn't waver from the glass of amber liquid.

"Killings?" The bartender's eyebrow arched. "Who would have it out for you?"

"The feds don't have a name," Raye replied, his voice a low rumble. "But if you're asking me, I wouldn't put it past the Warburtons."

The bartender paused mid-wipe, the rag in his hand twisting. "From what I've heard, you can't trust them either." He leaned closer, his voice dropping to a conspiratorial whisper. "As you know, this place sees all sorts come through those doors, and I've heard more than a rumor or two about that family."

Raye nodded slowly, absorbing the weight of the bartender's implications. Grizz knew about the murder charge that had been dismissed against Raye several weeks ago. Raye didn't feel the need to elaborate on why he thought a threat might come from Monty Warburton. Grizz got the drift. Raye ordered another beer and he and

Grizz talked about some of the stories that had circulated about the Warburtons over the years. Raye lamented that he'd done jobs for them and the evening wore on.

Much later, the chill of the night wrapped around Raye as he stepped out into the dimly lit street, leaving behind the dubious sanctuary of the bar. The suburban sprawl of outer-city Seattle spread before him, its streets quiet and seemingly innocuous. But tonight, the familiar route home was laced with an undercurrent of unease.

Raye's hand dipped into his pocket, fingers grazing over the smooth contours of the panic button. He had the disconcerting feeling that the agents had been right.

Each step he took was shadowed by doubt. Was their warning genuine concern or psychological manipulation? He wondered if those agents had another agenda. His mind flickered back to the Warburtons. Would they really come after him, now that the murder charge had been dismissed, even though he suspected they were the ones who had set him up for it in the first place?

The silence of the neighborhood was oppressive, punctuated only by the occasional distant bark of a dog or the whisper of wind. Raye couldn't shake a sense that the darkness was alive, watching him with unseen eyes.

A sudden movement – a fleeting shadow darting just at the edge of his vision – sent a jolt of panic surging through him. Raye stopped mid-stride, heart pounding. He spun around, searching the empty street for the source of his alarm. Nothing but the dance of tree branches in the glow of the streetlights.

He took a deep breath and resumed walking. Maybe he needed to give this nightly ritual of his trip to the bar a miss for a while. Just to be on the safe side. Or maybe he shouldn't be letting the anxiety get to him.

And then another darting shadow – a shape, swift and elusive, disappearing around the corner ahead. His instincts screamed at him to run, to flee the open vulnerability of the street, but a wobble in his legs held him back.

He forced himself to walk, each step quicker than the last, glancing from one darkened window to another, expecting at any moment to see a face peering back at him. The distance to his apartment, usually a short trek, seemed to take a hell of a lot longer.

By the time Raye reached the relative safety of his modest apartment, his breath came in shallow gasps – not entirely from the brisk pace he'd set. With a final glance cast over his shoulder, he slipped inside, locked the door behind him, and wondered if he was safe even in there.

Chapter Twenty-Six

I crept along the edge of the roof, my fingers curling over the gritty concrete lip. Far below, Seattle glittered like a box of jewels, the lights of skyscrapers and streets forming abstract patterns. Up here, it was just me and the stars of the night sky.

A police siren wailed in the distance. I paused, listening, muscles tensing. The wail faded as the police vehicle headed toward the other side of the city. The intensity of the siren reminded me of Judge Conrad's paranoia, powerful and all-consuming one moment, dropping away slowly the next as I distracted and calmed him. What had caused his paranoia to spike like that? I recalled his words. "I've had calls warning you were coming for me." Had he been receiving calls from like-minded activists, or was that just another aspect of his paranoia?

Even now, all these hours later, my confrontation with the judge had a lingering effect, putting me on edge, and I had given in to my secret addiction, taking to the rooftops.

Clearing my mind, I reached up and gripped the rusty fire escape ladder that stood where the roof on this level rose to the roof of another tier. I needed this – the physical challenge, the height, the complete focus of mind and body that urban climbing demanded. I'd climbed this building so many times I knew every handhold by heart. At the ladder's top, I stepped onto the flat roof, breathing hard. Seattle sprawled below, so peaceful from this vantage point. Up here, the problems of the city seemed small and distant and I did a slow spin, taking in the 360-degree view. The Space Needle pierced the sky, its halo of light brighter than the stars. The dark expanse of Puget Sound stretched to the horizon.

My eyes traced the jagged skyline and my thoughts were drawn back to the climb that had started it all. I was fourteen years old, trapped in the narrow confines of a box and consumed by panic. What my kidnappers didn't expect was that I would shift the heavy lid of the box and that I was crazy and desperate enough to attempt climbing the deep, body-width shaft that rose from the subterranean chamber to the world above. What I didn't know at that stage was that I was deep within an abandoned nuclear plant construction site. To this day I don't know how, with my heart pounding, my nerves at screaming point, and my body enveloped with sweat, I'd made it more than halfway up that shaft. I couldn't have made it much further and the fall would have killed me but FBI agents had found the spot and they arrived on the level above in time to get help down to me.

That climb was a memory to me that represented taking control. I'd started urban climbing, despite its illegality, and ever since, it gave me an exhilarating sense of freedom that only came from being high above the world. Here, I was untouchable.

I thought about the hour I'd spent with Will earlier in the evening. Our partnership at the UCU had brought us closer again on a personal level, a repeat in some ways to what happened years before when we'd been agents in the CCRSB – the Criminal, Cyber, Response, and Services

Branch – and I couldn't continue to deny that I was open to rekindling our relationship at some point.

But if that were to happen, there couldn't be any secrets, and the thought of revealing my hidden side filled me with a sense of dread. Will tended to see the world in black and white; gray areas, not so much, and my urban climbing was about as gray an area as you could get. It would also put Will in the difficult spot of having to report what he knew of my activities. I swallowed hard against the sudden tightness in my throat. This was one secret better left unsaid, and putting a stop to these climbs once and for all was the best – the only – real option.

I began my descent, leaving the rooftops behind and returning to the reality of the world below.

As my feet touched down on the pavement, I saw a hooded figure in the distance, standing at the entryway to the alley. I was certain they hadn't been there when I'd begun my climb down; I always scanned the immediate area to make sure it was clear. The figure was not beneath one of the streetlights so was hard to see clearly and they were clad in a heavy-duty jacket with a hood.

"Hello, Ilona."

My heart thudded in my chest. "Who is it?" I called out.

I started to advance but the figure's arm raised and I caught a glint of light touching the metal of a pistol in their hand.

The voice that replied was heavily muffled. "Freeze. Now."

I stood still. "You're threatening a federal agent."

"You won't tell anyone. Wouldn't do your career any good if your little urban climbing fetish got out." The voice was louder now and I could tell there was something over the mouth, maybe a heavy cloth or a voice-distortion device, making it raspy and unnatural. "Leave this case alone and no one has to know about your nighttime activities."

"You need to tell me who you are and what this is about."

There was grit in the tone. "Take this seriously. You won't like the alternative."

Still aiming the gun at me, the figure inched backward, past the entryway, and then turned into the street, disappearing behind the buildings.

I ran forward, slowing as I reached the alley's end, conscious I didn't have my Glock on me. Tentatively, I peered around the corner. The street was empty. No sign of the hooded figure, no sign of a retreating vehicle. Nothing except the lonely glow of the streetlights across the darkened street.

I swallowed hard. Someone knew my secret. And they knew exactly how to use it against me.

Chapter Twenty-Seven

Day Four

My phone buzzed and I grinned to myself when I saw the caller ID. "Hi, Joe," I said.

"Hey, Ilona, I know it's early but I thought I'd check in before you got immersed in all that FBI crap, and see where you're at."

There was something about Joe Christie, a fun-loving, thrill-seeking, larger-than-life presence I couldn't help but banter with. "I'm at home, about to leave for some FBI crap, and I don't *check in* guests."

"Not a hotel." He completed the joke with a hearty laugh. "I'll rephrase. Have you checked out those links I sent you?"

"A couple of them."

"And what floats your boat? The rock climbing, the mountaineering, the rope swing jumping?"

"All of the above," I said.

Joe ran an adventure sports club that took people out on weekends to learn a range of skills and indulge in extreme activities. The previous week I'd been along to one of the introductory lectures he gave to potential customers. If I was going to beat my dangerous and illegal urban climbing addiction, then spending some of my free time with Joe's outfit was possibly something that could fulfill my need. A different kind of rehab.

"Tell me more about the rope swing jumping, I'm less familiar with that."

"Well, firstly, it doesn't have to be as extreme as those YouTube links I sent, with crazy-ass guys, like me, rigging up ropes and swinging over chasms with thousand-foot drops. Mostly, we're swing-jumping across accessible spots with much shorter, non-fatal drops. However you do it, though, I can tell you it's a lot more fun, a much greater challenge, and a lot less dangerous than, say, bungee jumping."

"Then it ticks at least three boxes," I said.

"We can tick a whole lot more than that."

"Anyway, leave it with me, Joe. I need to give it some more thought and see how my time pans out. Right now, I'm in the middle of a case."

"Today, yeah. But on weekends, as well?"

"It's pretty much a 24/7 thing, at the moment."

"All work, no play. Scrolling through data, and sitting in cars drinking coffee."

"Sometimes we chase bad guys."

"Now you're talking," he said.

I ended the call, still smiling. I carried my breakfast coffee with me, over to my laptop, and clicked on one of those YouTube videos; this one from Joe himself, a tutorial on prepping ropes for a swing jump. Joe's operation might just be the ticket. Especially now, not only because of how I felt keeping a secret from Will, but because someone out there was threatening to expose me. I shuddered at the thought of those two things colliding.

I shut down the laptop, grabbed my keys, and headed out the door.

* * *

The stale scent of old cigarettes and dusty papers filled the air as I stood in Stan Avery's dimly lit office, Jill by my side.

"Alright, ladies, stand back," Reed said gruffly, his massive frame moving ahead of us toward the safe.

The FBI's best safecracker was an imposing man who looked like he belonged on a construction site rather than in this cramped office. He crouched down, pulling out an array of instruments that glinted under the overhead light. He expertly maneuvered his tools, the clicks and scrapes echoing in the small space. Moments later, I heard the metallic click of the final tumbler sliding into place and Reed stood up and stepped back, glancing at me.

"All yours, Agent Farris."

A man of few words. I nodded toward him as he headed for the door.

Eager and on edge, Jill barreled forward and squinted as she gazed into the open safe. There was just one single plain manila folder, unmarked, sitting on the steel base. Jill removed it and handed it to me.

Flipping it open, I found several grainy surveillance photos, all depicting the same sprawling country estate nestled amongst the trees of a manicured yard, behind a steel gate. In each of the long-range photos, two figures were talking on the front steps.

"What on earth is this about?" Jill wrapped her arms around herself, face pale. In that moment, she looked both confused and disappointed. "Vague photos of some country retreat?"

"Hold on," I said quietly. "There are handwritten notes here."

Jill's eyes were fixed on mine as I scanned the notes. "Listen to this," I said, and I then read aloud from Avery's handwritten scrawl. "I took up a spot to watch Jill's motel, in the hope I might spot whoever has been trailing her. And it worked. I sighted the white hatchback follow her back to the motel and then park down the street. The driver kept watch for a couple of hours. I saw Agent Farris come and go. When the hatchback left, I followed, keeping my distance, and these are the photos of the estate in Leavenworth it went to…" I paused, returning my gaze to the photo at the back of the pack, giving it closer scrutiny. And there I saw it, in the corner, partly obscured by a tall tree.

"What is it?" Jill asked.

A white hatchback. I put the photo in front of Jill, my finger pointing to the car.

Jill nodded, her eyes wide with alarm.

I continued reading from Avery's notes. "Unfortunately, I was unable to see the license plate of the car in the photo but I'm running a check for the listed owner of the estate."

"Is that it?" Jill said.

"Yes."

"Why would he leave his note at that point with nothing further?"

I clenched my jaw, trying to piece together what had been in Avery's mind before his death. "I'd say Avery printed off these photos and wrote that note to include in his case records, the night before our meeting, intending that by the following morning he'd know who the property's owner was."

"And he'd tell us that in person while showing us what he'd already collected," Jill surmised, "except…" Her mind veered off in a different direction. "Has he written down the address?"

"No."

"So, we only know this estate is somewhere in Leavenworth?"

"Taking a drive around that area, it shouldn't be too hard to spot the estate from these photos," I said.

Jill was breathless in anticipation that we were getting close. "I guess it's worth a shot."

"It's the best shot we've got right now," I said.

Chapter Twenty-Eight

The thick forest whizzed by as Jill sped down the winding country road. Evergreen trees towered overhead, their branches intertwining at regular intervals to block out the pale sun. Leavenworth was a picturesque area, nestled in the heart of the Cascade Mountains, but I didn't let the breathtaking scenery distract me from the task at hand. We were in my car but I'd suggested Jill drive while I compared the properties we passed with the photo on my phone.

"Damn it," I murmured, and not for the first time. "They all look so similar."

Jill nodded, her grip on the steering wheel tightening in frustration. "No argument here."

Two hours had passed and we were no closer to finding the property. As we followed the road around another sweeping bend, I gazed out at the forest, which seemed even denser here, as though it was casting a veil of protection over the place we were looking for.

"We might not be going around in circles but it sure feels like it," Jill said. "Maybe it's time to head back to Seattle."

"Maybe I was overly ambitious thinking I could make this work," I admitted, rubbing my temples, tiredness taking hold. "I expected it would take a while but I thought we'd be able to recognize the place from Avery's photo, but maybe it's not as simple as that."

I was about to instruct Jill to turn around but the words stuck in my throat. I wasn't quite ready to give up. Regardless of what case I was working on, I always thought that the next clue or sign lay just around the next corner, that methodically piecing together one piece of a puzzle after another would ultimately yield a breakthrough. "We've made this much of a commitment, Jill. Let's give it another half hour, surely there's a spot we haven't covered yet."

Jill sighed but I could tell from the determination on her face she didn't disagree, she was as intent as I was, more so, to find any clue as to what had happened to her sister.

Another five minutes passed, then ten, and my gut churned with anxiety. I'd wasted time and led both Jill and myself on a fool's errand. We passed a few more properties, stopping briefly, as I analyzed the frontages from different positions, but once again none of them matched the photo. I was about to call it quits after all, not just disappointed, but angry – angry at myself – when I saw we were approaching a side road.

"Let's take that turn," I said. "Looks like there are some estates along there." One last roll of the dice.

Jill turned onto the side road, but her tiredness had morphed into skepticism and it showed. As much as I hated to admit it, I'd let my defenses down and become emotionally involved in this search. Not just because of the distress that Jill was constantly under over the disappearance of her little sister, but because it was a stark reminder to me of the time when *I* had gone missing, kidnapped by men who blackmailed my father into releasing sensitive FBI information. The memory of those desperate hours was never far from the surface.

We hadn't traveled far along this narrow road when we were upon the wide frontage of another estate, and my eyes widened at the sight of the imposing iron gate marking its entrance.

"Jill, pull over," I said.

Jill brought the car to a stop by the side of the road. "What is it?"

"Those gates… the angle…" I showed her the photo as a reminder. "This looks like it could be it."

I stepped from the car, the scent of pine filling my nostrils, and walked forward, glancing at the frontage from a different perspective and eyeing the photo as I did. I walked back and got into the car. "That's the property."

Jill studied the frontage, glanced at the photo again, and then at me. I could see the uncertainty in her eyes. "You're sure?"

"I'm sure." I checked the GPS for the name of the road we were on, and glancing at the gates again, I could just make out the faded numbering on the gate, partially obscured by shoots of foliage. I reached for my phone and tapped Marcia's number. "Marcia, it's Ilona," I said as soon as she picked up. "I'm texting you an address and I need you to run a search on the owner."

I could hear Jill breathing heavily beside me, her eyes fixed on the house.

A moment later, Marcia was back on the line. "Got it. The owners are Monty and Oliver Warburton."

My next call was to Will's cell and I filled him in on the ownership of the country house Jill and I had located. "Will, given that Stan Avery was investigating Sam Reiberger's disappearance, suspected he was being followed by a white hatchback that he traced to a house owned by the Warburton family, and that Avery was killed by a sniper's bullet, I want to expand our folklore killer case to include Avery's murder and Sam's disappearance."

"Agreed," Will said. "I'll get Marcia to dig up as much background as she can on Sam's friends, colleagues, employment, the works."

"Great," I said. "The place here seems to be deserted so I'm going to take a look around the grounds."

"Ilona," Will said, "we need a warrant."

"I'd only be taking a cursory look around–"

"I'll arrange an urgent warrant and send backup. Stay in the car with Jill."

I was silent for a moment but, of course, Will was right. I said okay and ended the call but I didn't see any harm in getting out of the car and walking the perimeter for any view it might afford of how large the property was and whether there were any outbuildings further up the side or around the back. I told Jill to wait in the vehicle while I did a quick scout around. I opened the passenger door but as I stepped out, I heard a brief, sharp scream and there was no question it had come from the house.

"Wait here," I said to Jill.

I took a run at the gates and leaped, grabbing hold of a higher part of the grate and climbing up and over. I dropped down on the other side and drew my Glock. I was mentally prepared for the unexpected and I skirted around the side of the house. Peering around the corner to the back area, I saw two vehicles, one of them the elusive white hatchback, the other a nondescript sedan. I approached the back door, trying the handle as gently as possible. It was unlocked. The inhabitants hadn't anticipated any visitors at this remote spot and their complacency was my greatest advantage.

I took a moment to take in the rest of the property's back area. There was a workman's shed several feet to the rear northern side of the house. I sprinted across and peered in, scanning the interior. I saw what I needed, and a moment later I was back at the house's rear entrance.

Stepping inside, I found myself on an enclosed patio, with a wide window on the opposite wall, affording a view of the greenery outside. There were wide double doors, partly ajar, leading from the patio to another room. I took a deep breath and moved to a position from which I could see into that room. Through dim light, I saw a man tied to a chair, his face a mess of blood and bruising. He was shaking, his head lolling forward one moment and then snapping back to alert, his eyes wide with terror.

Two men stood in front of him, their backs to me. One of them was holding a pair of pliers and my nerves tightened.

"Okay, last chance to talk before we take this to the next level," the man with the pliers said. His accomplice stepped forward and gripped the prisoner's tied hands. "Shame about these fingernails."

"I don't have any answers," the man in the chair pleaded, his voice cracking.

Ignoring his cries, the accomplice forced the fingers of the prisoner's right hand onto a small, grimy table and the man with the pliers moved closer.

I stepped through the doorway with my pistol aimed at the two assailants. "FBI. Drop those pliers and turn around slowly, hands in the air."

The two men turned.

Narrowing his eyes, the man with the pliers said, "You don't want to get involved with this, girl. You have no idea who and what you're dealing with."

"Let me tell you who and what *you're* dealing with," I shot back. "A federal agent who is about to pull this trigger without any further consideration. So, let me repeat, one last time: drop those pliers, and hands in the air."

The room fell silent. Sweat trickled down my temple, and I swallowed hard, but I also took a tighter aim with my pistol, at the man with the pliers.

"Okay, okay." He bent forward, placing the pliers on the floor and then kicking them away. He and the man beside him raised their hands.

"Now, step back slowly and get down on your knees," I said.

The tension in the room was thick enough to choke on. The man tied to the chair breathed heavily, wincing in pain, watching what was unfolding with what looked like an expression of both relief and fear.

"*Now*," I ordered.

The two men began to step slowly back but then the pliers-man made a sudden move, grabbing hold of the small, grimy table and lunging forward, hurling it at me. I reacted instinctively, jumping back and raising my arm as a shield. The table smashed into me, knocking me off my feet and my gun went flying as I fell. I scrambled to grab it but as I did, the two men sprinted out the door.

Back on my feet, Glock in hand, I raced after them. They'd closed and locked the back door as they went. By the time I unlocked it and darted out, the men were in the sedan, rapidly reversing and then turning and screeching away, the electronic gates swinging open for them.

Before I'd entered the house, I'd used a hammer and nails I'd taken from the shed to drive nails through the walls of all four tires on both vehicles. It had taken mere minutes.

Now I ran to the front of the property, expecting – hoping – that the fleeing sedan wouldn't go much further than a mile or two along the road before suffering severe problems. But the wobble in the car must have been too obvious too soon as the sedan had pulled over not far beyond the driveway. The driver must have sussed what was happening and to my horror, both men had run from that car, back to the car I'd left Jill in.

I ran toward the vehicle, glimpsing as I did that one man took the passenger seat, the other the back seat, and with a knife pressed against the back of her neck, Jill was forced to drive off. I cursed myself for having left Jill alone like that.

I pulled out my phone, called Detective Radner, and rattled off what had happened, where I was, and the make and license plate of my car.

"Roger that," Radner said. "I'm sending units now."

I swore loudly at the impassive forest and strode angrily back to the house, where I approached the prisoner. "Who are you?" I asked, as I worked to untie his restraints.

"Danny… Gelfman," he stammered, flinching in pain as I removed the ropes.

"Have you any idea where those men might have gone?" I asked him. I told him that they'd stolen my car, kidnapped a woman, and the property's cars both had punctured tires.

Gelfman shook his head, but then, struck by a thought, he said, "There's a shed at the back."

"I know. I've been in there—"

"In the back corner, did you see a blue canvas covering?"

"Yes."

"There's a motorbike under there."

"Stay put, Danny, there's backup coming that will get you to a hospital," I said as I raced out the door.

I reactivated my ear comms as I raced to the shed and unsheathed the bike. "Zoe?"

"Yeah, Ilona."

I wheeled the motorcycle out to the driveway and hopped on. I kicked the engine into gear and sped off, onto the road. "Can you hear me?" I shouted.

"Just."

"On a bike, following the perps. Can you tell me if the Warburtons have any other properties in this area?"

"No," Zoe said, "but the property you were on is several acres and stretches over the hills behind it. There's a cottage at the rear of the property."

"Zoe, we're heading away from—"

She cut across me. "If you turn right at the next juncture, it takes you onto a road that winds around the hills and runs alongside the back end of the property. The cottage sits right there, not far off the road. If there are other vehicles there—"

"Makes sense to go there and change vehicles," I completed her thought.

The juncture was coming up. I slowed down to make the turn, my hair streaming out behind me in the rush of wind, and then gunned the accelerator so that I was practically flying. If those men had gone there and switched vehicles before I reached the cottage, then we would have lost them. I couldn't imagine the terror Jill must have been feeling.

Chapter Twenty-Nine

The woods on one side of the road gave way to rolling green fields and hills and I saw the cottage first as a smudge in the distance. As I drew closer, the details sharpened – a pristine lumber cottage and my car sat off to the side of the long driveway. I spotted the two men, dragging Jill toward another vehicle, a silver Toyota Camry.

The sound of the bike alerted them and one of the men glanced over, his eyes narrowing as I throttled down, bringing the motorbike skidding to a halt, loose gravel spitting under its weight.

I leaped off, and raised my Glock with both hands. "On your knees and hands in the air," I shouted.

The men froze but only for a few seconds. The pliers-guy reached into the car and pulled out a rifle, whirling around to point it straight at me.

Weapons stashed at the cottage. Of course there were.

Stupid. Never assume.

Time seemed to slow as the man's finger tightened on the trigger. I hit the ground and rolled as a deafening shot cracked over my head, bits of dirt stinging my cheek.

I came up, crouching, taking aim, but the cowards were using Jill as a shield. I steadied my aim, finger hesitating on the trigger. I couldn't risk it, not with Jill in the line of fire.

"Move!" the shorter of the two men barked, shoving Jill into the back seat with a force that was more panic than it was control.

The engine roared to life and the sedan jerked forward, charging to the end of the driveway.

I had mere seconds to try and stop this. I took aim with the Glock, my Quantico training clicking in, zeroing in on one of the back tires. There was a split second when the car slowed as it fishtailed onto the road, spraying gravel. I squeezed the trigger and prayed that it would pierce the rubber. The car was moving off then as I aimed at the other back tire. I peeled off a series of shots and then I ran back to the motorbike, swinging my leg over the bike, gunning the engine, and giving chase. Again.

If I'd hit the tires, and I was fairly certain I had, then one or both would either deflate or blow out, causing the car to become erratic and slow down. And that was on a good day.

The car was already a speck on the distant road, vanishing into the shadows cast by another stretch of woods.

I leaned low over the handlebars, the wind whipping at my face as I accelerated and it was less than a minute later that I saw I was rapidly closing the gap. As I got closer, I saw that the vehicle was veering from one side of the road to the other, shuddering as it decelerated, showing the impact of damaged tires. It came to a stop by the side of the road.

I increased my speed, but even as I did, the two men leaped out of the car, one of them pulling Jill with him in a vice-like grip, and they plunged into the thickets that bordered the road.

I braked, bringing the bike to a halt a few feet from the car, the dense woods looming ahead of me as I demounted and, pistol in hand, I pushed forward through the foliage, every muscle and nerve end coiled, driven by nothing more than sheer determination that I wasn't going to let Jill become another casualty of this investigation.

I weaved through the undergrowth, branches scraping the fabric of my jacket, straining my ears for any sound. I couldn't be sure which direction they'd taken once they were under the cover of the forest.

I paused for a moment, listening intently, eyes scanning the lush green surroundings, and then I picked up on it. The snap of twigs, the crunch of leaves underfoot. Coming from my left. I pivoted and moved forward at a fast pace, the woods ahead of me thinning out a little.

Movement caught my eye – a flash of color through the trees. I sprinted ahead and there they were, coming into clearer view, the two men, pressing forward, the barrel of the rifle still pressed against Jill's temple.

I stopped and squinted, raised my Glock, and focused on the legs of the man closest. I squeezed the trigger, the shot exploding like a crack of thunder, reverberating through the quiet forest. The kidnapper howled in agony, his leg buckling and he crashed to the damp earth.

My gaze was on the other man – the plier guy – and he whirled around, still with an iron grip on Jill, but he maneuvered the rifle to point at me.

My words rang out across the space between us. "Listen to me, your car is finished, your partner's down, and the cops are on their way. Your best bet is to give yourself up and cooperate. You don't owe the Warburtons anything."

For a moment he hesitated, the rifle wavering, but the gleam in his eyes was pure desperation. "You come anywhere near me, I blow her head off."

Jill's gaze met mine, her face frozen in panic, her eyes pools of terror.

I didn't move a muscle. "Think this through," I said. "You know what your best option is."

He glared at me with the expression of a cornered animal. But then, in a sudden burst of motion, he pushed Jill away from him, so hard she stumbled before catching herself. Keeping his rifle aimed at me, he began to back away, his eyes darting left and right, seeking the easiest escape route through the woodland.

The sound of sirens filled the air.

"You're making a big mistake," I called after him.

With a final glare, he turned and bolted into the shadows of the forest.

I sprinted across to where Jill stood, shaken but upright. My eyes raked over her, searching for injury.

"Jill, are you okay?'

She nodded, her eyes still wide from the horror she'd experienced but her voice was steady. "I'm okay."

The wounded man on the ground cried out. "Help me."

"Help is on the way," I said coldly, my eyes locking on his. "You'll be looked after, which is more than you would do for anyone."

The sirens had stopped, and coming from the direction of the road, we heard the rustle of leaves and the sounds of feet crashing through the undergrowth. I turned back to Jill, whose breaths were coming in short, sharp bursts.

I inclined my head in the direction the other man had fled. "Don't worry about him," I said. "He won't get far."

Chapter Thirty

The interrogation room at the SPD was stark and small, with a narrow table and two chairs on either side. Monty Warburton sat on the far side, his expression unreadable. His lawyer, Garrett Parsons, a gaunt man with thinning hair and calculating eyes that took in every detail, sat beside him.

Will and I had been on our way to the interview room when Marcia had come running up to us. "Something you'll want to know about Sam Reiberger's employment."

"What is it?" I asked.

"The laundromat she was working for is one of a chain, owned by the Warburtons."

Will and I exchanged a glance and then, thanking Marcia, we headed into the room.

"Mr. Warburton," Will began, his voice steady and commanding, "we have your son, Oliver, in an adjoining room, and two of your employees are back in their cells after being interviewed."

"Full house, then," Monty Warburton said.

I was sitting beside Will, and Detective Radner stood behind us, by the door. I studied Monty: he appeared unfazed by the news. He was a bulky man, with broad shoulders and a square jaw, clean-shaven and well groomed. Everything about his inscrutable eyes implied power and control.

"Here's the situation," Will continued, leaning forward. "Your accountant, Danny Gelfman, was found at your Leavenworth country estate. He'd been tortured by your two employees, both of whom were apprehended. They're both singing like canaries, and the word is that you had given the order. You and your son suspected him of stealing from you and you wanted a confession."

My stomach churned at the memory of those pliers being moved closer to Gelfman's fingers.

"Mr. Gelfman believes your men were going to kill him," Will added, staring directly into Monty's eyes. "He and the other two employees are all prepared to testify against you and Oliver in court."

"Is that so?" Monty said. The nonchalance in his voice was infuriating but I couldn't let that get to me.

Parsons leaned over to whisper some advice in his client's ear. Monty barely registered his lawyer's presence, instead glaring defiantly at Will and me.

"Mr. Warburton," Parsons said, addressing us all, "doesn't have to answer your questions."

"I haven't asked any questions yet," Will countered, "but let me start now. Mr. Warburton, do you deny the allegations that have been made by Danny Gelfman?"

Parsons tensed. "I repeat, my client doesn't—"

"Relax, Parsons," Monty cut him short, waving the advice aside. He hadn't averted his steel-like gaze from Will and me. "I haven't been out to that property for quite some time. I allow certain employees and trusted business associates to use the estate as and when they need it. Whatever those people have been getting up to isn't something that I'm aware of."

"Let's talk about the white hatchback found on the property," I said, not giving Warburton the chance to further deflect. "We have evidence it was involved in the surveillance of a private investigator, Mr. Stan Avery, before his murder. Who was driving it?"

Monty Warburton shrugged and tightened one side of his mouth. "Again, I don't have any knowledge of that. I let my guests use the hatchback as they please. It could have been any one of my associates who had access to the estate recently."

"One of the men who was assaulting Danny Gelfman — Blake Carson — tells us he was ordered by you and your son to follow Stan Avery and his client, Ms. Jill Reiberger, for several hours a day, one after the other, at random intervals."

"He's talking crap," said Monty.

"What was it you were afraid they'd find out?" Will pressed.

Monty was silent, lifting his brow in irritation.

"My client does not have to answer any of these absurd questions," Parsons said.

Will's gaze was intense. "As it turns out, Mr. Warburton, your man's surveillance was incredibly sloppy and he was spotted by both Mr. Avery and Ms. Reiberger, and it led Mr. Avery back to your country estate."

Monty's glare was icy but he didn't take the bait, remaining silent.

"It's going to play a hell of a lot better for you," Will said, "if you stop playing this game and come clean. These employees of yours might've acted tough when they were around you, but now that they've been caught red-handed, they're giving up what they know to save their skins."

Monty's continued silence made his answer obvious. He wasn't going to be cooperating with us anytime soon.

"Did you also instruct your men to follow me, or Agent McCord, or any other Federal agents?" I asked, avoiding Will's questioning glance.

"No," was all Monty said in response.

"Let's move on, then," Will said. "Stan Avery was investigating the disappearance of one of your laundromat employees and his client's sister, Sam Reiberger. What do you know about Ms. Reiberger's disappearance?"

"Sam Reiberger was engaged to my nephew, Liam," Warburton said matter-of-factly. "They argued and I presumed she broke off the intended nuptials and took off somewhere."

I stiffened at those comments. Sam engaged to Monty Warburton's nephew? That would come as a hell of a shock to Jill. Neither she nor Avery had known about that.

"No one has been able to find any trace of her," I said, glaring at Monty, my fists clenched, my voice rising. "Do you know where she is?"

"No. I don't know anything about the young woman."

Will referred to his notes and read off the names of the five murder victims and some of the details of the murders. "Each of these people had been missing for varying lengths of time before their bodies turned up. What do you know about these killings, Mr. Warburton?"

"Ah, I see why the FBI is involved. You're hunting a serial killer, it seems. But I've never heard of any of those people," Warburton said. "What has any of that got to do with me or my employees' activities at Leavenworth?"

Again, Will ignored Monty's question. "We've enough initial testimony from Danny Gelfman and the other two men to have obtained a search warrant for both yours and your son's homes and offices, so if you have anything to declare, now would be the time."

Monty stiffened at this, the first slight sign I'd detected that he was on edge. "You're wasting your time, Agent McCord."

Before we'd come into the room, I'd promised Will I would keep my cool, despite my close connection to the Reibergers. No problem. Except, as it turns out, it was. I leaned forward suddenly, my face inches from his, my voice rising again, my eyes boring into Monty's. "Where is Sam Reiberger, Monty? It's in your best interests to tell me *right now* what's happened to her."

Monty stared back. Unflinching. "I've no idea."

I leaned back in my chair again, my eyes not leaving his. That was when I caught the slightest twitch at the corner of his right eye.

I had the oddest sensation. For whatever reason, I believed at that moment that Monty Warburton was telling the truth about Sam. Call it intuition. Call it what you want. But at the same time, I had the unmistakable feeling that there was something else, something entirely different from any of this, that he was keeping to himself.

* * *

"I didn't know you were going to go all bad cop in there," Will said to me as we made our way to the next interview room along the corridor.

"I know I said I'd keep my cool—"

"Maybe it's just as well you breathed a little fire. It was the only thing that made him squirm, even if it was barely noticeable. What did you make of his comment that Sam was engaged to his nephew?"

"It certainly wasn't what I was expecting to hear."

We entered the next room, where Oliver Warburton sat, lounging as though he didn't have a care in the world. His was the kind of arrogance that made my blood boil and I knew it would have the same effect on Will.

Radner followed us in; he was purely acting as an observer on behalf of the SPD at this stage. Parsons, who represented both father and son, came in and took a seat next to Oliver.

"Mr. Warburton," Will said, "we have testimony from Danny Gelfman and the two men who were assaulting him that the orders to do so came from you and your father. What's more, Blake Carson has told us that you and your father ordered him to keep surveillance on Stan Avery and Jill Reiberger. Care to explain what this is all about?"

"They're lying," Oliver scoffed.

He was very much a younger version of his father – broad-shouldered, bulky, dressed in a designer-label suit. There was no warmth in his demeanor, just a sense of entitlement, and his eyes had the same cold, calculating look as his lawyer.

"Why would they do that?"

"I've no idea what those guys have been up to in their spare time."

Will looked at me and I acknowledged the look, weighing in with another line of questioning. "Maybe all of this has something to do with Sam Reiberger?"

His eyes contracted. "What about her?"

"I understand she was engaged to your cousin, Liam Warburton."

"What's that got to do with anything?"

"What do you know about her disappearance?" I asked.

He gave an irritated shake of the head. "Why would I know anything about that?"

"Maybe because Sam found out more about your family's business dealings than you and your father wanted her to know."

"Maybe you should be talking to Liam. He and Sam had some kind of tiff and she broke off their engagement and took off. Maybe she's avoiding Liam, who, by the way, is a loser, who didn't want to let her go. Maybe she doesn't want to be found or maybe Liam had something to do with her so-called disappearance. What the hell do I care?"

"Where is Liam Warburton now?" Will asked.

"The crybaby was so hurt by the breakup, that he told my dad he needed time off from the business. As far as I know, he's staying with some friends on a ranch in Montana. And no, I don't know their name or address, I don't think any of us do."

"It sounds to me, Oliver," I said, "that you and your father have sent Liam away so that he won't be able to complicate matters further with a slip of the tongue when questioned. But you are prime suspects in the murder of Stan Avery and because of that, in the disappearance and murders of those others as well. We have enough evidence right now to charge you and your father as accessories to aggravated assault and stalking of private citizens, and there's no telling what we'll turn up in our search of your premises. So, maybe it's time to stop acting churlish and speak up."

His silence was both expected and deafening. He shared at least one other characteristic with his father, a twitch at the corner of his eye when I mentioned the search.

Chapter Thirty-One

Danny Gelfman was sitting up, propped against his pillow, when I entered the private hospital ward. His face was black and blue and swollen, but he managed a lopsided half-grin when he saw me. "Agent Farris. My savior."

Will had returned to the UCU and I'd made this trip across town because I had something specific about which I wanted to ask Gelfman. There would be time for a more comprehensive interview with him, by Will and myself, once Gelfman was out of the hospital.

"I hear they're keeping you in overnight for observation."

"Yeah. And then it's off to the comforts of a holding cell at the local." He gestured feebly to the police guard stationed at the doorway. "They really don't need to lay on all this SWAT-type crap. I'm not going anywhere. I'm happy to cooperate with you guys and accept whatever plea bargains are on offer, and do my time."

"Glad to hear it, Danny," I said.

"But you're not here for a social visit."

"I'm looking for a Warburton employee who went missing six months ago. A young woman named Sam Reiberger. What do you know about her?"

"She's the one who got engaged to Monty Warburton's flaky nephew, Liam. I heard on the grapevine the big man wasn't happy about that, didn't trust her, so no surprise she vanished."

"What happened to her, Danny?"

"No idea. I don't expect it would be too pretty, though." He raised his hand to his face. "Just take a look at me."

"Do you think Liam Warburton was involved?"

"Liam? I only met him a couple of times. He didn't visit the head office very often. No, Monty and Oliver wouldn't let him in on anything. They saw him as a weak link. And he was always getting obsessed over some new fad or other. Last I heard, he'd been hanging with some group of pagan guys who thought they were warlocks or some such garbage. *Wiccans*, I think they're called."

"Could he be with them now?" I asked. "In Montana?"

"I wouldn't know." Gelfman shrugged. "But he's a Warburton, you know, so they kept him on a leash, gave him crap jobs to do." He forced a ragged breath, a look of remembrance passing across his eyes. "But…"

"But what, Danny?"

"Liam's got a sister, Shailene, or Shaley as she's known. Totally different piece of work to her younger brother. Smart, feisty, isn't afraid to talk back to her Uncle Monty. She does a lot of work for him, and runs a business of her own as well, though I never was clear what that was. Financial consultant for businesses. What the hell is that, anyway? But she was nonetheless very protective of Liam, and I know she spent a bit of time with him and Sam. Wouldn't surprise me if she knows something; I always had the idea that she knew a lot more than she ever let on."

"Any idea where I'd find her?" I asked.

"I haven't been there myself, but I heard she has some pretty impressive digs across the bay, on Mercer Island," he said with a shrug. "And maybe, seeing as how I'm being so helpful, you could put in a good word for me?"

"Thanks for your help, Danny," I said. "I'll be talking with you further, with my colleagues, about the Warburtons, so you take it easy."

He could take that response any way he wanted. I didn't care. Right now, I needed to follow whatever trail I thought could lead to information about Sam Reiberger.

* * *

It didn't take long for Marcia to send me some details, and an address, for Shailene Warburton. The sun dipped below the horizon, casting an orange glow over the water, as I drove across the bridge onto Mercer Island. This expensive, upmarket suburb was home to some of the wealthiest individuals in the city and the meticulously maintained streets, lined with tall, mature trees, were a testament to that. Sprawling homes stood on large, landscaped plots of land.

Shailene Warburton ran her business consultancy from her home. I pulled into the long, sloping driveway of the house, a sleek, modern design, flanked by a manicured yard. As the niece of Monty Warburton, it seemed she'd leveraged her family connections to do very well for herself, and yet, as I understood it, she was a single woman, so this home was much larger than she'd need. Was it all for show, for ego? The exterior of the double-story house was a mix of glass, steel, and lattice brick, creating a sense of cold sophistication that seemed to mirror the thirty-ish woman who opened the front door as I approached.

"Agent Ilona Farris, I presume," she said as she ushered me through the doorway, her voice carrying a confidence that bordered on intimidation. "I gathered, with my uncle Monty and cousin Oliver in custody, it was only a matter of time before the FBI came knocking, though I admit this is sooner than even I anticipated." The smile on her face could have been plastered on.

"You know of me?" I said.

"I was told of your interrogation of my uncle, and on that occasion, I googled your name. You have quite the law enforcement profile given your recent cases. Even as a schoolgirl, I was best in my class at doing my homework."

The interior of the house was as impressive as the outside, with strategically placed minimalist furniture and modern art pieces, their sole purpose seeming to be to convey wealth and privilege. There was hardwood flooring throughout the main living area, leading to French doors that opened onto an expansive deck.

"I'm not here about Monty or Oliver, at least not regarding the charges they're currently facing," I said. "I'm here to ask you what you might know about the disappearance six months ago of your brother's fiancée."

"Sam?" She sat on a lounge chair and gestured for me to sit opposite her on a two-seater. She was dressed in a pantsuit, her sharp, angular features accentuated by carefully applied make-up, framed by coiffed, platinum-blond hair. "Well, it was no secret in the family that my uncle didn't want her to marry my brother. She was a trashy type and he thought she just wanted to marry into a moneyed family. But what became of her, after she broke off the engagement, your guess is as good as mine."

"Do you think your uncle had anything to do with her disappearance? Anything you saw or heard, however seemingly insignificant at the time, could prove useful."

"Agent Farris, do you honestly believe my uncle Monty would have Sam hurt, or worse, just because he didn't want her in the family?" she asked rhetorically. "That's not his style. If anything, he'd try to buy her off. He certainly wouldn't risk drawing police attention to himself or his beloved business, and now, with his arrest today, you know why. I always had a sneaking suspicion that there was a hidden underbelly to his business operations, though he kept it well hidden from me."

"You say Monty wouldn't do anything to attract attention to his business, but he and your cousin had no problem having their accountant, Danny Gelfman, held and tortured on one of their properties. I've just come from visiting Danny in the hospital, and it was he who suggested that if anyone knew anything about Sam, it might be you."

"The situation with Danny would've been completely different. An employee, who wouldn't run to the police, whom my uncle knew to be stealing from him. My uncle's an arrogant man, he'd want to have dealt with that situation himself."

Floor-to-ceiling windows offered an unobstructed view of the bay but Shailene kept her eyes leveled directly on mine. I studied her face, searching for any telltale signs of deception. Despite her intimidating presence, something in her words about Monty rang true, though they also gave me the sense that there was something else entirely that she was keeping locked away. I'd had the same uncanny sense when I'd interviewed both Monty and Oliver.

"What about your brother?"

"What about him? Liam's a softie, not cut out for the Warburton style of business. He wouldn't hurt a fly, and he was besotted with Sam. He was out of his depth in our uncle's business." Her gaze drifted for just a moment, as she glanced at her phone. I heard a muted buzz.

"You, on the other hand, don't seem out of depth in the business world."

"I've thrived, using our family connections. I have an MA in Business Studies. I ran one of Monty's supermarkets for a while and advised him on investments and the like. Nowadays, my consulting firm advises not just Monty but many of his business partners as well. All above board, of course."

"And Liam's spending time with friends in Montana?" I said. "Possibly some bunch of neo-pagans who are into witchy stuff?"

She rolled her eyes. "One of his fads. They don't last long. I don't know where he took off to but at least he's away from all his uncle's crap at the moment."

"Danny told me you spent a bit of time with Liam and Sam. Did Sam say or do anything to make you think, in hindsight, that she intended to take off, or that she was in any kind of danger?"

There was a moment of reflection, her gaze narrowing, and then Shailene said, "Now that you mention it… yes, maybe."

"Maybe what?"

"I recall her once, in confidence, telling me she'd had a couple of instances when she was out, and she had a sense that someone was watching, or following her. She wondered if it was Liam's relatives, she knew they'd told Liam he should dump her."

"And what did you say?"

"I told her, as I've just told you, that it wasn't Monty's style, not for a domestic matter. I thought she was imagining this phantom stalker, whom she never actually saw, but maybe…" She took a breath. "Maybe there was something in it. But Agent Farris, I really can't help you, and" – she glanced at her phone again – "I have an important conference call, there's no nine-to-five in my line of work." She rose, a clear signal she didn't have any more time.

I nodded my understanding and she hurriedly showed me to the front door.

As I stepped outside, I couldn't shake the feeling I was missing something vital.

On my way in, I had noticed there were two vehicles parked in the extended driveway, one of them a Mercedes, yet another sign of her affluence. My car was parked further back on the driveway, blocking them.

I turned the car around and drove up the long driveway. As I turned onto the road, the sudden glow of headlights from one of the cars back by the house caught my attention. The Mercedes had just been remotely unlocked, and in the rearview mirror, I glimpsed a figure by the front door, distinctly different in shape from Shailene.

I quickly pulled over to the side of the road, out of sight of those on the property, and killed my headlights. Someone had been in the house all along, without Shailene making mention of them. I stepped from the car and quickly moved stealthily to a point from which I could look down the driveway, from an angle that hid me from view.

I saw Shailene kissing a man passionately. The man then climbed into the Mercedes and headed up the driveway with Shailene watching from the doorstep. It was clear that, for whatever reason, he'd needed to be somewhere else, and my car had been blocking his. The muted buzz I'd heard on Shailene's phone must have been a text, sent by the man from somewhere else in the house, hurrying her along. But why not just introduce him, and ask me to shift my car? What was with the big secret?

As the Mercedes exited the driveway, I ducked behind a tree, holding my breath as it passed, and making a note of the license plate.

I slipped into the driver's seat of my car and phoned Marcia.

"Girl, you need to occasionally switch off."

"Soon," I said. "Right now, I need you to run a number for me." I read the plate number to her.

"Give me a moment." Less than a minute later, Marcia said, "A Mercedes. Belongs to Ryan Selworth and I'm pulling in data on him now." I didn't have to wait long. "He's a prominent business owner and property investor," Marcia said. "Interestingly, he shows up as an adversary of the Warburtons."

"How do you know that?"

"There are records of legal complaints they've filed against each other, for fraud, misuse of funds, misrepresentation of data, that sort of thing."

"Has any of it made it to court?"

"No. Not yet, anyway. It would appear these two firms are fierce competitors for buying up certain businesses and properties, and they're not above hurling accusations against each other. Why do you want to know about this Selworth guy?"

I told Marcia what I'd seen.

"Just checking on some personal info," Marcia said. "Okay, Selworth is married with two kids and lives in Bellevue. That would explain his staying out of sight in the house. He wouldn't want it known that he was having an affair. And Shailene wouldn't want it known that she's in a relationship with Monty's biggest business rival."

"Okay."

"You coming back in here or heading home? The latter, I hope."

"Neither. I need to pay Danny Gelfman at the hospital another visit."

"Why?"

"Something niggling at the back of my mind about all this," I said.

Chapter Thirty-Two

Danny Gelfman showed his surprise when I walked back into the ward. "Didn't expect to see you so soon, Agent Farris, but I guess you went to see Liam's sister and you saw a bit of what I've seen."

I pulled up a chair beside the bed. "And what would that be, Danny?"

"The big house on Mercer, the cars, the clothes, the art. Always thought she was a bit of a pretentious bitch. She's done incredibly well, you'd have to agree, from running one of Monty's supermarkets and then becoming a big-time financial advisor, all because she's got some college degree in commerce."

"Good to know you don't harbor any bitterness, then."

He shot me a quizzical look, confused.

"Danny, you're Monty's in-house accounts guy, among other things, I gather. This is one of the questions I would have put to you once you were released from the hospital, but, well, I'm back here now, so let me ask you, why did Monty think you were stealing from him?"

"He claims I skimmed money off his various accounts and deposited them in a secret account of my own. Which I never did."

"Did he locate this alleged secret account of yours?"

"He seemed to think he'd found the trace of an account but it had been closed and the funds diverted. The trail was cold, so there's no evidence, and I never moved any money so it has to have been system glitches, like what happened with that Post Office systems error in England. You heard about that famous case?"

"Let's not get off topic, Danny," I said. "Shailene was a financial advisor to Monty's various businesses, so did she ever have access to the accounts on your PC?"

"No. And it's password-protected, anyway."

"Did she ever sit beside you at your PC, to look over the company's accounts?"

He gave this a moment's thought. "Well, I guess. Not recently, but I vaguely remember a few instances, going back a couple of years."

"Could she know your password?"

"No way."

"But it's not inconceivable she could've seen you put your password into the network."

"It's encrypted, it doesn't show on the screen."

I wasn't about to press the matter with Danny Gelfman any more than that, but I did voice my thoughts when I was outside and back on the line with Marcia.

"When I discovered Shailene was having an affair with an enemy of Monty's, and I factored her financial role and her accumulation of wealth into the picture, my suspicious mind went into overdrive. She's clever enough to have watched the keys Danny hit on his keyboard and memorized them. Which means if she manipulated his PC remotely – not hard given she's the company's financial advisor – then she could've accessed his PC and made certain transactions."

"You think she's robbing Monty and giving to Ryan Selworth?" Marcia read my mind.

"She's in bed with the enemy and I don't think it was Danny stealing that money. Like most of Monty's hirelings, he's not that bright. Maybe Selworth is planning to leave his wife, hook up permanently with Shailene, with the two of them ruling like czars over a business empire partly funded by Monty's money."

"One way to find out if you're on the right track," Marcia said. "The SPD and the FBI are both now looking through all the Warburton company's finances. If Selwood had anything to do with that secret account that's now closed, we should be able to locate that data."

"My gut tells me we're going to find evidence that brings charges against Shailene and Selwood. But" – I bit down in frustration on my lower lip – "none of that gets me any closer to finding out what happened to Sam Reiberger."

"You're not going to get any closer tonight, and tomorrow's another big day. Now are you going to head home and get a little rest?"

"I'm heading into the office," I said.

Chapter Thirty-Three

Zach was scrutinizing the photos that had been taken in Rodwell's house as part of the warrant-approved search. "There is a whole heap of books on folklore and history," he said to Zoe, "but there are also these." He zoomed into a section of one of the photos that included a bookcase. The enlarged image clearly showed the spines of several books.

Zoe wheeled her chair alongside his. "And?"

"There are several books on witchcraft and the occult, including this one by Aleister Crowley, who was a well-known and controversial occultist—"

"I know who Aleister Crowley was," Zoe said.

"Crowley believed that the natural energies of the universe could be harnessed to bend reality, that what was thought of as supernatural was simply those energies not yet understood. The same belief held by some of those who practice modern witchcraft, including those on an occultist site run by a woman named Jessica Saville. Reading through Rodwell's social media, I saw that he's frequently posted comments to that site."

Zoe shook her head. "Where are you going with this?"

"As I pointed out before, in Grimms and other folkloric tales, people are turned into birds and frogs, or made to vanish. Let me give you an example of just one. In *Frau Holle*, a young woman fetching water falls into a well and finds herself transported to another realm. In many of the tales from that era, witches make people disappear and sometimes reappear later. What if those tales were drawn from, or inspired by, observations of real-world practitioners of witchcraft, who'd discovered how to bend reality, in a way similar to what Crowley theorized?" He gestured. "Let's look at what we know about this case. We've got five people who vanished and then turned up years later, the victims of a sniper. We've got pages ripped from nineteenth-century German editions of Grimm books, and silver buttons from a similar era. And this oddball Rodwell, a Grimm enthusiast who studies and partakes in the occult."

"Are you implying that those murder victims were shifted to hidden realms and then back again?"

"Well, when you put it that way, I know it sounds crazy—"

Zoe cut across him. "It doesn't just *sound* crazy, Prof, it *is*. Actually, no, it's more than that. It's absolutely bonkers. Even for you."

Zach grinned. "Good to know I haven't lost my touch."

"You haven't."

"Humor me," Zach pleaded. "We know there is something very strange going on. And Rodwell's a person of interest for very good reasons. He also wasn't able to supply much of an alibi to Will and Ilona for the times the bodies were dumped. He was at home with his mother, and she can't be relied on to verify anything. And none of the friends he visited in Tacoma can account for his whereabouts at night. I see from the reports that his delivery route was close enough to where Avery was shot that he could have stopped there. And I know from his posts that he's attending one of Saville's witchy worship meetings later tonight."

"Let me guess. You want to wander onto a remote field at night, into the midst of a bunch of people who think they're witches?"

"Supposedly, they're open to newcomers. I want to see if there's any unusual activity, or if Rodwell or anyone else lets slip something that we could link to our case."

"And, of course, you're hoping to stumble upon something otherworldly to prove your theories."

"Always hoping for that," he said with a smirk.

"If you're insistent on going along to this thing," Zoe said, "then I'm stepping in and making certain it's done safely and smartly."

"I was hoping you might say that." He proffered a sheepish grin.

"Let me take a look at the location," Zoe said. "If Ilona and Will agree, and if I can figure a way of watching from afar, unseen, then that's what we do. Not because we're going to see people vanishing, but because we might observe something incriminating in Rodwell's actions. Agreed?"

Zach gave a mock salute. "Yes, boss."

"I'm not your boss but I *am* starting to wonder if I'm a little crazy going along with this."

* * *

I wasn't the only one who hadn't headed home yet for the evening. Zoe called for Will, Marcia, and me to join her and Zach in the ops room.

"Zach and I have been taking a closer look at the photos of Rodwell's home," she said. She told them about his books on the occult. "We've also been trawling through Rodwell's social media and something else has come up. Several interactions with a woman named Jessica Saville, who runs a site called Witchcrafting."

"What's that?" Will asked.

"A Seattle-based group of men and women who study witchcraft."

"Men as well as women?"

Zoe laughed. "You haven't been keeping up with your occult studies, Will."

He rolled his eyes.

Zach chimed in. "The term 'witch' isn't gendered. Yes, men and women practice it, with Wicca being the most popular and fastest-growing form, representing the worship of Mother Earth and the spiritual connection between people and the natural elements. There are over 700,000 people across the States, from all walks of life, who consider themselves Wiccans, with dozens of different branches and, in some cases, breakaway groups. Some of those breakaway groups hark back to the medieval-era belief in witchcraft as being a portal to the supernatural."

"Not this supernatural bent of yours again." Will expunged a breath in frustration. "Is Rodwell a member of this Saville woman's group?"

"That's not clear but it appears to be the case," Zoe said. "Most of her posts are general reflections on her beliefs but there's one that states the group's next worship meeting is later tonight."

"Where?" I asked.

"On an open field in the country, not far from her home."

I was expecting Will to tell Zoe and the professor that going out there was a waste of time. Once again, as he had more than a few times just lately, he surprised me.

"Zoe," he said, "just make certain the professor doesn't get himself, or you, into any trouble."

Zoe grinned and rolled her eyes. "Easier said than done."

I looked at Will. "Danny Gelfman told me that Liam Warburton had got involved with a Wiccan group," I said.

Will pursed his lips and then turned to Marcia. "See if you can track down any of Liam's other friends. Maybe someone else who knows him might know where he's staying."

Chapter Thirty-Four

The field was at the base of a wooded hill. Positioned on the hill, under the cover of both the night and the pines, Zoe and Zach took up a spot that afforded a clear view. Zoe had organized infrared night binoculars and a zoom-lens, long-distance camera. At various intervals, she took photos.

The meeting in the field lasted an hour and a half and consisted of the group sitting, holding hands, and chanting. On occasion, they stood and swayed together in a slow, rhythmic movement, their faces upturned to a sky illuminated by a full moon. That, Zoe guessed, was the reason this night had been chosen. If nothing else, the full moon cast an ethereal light that graced the tops of the pines in the distance.

When the meeting ended and the group left the field, Zoe turned to Zach. "I'm afraid that was a waste of time, and what's more, no teleportation."

Zach had a crestfallen expression. "Even so, my gut's telling me there's something more to this."

"This whole exercise hasn't even made me tired," Zoe complained. "I'm wide awake."

"Seems to me that's your natural state of mind this time of the evening."

Zoe gave him an impish grin. "You got a point?"

"Let's go grab some late-night coffees and take a look at those photos," Zach said.

* * *

I stood at my window, watching the shimmering lights of the city. I was restless and anxious, feeling the familiar itch for an adrenaline rush. But I couldn't risk going out climbing. Not now that I knew someone had seen me and had warned me off the case. I knew Monty Warburton had ordered his man, Blake Carson, to keep watch on Stan Avery and Jill. I had thought it was Carson who'd confronted me in the alley. But Monty denied it, and even Carson himself, spilling the beans on everything else, had declared he hadn't been following me or any of the others on our team.

So, who was it?

My phone buzzed, yanking me from my thoughts. A text from Zoe, updating me. I texted her back, asking her to send me the photos she'd taken. I didn't expect them to mean anything to me but scrolling through them would be a welcome distraction.

'Sending them now,' she texted back.

I tapped the screen, keen to see what Zoe had captured. I scrolled through the photos, of which there were a dozen or so. Row after row of robed figures, some in hoods, some not, standing and sometimes sitting around a bonfire. The flickering flames cast grotesque shadows across their faces. I scanned the faces, looking for Thomas Rodwell. He was in a few of the photos, his face clear in one of them, his expression intense.

And then my gaze fell on another face, instantly recognizable.

She stood among the others, her stern expression illuminated by the glow. It was unmistakably her.

I tapped Will's number, pacing back and forth from the window as it rang. As soon as he picked up, I blurted out what I'd seen.

His voice crackled with disbelief. "Tranter? Are you sure it's her?"

"Positive." My fingers drummed against the windowsill. "Of course, as Zach pointed out, it's not considered weird in this day and age to have an interest in Wicca, even if you're a police officer, and it doesn't mean she's met or knew Rodwell before this, but the simple fact they're involved with this same group seems odd."

"Let's discuss strategy first thing," Will said. "I'd say we need to question Tranter as to whether she's had any dealings with Rodwell, but at the same time, we can't go casting aspersions on a senior detective simply because they attended a perfectly legal special interest group. At this point, we also don't know whether Rodwell has been along to any previous meetings of this group."

I knew he was right. But seeing June Tranter in those photos hadn't been the distraction I was looking for, and if anything, I was more wired than ever.

My inner voice was whispering in my ear that something wasn't right about this.

Chapter Thirty-Five

If she cast her mind back, she remembered that when she first saw the light, it temporarily blinded her. So bright. So intense. As her eyes adjusted, she'd seen that the light was in the shape of a doorway, in the distance, and there was a dark smudge within that luminescence. A shape.

A human shape.

Should she go toward it? Was it a way out of this… whatever this was?

She waited. Uncertain. Fearful. Her eyes adapted further, the light spilling through the door-shaped portal, and the figure stood still and silent.

She squinted, the light hurting her eyes, and then the figure placed something on the ground. And beckoned.

She walked slowly, tentatively, toward the light. As she did, the figure stepped back through the portal as it closed and the light vanished, plunging everything into total darkness again.

Her head was throbbing, her breath coming in ragged gasps. In the back of her mind, she kept hearing what had been the last words she'd heard before all of this had begun. "Turn back, turn back, thou pretty bride…"

She wished she'd turned back. But turned back from what and where? She still couldn't remember where she'd been or what she'd been doing before all this, although she had started having brief, random memories of… something familiar.

She reached the spot where she believed the light had been and she knelt, feeling around for the object she'd seen being placed on the ground. Her mind was fighting disbelief and burning with just one thought:

What the hell is happening?

PART TWO

Chapter Thirty-Six

Day Five

A 6 a.m. call with Detective Paul Radner's name displayed could only mean one thing. Another body had been found. I answered the call with a single word. "Where?"

"A narrow road that runs alongside the zoo."

"Which doesn't have CCTV," I assumed.

"No."

The next call, immediately after, was from Will. "I'll pick you up," he said.

My worst fear had been realized. The sequence of bodies being murdered and dumped had increased and was gaining even more momentum. Why? Was the killer getting off on this now that it was known that both the SPD and the FBI were on the hunt? If this continued, and that now seemed to be the case, then Sam Reiberger, if she was still alive, was next, and her murder was imminent. I felt the tension like a band wrapped around my head. Where was Sam? We were still no closer to discovering what had happened to any of these people after they vanished.

I was in no mood for make-up or styling my hair. I slipped into my blouse, pants, and standard-issue FBI jacket and headed downstairs to meet Will.

The pale light of morning barely skimmed the sky as we arrived at the crime scene. It was located down a narrow service road used by staff to enter the zoo from the rear. The animal scent was heavy in the air as Will and I stepped from his car and we made our way down the service road. Crime scene tape wavered in the breeze and the forensic officers were already going about their tasks. Detective Radner and the medical examiner, Marla Lui, greeted us as we approached.

"Morning," Radner said without any warmth, his gaze shifting from us to the woman's body splayed by the side of the road. "Early morning shift worker found her when they arrived for work."

"Maria Corvici?" I asked.

"Her ID says so," Radner confirmed, his voice heavy.

A fourth murder victim in less than two weeks was a toll even a seasoned homicide detective would feel. Formal identification would come later but this was the victim we'd expected would be next.

"Single gunshot to the head," he said, "like the others."

Dr. Lui stepped forward. "There are postmortem burn marks covering most of her body," she explained, "and bites from small animals."

Her voice wasn't quite as clinical and detached as usual. I wondered if that was because she'd now encountered Will and me at more than a couple of these scenes, or whether the enormity of all this was getting under her skin. Medical examiners are rarely confronted with the victims of a serial killer, let alone over such a short period, and so early in their career.

"Can you conclude what kinds of animals?" Will asked.

"I'll need to conduct further analysis back at the lab," Dr. Lui said, "but the bites are consistent with rats."

Rats. My stomach churned at the thought. "And the same items in the hands?"

"Yes. A silver button in one, a page torn from a book in the other."

Radner's eyes found mine. "Another victim, I gather, who has been missing for some time?"

I nodded. "A little over two years ago, and she was an employee of the zoo."

Will and I scouted the area. We didn't expect to find anything useful or incriminating, and we didn't. Once again, the time, the place, and the presentation of the body, all had been meticulously planned and carried out in perfect symmetry with the *Brother and Sister* tale's narrative found on Ryan Moreton.

Will and I headed back up the service road to his car and I had an unnerving sense of déjà vu.

* * *

There was a tense atmosphere in the office when Will and I got in, the energy in the air palpable. Marcia and Zach had arrived and Zoe was poised like a panther at her console as though primed and ready to pounce on every line of data that graced her monitor.

She swiveled to face us as we walked in. "We know Maria Corvici's housemates died and she was suspected of arson," she said. "She disappeared a few months later and I've been going over the missing person report, and there's something that's buried in there, just a brief note, that could be of interest."

"No doubt something else Detective Caulfield didn't share with us," I said.

"After the arson investigation, Corvici told her mother that one of the fire victims had a boyfriend who wasn't happy that Corvici wasn't charged with murder. He made threats against her. Corvici's mother reported this to Detective Caulfield after her daughter vanished but there are no further references to it."

"Who is this guy?" Will asked.

"His name's Ed Slater. Anyway, I've run a search on him and this guy has a history of domestic abuse. After he lost his girlfriend in that fire, he hooked up with someone else but that didn't end well. He was reported for domestic assault and he's been on a good behavior bond." She swung back around to her PC and brought up another document. "This is his mug shot."

Will and I moved closer to her desk. Ed Slater had one of those insolent expressions that intimated something darker. His cold, unyielding eyes glared at the camera. "Even if we were to consider him a person of interest for Maria Corvici's murder," I said, "it wouldn't tie in with the other murders."

"Except that the abuse charge wasn't the first. There's a record of a similar complaint and a civil anti-harassment order being taken out against him six years ago."

"Good work, Zoe," Will said. "With a history of violence and a motive for wanting Corvici dead, he's worth us checking him out further."

Zach had remained in his spot but he spoke up, his voice calmer and more measured than was normal for him. "Motive is the key. Whether it's Slater, Rodwell, or someone else, vigilantism is almost always driven by something intensely personal, something traumatic in the killer's history."

It certainly wasn't Zach's style to be subtle about anything, but I sensed immediately that there was a subtext to his words: the observation that we hadn't come close to discovering what it was that drove this killer's obsession in delivering their own brutal form of justice.

* * *

Ed Slater's inner-city apartment was housed in a grimy, red-brick building. Will and I climbed the worn staircase to the third floor, the creaks echoing through the dimly lit hallway. Muffled traffic sounds drifted up as Will rapped on the door.

After several minutes, the door swung open to reveal a man in his mid-thirties with an unshaven face and unkempt hair. The insolent expression across his features was unmistakable.

"Ed Slater?" Will asked, flashing his badge.

"Who's asking?" His voice was low and gravelly and he was clad in a stained white tank top and faded jeans.

"Special Agents McCord and Farris, FBI." As Will spoke, I surveyed the cramped living quarters visible behind Slater. Piles of clothes lay haphazardly strewn about.

"Look, if this is about my good behavior bond, I've done everything by the book," Slater said defensively.

"Actually," I said, "we're here to talk to you about Maria Corvici."

A flicker of recognition crossed his face, followed by a dismissive sneer. "What about her?"

"It might be best if we could come in for a moment," I said.

He stood aside and we stepped into a cluttered and musty atmosphere.

"Maria's body was found earlier today," I said.

He didn't react, he simply stared back at me. "Where had she been all this time?"

"We don't know, but she'd been shot and her body was left on the service road to the zoo where she used to work."

Slater sat down and ran his fingers through his straggly hair. "Jeez-us!" He took a deep breath. "Well, what can I say? Seems like the bitch finally got what she deserved."

"Mr. Slater, can you account for your whereabouts last night and early this morning?" Will inquired, his tone sharp.

"Here. Asleep." Slater folded his arms across his chest.

"Can anyone corroborate that?"

"Who the hell would be here to watch me sleep? No, I don't have an alibi, if that's what you're asking, and I didn't have anything to do with Maria's abduction or murder."

"What makes you think she was abducted?" I asked him.

"Well, I don't know, she went missing, and…" His voice trailed off. He looked a little shaken.

"She could have simply run away because she felt threatened by you," I said, my hackles up.

"Why would she have felt threatened by me?"

"There is a report that you'd threatened her and you have had arrests before for domestic abuse."

"Those are misunderstandings," Slater said with a childish air of defiance.

"Why did you assume Maria had been abducted two years ago?" I pressed. "Do you know something about her disappearance?"

Slater unfolded his arms and puffed his chest out. "No, I don't."

Will interjected. "If you know anything about what happened to Maria, Ed, then it's in your best interests to speak up now."

"I can't help you."

Will handed him his card. "My number, if you do happen to remember anything."

There was something about this man's manner, not just his usual face mask of insolence. It was the shift in his eyes and the way he scraped his hand across his stubble.

Will and I headed for the door and let ourselves out. Will headed to the stairwell but I held back. "Will?"

He turned. "What is it?"

"This guy seemed rattled when I asked him why he thought Corvici's disappearance was because someone kidnapped her."

"I noticed that."

"He's not the smartest guy. I think I can trip him up."

"Trip him up how?"

"Just bear with me."

I rapped on Slater's door and he opened it with a bemused expression. "What now?"

"Just one other thing, Ed, that we forgot to ask. If you know anything about the white hatchback from that night—"

"I don't, but I thought it was an SUV someone reported seeing."

"A white SUV?" I asked.

He screwed up his face. "I thought it was black, but whatever."

Will glanced at me in astonishment.

Slater stepped back as I pushed my way back into the apartment, my face just inches from his. "How do you know about a black SUV?"

Fear etched its way into every line on his face as he realized he'd slipped up. "What do you mean, it was… it was on the news back then."

"No one saw Maria after she left work that evening. No one ever reported seeing her abducted or seeing a black SUV. But you saw it, didn't you?"

"You're crazy—"

"What happened that evening, Ed? You know what I think? You were furious that Maria hadn't been charged with the murder of your girlfriend over that house fire. I think you went to confront Maria that evening when she finished her shift at the zoo. But before you reached her, you saw her grabbed and bundled into a black SUV. You just shrugged and walked away, never reported it to the police, and even after she was reported missing, you never said anything, you just figured she got what she deserved."

"No—"

"That was vital information that would have assisted investigators at the time."

"This is bullshit, I didn't realize it was an abduction—"

And there it was.

I grabbed him by the shoulders, spun him, and pushed him against the wall. "Ed Slater, I'm placing you under arrest on suspicion of obstructing the course of justice, you have the right to remain silent…"

Will phoned Detective Radner. Slater would be the SPD's problem now. I heard Will bring the detective up to date, and a moment later, saying, "Okay, thanks." He ended the call and said to me. "Radner's sending a couple of his guys to take him into custody. But Radner's heading over to our building, he says he needs to speak with us pronto."

Chapter Thirty-Seven

"I've always been awed by your intuition," Will said as we headed back to the UCU, "but that, back there with Slater, that was… next level."

"Not really," I said. "You must have guessed as well that Slater was hiding something. He couldn't have been more shifty if he'd tried."

"Sure. I figured maybe he had something in the apartment he didn't want us to go snooping about and find. Like drugs, or stolen goods, but not what you sussed out."

I shrugged.

"I'm afraid it still won't be easy to prove in court that he observed Corvici's kidnapping if he recants," Will said.

"Radner's team will go over Slater's place with a fine-tooth comb. I think they'll find more than a few things that'll bring a raft of charges. No good behavior bond this time."

Will drove into the FBI parking station. Even though my anger at Slater was seething under the surface, it wasn't front and center in my thoughts. My mind was still racing with thoughts about June Tranter's involvement with the Wicca meeting, and the mysterious observer I'd encountered in the ally two nights before but I needed to put those to the side and focus.

Will and I headed straight to the UCU conference room. Marcia and Zoe were already seated, and Radner was pulling up the chair beside Marcia. Will and I took seats opposite Zoe.

Radner didn't waste any time on niceties and his voice was grave. "In our search of the Warburton premises, we found detailed files on a large number of people, most of them public officials." He cast his gaze over everyone at the table, his eyes settling on me. "But nothing on any of the missing people who turned up as murder victims."

"Damn." I frowned, disappointment gnawing at me.

"But we did find a file with personal details and stats on Sam Reiberger's sister, Jill, and a burner phone that had been used to make numerous calls to her number."

"Jill?" I echoed, trying to keep my tone neutral, but inside, gears were turning furiously. Sam, troubled and vulnerable; Jill, fiercely protective. What the hell was this all about?

"Anything else?" Will's question pulled me back from a torrent of confused thoughts.

"Rough notes, in Monty Warburton's handwriting," Radner said, and my stomach knotted. He pulled out a sheet of paper from his briefcase and handed it to Will. "It details a plan for setting up Sam so that it would appear that she had given her friend the drugs he overdosed on. Monty didn't want her in the family, and setting her up for this was intended to stop her wedding to his nephew."

Will handed me the sheet of paper and the floor seemed to tilt beneath me as I read through it.

"The evidence we've got against Monty Warburton keeps mounting," Marcia commented.

Radner turned to me. "And I've had our guys combing through the Warburtons' books looking into the matter you raised about those diverted funds," he said. "They've traced the funds to the offshore accounts of various shell company hubs, all of which have a link to one or another of Ryan Selworth's businesses."

"Enough to lay charges?"

"Yes, and we've got a warrant to search Selworth's premises and accounts for anyone and everyone else who can be implicated. As Shailene Warburton is a registered advisor to her uncle's businesses, that warrant extends to her online transactions, as well. Now, while there's no guarantee we'll find anything incriminating—"

"Hopefully she'll have slipped up somewhere," I said. When it came to using her charm to manipulate others, and her smarts to cover her tracks, I suspected Shailene had long since not only matched her uncle in those respects, but overtaken him. And while bringing down the Warburtons' criminal enterprise would be another feather in the UCU's cap, I was increasingly conscious that our main focus, the vigilante killings, didn't fit with what we knew about them. Monty was all about making money from his seemingly legit businesses while using them to launder money for drug gangs. He wasn't interested in the drug-running himself. Too dangerous, too much competition. He preferred to stay out of it and instead, provide the money laundering services. I was reminded again of Shailene's own words. "Agent Farris, do you honestly believe my uncle Monty would have Sam hurt, or worse…? He certainly wouldn't risk drawing police attention to himself or his beloved business."

Zoe remained quiet, listening intently.

I directed my gaze to Will. "I need to go and talk to Jill," I said.

"Before you do," Marcia said, "quick update. No luck tracking down anyone who might know where Liam Warburton is. He's got few friends, if any. Also, I've translated the page found on Maria Corvici and I sent it to Zach. I've just received a message saying he's on his way in."

I couldn't wait around. "Get him on a video call," I said, "and put it up on the big screen."

Marcia made the call and a moment later, the larger of our screens above the Themis console came to life with Zach's head and shoulders. "Just heading to my car," he said.

"What can you tell us about the text on that page?" I asked.

"It's from the 1857 Grimm version of *The Robber Bridegroom*. To briefly summarize, it tells the tale of a miller's daughter who is engaged to a man she barely knows. The bridegroom gives his fiancée the address of his house in the woods and asks her to visit him there. When the woman goes there, she finds she has been tricked. This is the house of a group of thieves and murderers, who plan to chop the young woman up, cook her, and eat her. I know, I know, another nice and cozy Grimm fairy tale." His grin seemed to fill the screen. "Helped by an old woman, the young bride-to-be escapes the house and later, on the day of her wedding, she exposes the bridegroom as one of the murderous robbers. The page Marcia translated is from a passage where the young woman is heading through the forest to the house and encounters a bird in a tree that sings her a warning."

"Thanks, Zach."

Marcia ended the call and I stepped across to look at the translated words on her monitor. My attention was drawn to the rhyming words of the bird's warning that had gone unheeded, and its parallels to Sam. I read the words of the verse out loud.

> *Turn back, turn back, thou pretty bride,*
> *inside this house thou must not bide,*
> *for here do evil things betide.*

I turned to the others. "Sam was engaged, so the pretty bride line could be a reference to that. The house in which you must not bide could be seen as the Warburtons' house."

Zoe repeated the final line. "The evil that betides there fits the Warburtons' criminal dealings. But how does the whole fairy tale fit the killer's pattern?"

I shivered at the thought. "Maybe by cutting up parts of the body as the robbers did to their victims."

The tension was like a vice tightening around my skull. How long did Sam have before she became the next victim, if she hadn't already?

* * *

A short while later, after Ilona had gone to see Jill Reiberger, Zoe was hunched over her sleek monitor, fingers flying across the keyboard, absorbed in her digital domain, when the UCU's entry door slid open. She looked up, as did Marcia, and Zach strode in, his lanky frame nearly bouncing on the balls of his feet.

"Guys," he said excitedly, "I've come across something intriguing I want to run by you."

Zoe smiled, amused as she always was, at how Zach's enthusiasm seemed to lift everyone's energy levels when he entered a room, but her expression was also one of skepticism. She was expecting another one of Zach's supernatural theories and right at that moment, she wasn't in the mood for that kind of speculation. "Go on," she said, with a tinge of weariness.

"I've been searching through university archives for anyone with a heightened interest in German folklore and justice or vigilantism." Zach's eyes widened as he continued, his words tumbling out in a rush. "I came across a student from the same college where I lecture. Mandy Rutledge. She wrote her thesis twenty years ago on Grimm folklore and its parallels with law and justice and society's perceptions of justice at that time. I was curious, so I looked for further details on her, and get this, I found news reports that she was murdered in a street mugging gone wrong not long after she sat for her final exams."

This wasn't remotely what Zoe was expecting him to come out with.

"That's awful," Marcia said, her brow furrowing, her calm demeanor in stark contrast to Zach's nervous energy, "but I'm not sure if it's relevant to what's going on with this case."

"Neither was I," said Zach. "But there's more. I read her thesis last night. Mandy was an enthusiast for all things from Germany in the era of the Grimms. She vacationed in Germany and while there, she purchased nineteenth-century editions of the Grimm books and other collectibles from the era, and that included jewelry, and the silver buttons popular at that time."

"Silver buttons…" Zoe's eyes narrowed. "Now you've got my interest."

"And mine," said Marcia. "Do you know what happened to her killer?"

"No, but I'd like to know a lot more about Mandy, her killer, her family and friends, and, in particular, what became of those collectibles."

"I'll get Themis to run a search on every piece of data out there that connects to Mandy Rutledge," Zoe said. "Let's see if anything of further interest crops up."

She programmed the necessary prompts into the AI.

Within minutes, streams of data zipped across her monitor, with Themis highlighting key points.

Leaning forward, with her brown eyes fixed on the screen, Zoe said, "Her father had a history of alcohol and drug abuse. Did a few stints in rehab. By all accounts, he drifted from job to job and was divorced from Mandy's mother, Victoria, soon after Mandy was born."

"Is he still around?" Zach asked.

Zoe tapped a few more keys. "No. There's a death certificate from a few years ago."

"And Mandy's mother?" Marcia probed.

"Victoria Rutledge. Let's see what Themis can find on her."

"Victoria Rutledge?" Marcia repeated, rising from her chair, the motion smooth and deliberate. "That name rings a bell." She watched over Zoe's shoulder as pixels coalesced into profiles and records.

"There are quite a few media references to her," Zoe said. "After her daughter's death, Victoria became a well-known and oft-quoted activist for justice, wanting stronger laws against violence, and greater rights for the victims and their families, but she's been off the scene for over ten years now."

"We should speak with her," Zach said.

Zoe nodded. She reflected for a moment on the legacy of a student long gone, her connection to the case tenuous but undeniable, opening up a new line of inquiry.

"Oh, my God," she said suddenly, her focus drawn to a specific line in one of the news articles.

"What is it?" Marcia asked.

"Mandy was stabbed multiple times and she was taken to a hospital where she died in the emergency room," Zoe's voice was a whisper, the hairs standing up on the back of her neck. "The same emergency room where her mother worked as a nurse."

Chapter Thirty-Eight

As I drove to Jill's motel room, I couldn't shake the sense of unease that had settled into my bones like a cold chill. Each new step in the investigation seemed to unearth a piece of information that sent us veering along multiple paths. It made no sense. None at all.

Jill answered the door on the first knock and was pleased to see me, ushering me in. I started by telling her about the evidence we'd uncovered that proved Monty Warburton had set Sam up for the murder charge. She listened intently, nodding, but then her face paled as I told her about Monty's burner phone and the multiple calls that had been made to her.

The silence that followed cast a pall over the two of us. It was as though time had trickled to a stop.

"Jill, did you know Sam was engaged to Monty Warburton's nephew?"

She hesitated, then nodded her head slowly.

"Why did Warburton phone you?" I prodded. "Jill, what's going on? Speak to me."

A haunted look passed over Jill's eyes and I saw the shake in her hands. "When Sam was arrested in DC for involvement in the robbery, I knew she was guilty and there was enough circumstantial evidence to see her convicted." She cleared her throat. "Sam would have been behind bars for at least five years. I was terrified for her, Ilona, I didn't believe she would survive, not with her attitude at the time. She would've ended up with a great big target on her back in the prison yard."

"What did you do?" I asked quietly.

"Monty Warburton approached me. He said he had an underling who was already on a similar charge and facing jail time. He'd persuaded this employee of his to take the fall for Sam by admitting to her crime. The Warburtons would further back that up by giving Sam an alibi, that she was in Seattle at the time interviewing for a job with them. All Warburton wanted from me in return was to do him just one favor – to remove a piece of evidence that the prosecution in DC had against an associate of his, evidence that was held by the department I worked for. It wasn't a case I was working on, but I could gain access to that evidence. I don't know, to this day, why I agreed to it. I'm totally opposed to any form of corruption but in a weak moment, terrified for Sam, I gave in. Weak, pathetic, and beyond that, so incredibly *stupid*, and I am so sorry, Ilona, so sorry. I wanted to come clean to you about it, and I never wanted you to find out like this."

Just listening to her confession, I felt numb. "But that wasn't the end of it," I said.

She shook her head slowly. "He came to see me again a while later, all the way from Seattle, for just one more favor. Last one, he promised, but I knew by then there would be no last one. I said no and he threatened to expose what I'd done for him the time before. He had proof, he said, and that would be just the tip of the iceberg, and that Sam would rue the day I'd refused him."

"What evidence did he have?"

Jill shrugged. "I never knew. He wouldn't say. Maybe he'd recorded our earlier conversations. Or maybe he didn't have any evidence, maybe that part of it was a ruse."

"You still didn't agree?"

"I didn't. I told him I would accept the consequences. I knew it would be the end of my career, and that I'd face serious charges, but I was in a dark place and I figured it was all over for me anyway. It was the only way out of being beholden to Warburton for the rest of my life."

"And?"

"He didn't leak to the cops what I'd done for him. Maybe he had no proof after all, but it was immediately after this that Sam moved to Seattle, took up a job in a laundromat that I later learned was owned by Monty Warburton, and not long after that, way too fast, I thought, she got involved with Warburton's nephew, Liam, and they got engaged. And then a short while later, she was arrested again, this time for a murder in Seattle. You know the rest, the charges were dropped, and then she vanished."

"You didn't think it strange she went to Seattle, the home base of the Warburtons, after that robbery charge against her in DC, was dismissed?"

"No. She knew what I'd done for her, but she didn't know the Warburtons personally and had no reason to have any contact with them. It wasn't until I hired Stan Avery and he discovered the firm she was working for was owned by the Warburtons that I realized they'd lured her here with a job offer. The last thing I knew about her life here was the murder charge."

"Do you think she knew the Warburtons were behind the job offer?"

"No, the offer was via their laundromat manager. They wouldn't have wanted her to know their intention of using her as leverage to get me to do their bidding."

"Then how did Sam come to meet Liam?"

"One of his jobs for his uncle was overseeing the chain of laundromats."

"Okay. And you believed the Warburtons had something to do with her disappearance?"

"I received a call from Oliver Warburton. He said he had a message for me, that they'd be wanting my help soon, and when they asked for it, this time they were sure I'd comply."

I mulled this over for a moment. It would be much easier for the Warburtons to kidnap Sam if she was in their home state. "Implying they were holding Sam as collateral."

Jill sucked in a deep breath, her hands shaking. "Yes."

I wasn't certain this made sense. "But Sam had become engaged to Liam."

"Yes."

"Do you think Liam was involved in Monty Warburton's criminal activities or Sam's disappearance?"

"I tried getting in touch but he never returned any of my calls, and as you know, he's since taken off for parts unknown. I've asked around and yes, he was suspected of being involved, although kept at arm's length by the family. He wasn't highly regarded by them when it came to his competence."

"Why did you think they would want to do any harm to a girl engaged to one of their own?"

"These are not normal people, Ilona; you, more than anyone, as an FBI agent, would understand that."

"But you've heard nothing from the Warburtons since?"

"Not since I last spoke with Monty and he assured me no one in his family had anything to do with Sam's disappearance. I didn't believe him and in the meantime, I came here and employed Stan Avery."

And that, I thought, would explain why the Warburtons had had Jill and Avery watched. They didn't want the PI stumbling on any proof of their suspected criminal activities.

"Jill, it seems unlikely the Warburton family kidnapped Sam for that reason and that six months later, you've heard nothing further. There may be something else going on, something different to what you're thinking."

Her expression darkened further. "What do you mean?"

I told her about the UCU's investigation into the sniper/folklore murders, and how Sam's dropped charges matched similar circumstances to the other victims.

"You think Sam could be one of the sniper's next kills?" Her voice was hoarse.

"I'm afraid it's a high probability, Jill. We're doing everything we can to find this sniper and Sam."

"But the call from Oliver Warburton? If they kidnapped Sam, they're not going to kill her if they want to use her as a bargaining chip."

"If that's the case, she'd be safe."

"But if the Warburtons didn't kidnap Sam, then where is she?" Jill's head dropped, a single line of tears glistening on her cheek. "I'm so ashamed of what I did, Ilona, I could never forgive myself if anything happened to Sam…"

I placed my hand on her shoulder. "As you said, you were in a dark place when you made an out-of-character decision." I didn't voice my deeper thoughts, that none of us could ever know what we might do if we were faced with the same choice. My memory flashed back to my teenage kidnap and how my father had agreed to my kidnapper's demands. My father released confidential FBI information to the general public, a move that led to the end of his career.

I've never regretted what he did but whenever he and I had spoken of the Bureau and his career, the sorrow was always there behind his eyes.

Jill's voice was a croak. "What happens now?"

"We find Sam," I said.

Chapter Thirty-Nine

I walked into the UCU and stopped in my tracks. The air felt charged, and all eyes turned to me. Will and the others were grouped around the main Themis console.

My heart skipped a beat. "What is it?"

Marcia brought me up to date on what Zach and Zoe had found out about a student named Mandy Rutledge, murdered twenty years ago.

I wasn't sure where they were going with this but I took a deep breath and pulled up one of the empty chairs. "Go on."

"Themis has run a facial recognition search on Mandy Rutledge's college photo," Zoe said, "cross-referencing it with social media from around that time. We're looking for connections Mandy had before her murder."

"And trying to trace what happened to her antique books and the silver buttons," Zach added.

I nodded, my mind racing with the possibilities.

"Themis has cataloged a bunch of photos," Zoe said, zooming in on an image. "I'd just pulled this one out of the pack and you'll see why. It's Mandy, and another girl, dressed in very witchy-type outfits, with a caption saying they've discovered the wonderful world of a Wicca breakaway group."

Zach shot me a half-grin at my reaction to the word 'Wicca.' He raised an eyebrow and pointed to it. His ongoing idea again that I continually raised my right eyebrow to convey a thought. *His* in-joke, not mine. As I usually did, I ignored the inference.

Instead, I stared at the image on the screen, and as I did, felt a chill crawl up my spine. The other girl in the photo looked like she could be a younger June Tranter. "Zoe, let's prompt Themis to access any college photos of Detective June Tranter from that period."

Zoe's fingers did their dance across the keyboard. A moment later, a photo of a young June Tranter, at the time of her graduation from the police academy, appeared.

Zoe gasped. "It's her. And you recognized Tranter in one of the photos I took of the Wicca meeting last night."

I swallowed hard, my throat dry. "Let's view all the Mandy Rutledge photos Themis has collected."

There weren't as many as I might have expected. Some more college shots. Some happy snaps, teenagers skylarking for the camera. And then a shot of Mandy with a young man, his arm slung casually around her shoulders.

"Rob Caulfield," I said, a stone dropping in my stomach. His youthful, carefree smile in the photo was a far cry from the cynical, jaded expression he wore when he'd met with Will and me.

"Before he became Detective Caulfield," Will said, his eyes meeting mine with an urgency. The room seemed to constrict, the weight of implication heavy in the air.

"Before," I echoed, my mind spinning. How deep did this connection between Caulfield, Tranter, and Mandy go, and how did any of that, or the girls' witchcraft involvement, connect to our investigation?

I thought about how Caulfield and Tranter had both known Mandy, how they'd both gone into law enforcement and had investigations that linked to some of the missing people who'd later become murder victims. I thought of how Mandy's collectibles were similar to the items found on those victims, and how June Tranter and Mandy Rutledge had been part of a Wicca group. What, if anything, could any of that have to do with the Warburtons and Sam Reiberger's disappearance – unless it was somehow linked with Liam's interest in Wicca? I had never known so many aspects of an investigation to be as shadowy as this, fading like ghosts before my eyes the moment I found potential links between them. The thought of entertaining Zach's theory about hidden realms was too out there for me to take seriously. There was nothing rational about any of this, but I was certain there had to be a rational explanation.

"There seems to be a pattern to all this," Will said, "though of what exactly, I'm not sure. But Ilona, you and I need to speak with Caulfield and Tranter again."

I nodded. "Anything on Mandy's killer?" I asked Zoe.

"There was a charge but it was dropped. We're hunting down more info on that."

"And what do we know about Mandy's mother?"

It was Marcia who replied. "I thought Victoria Rutledge's name seemed familiar when I first heard it, and, of course, we've since learned she became quite the activist after her daughter's death, often appearing in news reports. Very outspoken campaigner for a stronger form of justice in the courts. From what I've been able to find out, she's a widower and long since been out of the limelight. She's in a nursing home now. Dementia, I'm afraid."

Zoe navigated to the most recently known photo of Victoria, from her activist days over ten years earlier. An older woman with graying hair appeared on the screen. Her eyes were hard and determined, and there was a fierce intensity about her, fighting for a cause that must have left her in despair for most, if not all, of the time. An intensity that would have been sucked away now by a cruel disease.

"Where is the nursing home?" I asked.

Zoe rattled off an address south of the city.

I turned to Will. "Before we speak with Caulfield and Tranter, maybe we should see if Victoria is still capable of communicating. Even if only a little. If she's able to give us any idea what became of those early edition books and collectibles, it might point us in the right direction."

Will agreed. "First port of call, then."

* * *

But the frail figure that sat hunched in a plush armchair, in the nursing home, was barely able to speak, let alone understand. When the nurse led us into Victoria Rutledge's room, she told the old woman she had visitors and introduced us. The air was thick with the scent of lavender and antiseptic, mingled together, and sunlight filtered through sheer curtains.

Victoria remained immobile, her eyes staring vacantly ahead. The flickering light of the TV reflected off her thin glasses, emphasizing the deep lines etched into her face, lines that bore the markings of a long life no longer remembered.

Will and I both tried speaking with her to no avail. It was then, as we prepared to leave, that Victoria shifted in her chair, the soft fabric rustling beneath her. The eyes that were vacant a moment ago focused on me with a curious intensity.

"Did you know my daughter?" she asked, her voice trembling with a mix of hope and uncertainty, the words carrying a weight that seemed laden with history and longing.

For a moment I was taken aback, her question catching me off guard.

"I'm sorry, no, I didn't know Mandy," I replied gently, kneeling before her. "My name is Ilona and this is my friend, Will. We were just stopping by to visit some of the residents here. We were wondering if you were able to tell us a little about your daughter and her studies?"

Victoria's face remained blank, but there was the slightest glimmer of recognition in her eyes as she looked at me. But it wasn't my name that left her lips. "My daughter…" she repeated softly.

I smiled at her, hoping to forge some sort of connection and I decided on another approach. "Hello, Mandy's mom, it's good to see you."

Just saying that word brought a flood of memories that I couldn't afford to give in to at this point. There wasn't a day that went by when I didn't think about my mother, lost to me when I was just a little girl. I quickly refocused on the here and now but I couldn't help the catch in my throat.

"I was wondering, Mrs. Rutledge, what you remember about Mandy's folklore studies and the collectibles she bought in Germany?"

The old woman's eyes bore into me, as though trying to understand what I was saying. There was a long silence, and just when I thought Victoria was about to sink back into this strange mental oblivion, she suddenly cleared her throat, and as if the previous conversation hadn't taken place, she repeated, "Are you my daughter's friend?" Her eyes watered. "It is you, isn't it? Thank goodness... You must never tell anyone the truth, you know. Never... tell..." Her feeble voice trailed away, her eyes drooped, and a moment later she was in a deep sleep.

Will and I exchanged glances before signaling to the nurse and making our way out of the room.

As we walked down the hallway to the exit, I couldn't stop thinking how different this Victoria was from the strong-willed campaigner who had championed the cause for greater justice. Seeing her in such a fragile state was both heartbreaking and unsettling.

Will noticed my troubled expression and he put a reassuring hand on my shoulder. "Are you okay?"

I sighed. "It's incredibly sad to see someone like that."

He nodded, his eyes conveying much more than any words might have at that point, but they also reflected that he had the same question as I did buzzing in the back of his mind about Victoria's rambling words.

You must never tell...

Outside the nursing home, dark clouds loomed overhead as the first drops of rain fell. We were heading for Will's car when both our phones buzzed simultaneously. Exchanging quizzical looks, we both looked at our screens.

The panic button we'd given to John Raye had been activated.

Chapter Forty

"Headed in the direction of Leavenworth," I said, glancing at the dot on the screen's map as I slid into the passenger seat of Will's replacement Ford.

"We'll take the US-2." Will fired up the engine and the tires screeched against the slick asphalt as we sped off.

We were closer than any of the federal or police units we could get on the road. I phoned Marcia and told her Will and I were in pursuit. She, Zoe, and Zach were all looking at the same map on the monitors at the UCU.

"We've got Themis hooking up to the satellite over that area," Zoe said. "I'll update you when we've matched the aerial with the panic signal."

We made the decision not to phone Raye's cell, in case he'd been kidnapped, which we assumed must be the case.

As Will and I raced toward Leavenworth, the world outside blurred into a watery late afternoon haze of shadow and light. The drive seemed to last an eternity. By the time the quaint Bavarian-village-themed town came into view, my nerves had worked themselves into a frenzy. The rain had subsided and twilight was spreading. In the distance, the Cascade Mountains were like an apparition in the mist. The GPS dot had come to a stop in an area beyond the town, further into the countryside, but more alarmingly, Marcia phoned back to tell me that the live satellite view of that spot did not show any vehicle, just empty tracts of Douglas fir and pine forest.

The rain had stopped and the sun was low on the horizon, brushing the sky with streaks of crimson and gold. Will parked the car by the side of the road, in the spot where the panic button had last transmitted. The flat land here was peppered with groves of forest, their branches reaching out like gnarled fingers in the dying light. There was no sign of another vehicle hidden under the tree canopies along here, no trace of what might have happened to John Raye.

"Where the hell is Raye?" I muttered, my thoughts drifting back to Zach's wild theories about unseen realms. I shook my head. "The panic button could have been discovered by his abductors, dropped here, and they've driven on," I suggested to Will.

He nodded. "Or Raye thought the button was about to be discovered and got rid of it, leaving it as a beacon leading into the woods."

"But there's nothing here but empty land."

Will's reply chilled me. "Unless his body's been dumped here. Either way, we've not got much choice now than to check the area out."

We switched to our earpiece comms, drew our pistols, and stepped from the car. A fence, weathered and overgrown with wild brambles, marked the perimeter of the property along this stretch.

There were small gaps in the wire fence. Will located one that was large enough to squeeze through, its thin metal twisted and gaping like a wound. He inched through, lowering his head where the higher line of the wire drooped, and I followed, the scent of pine and wet earth rising to meet me. I studied the ground ahead and around us. No bootprints on the wet earth, no sign of the underbrush being tramped on.

"Doesn't look like we're going to find anything here," Will remarked. "We'll have to get a team out here in the morning to give the whole area a thorough search." His voice dripped with disappointment.

My gut squirmed at the thought of what might have happened to him.

There was an eerie stillness to the forest and I had a sense that it was disappearing around us as the lengthening shadows swallowed it up. The silence grew heavier with each of our steps, except for a crow's lone caw, which sounded more like a warning cry than anything else. And then, all of a sudden, something materialized just ahead of us, like a specter from another time – a large, dilapidated, single-level brick building, half eaten by a forest intent on claiming back every patch of earth as its own.

The forest seemed to inhale deeply, as though holding its breath along with mine, as I scanned the brick structure.

"What the hell…" Will began, his voice a whisper, stopped short by the crackle that came over our earpieces.

It was Zoe. "We've gathered some data on the area where the panic button went dead," she told us. "There was an old abandoned military outpost there in the middle of the last century. Army docs and local press of the time indicate it was sold to a private investor who had the non-forested part of the land cleared of buildings."

"Not totally cleared," I said. I told her about the building Will and I had stumbled on.

"Sounds like it must have been one of the barracks," Zoe said. Her voice was starting to break up.

"Who's the owner, Zoe?" Will asked.

"We're tracing all the documentation now."

"Keep us posted," Will said and Zoe signed off.

The building before us was dark and silent and Will's gaze was intense. "Let's take a look. Very, very slowly."

I nodded, my hand instinctively resting on the grip of my pistol.

The paint was peeling from the front door and the handle was rusted. Will turned it, slowly, cautiously, and then pushed the door open. With his pistol raised and aimed in front of him, he peered inside and then, satisfied, stepped through. I followed.

We were in a small room that was thick with dust and decay. There was some aged, rotting furniture pushed against one wall and a spiral of cobwebs in the corners and trailing across the ceiling.

Will approached the doorway at the far end of the room. He looked back at me. "There's a larger area beyond this," he whispered.

No matter how stealthily we crept, the floorboards creaked.

We stepped through and the long, wide room here was like nothing I'd ever seen. The walls were stark, moss growing up in smudges of green slime. The floorboards had been ripped away, exposing the bare earth beneath. In that exposed ground gaped a broad hole, covered by a metal hatch that had been left standing open.

"A bunker?" I whispered.

We edged forward, peering down at a metal ladder that descended into darkness. What was this place?

That was when the sound of a gunshot pierced the silence.

Chapter Forty-One

"I've tracked down a news article on Victoria from fifteen years ago," Marcia told Zach and Zoe, as they joined her at her desk. "It's a profile piece. An interview with Victoria about her memories of Mandy. There's a comment here that Victoria took Mandy to Germany to seek out some of the historical places associated with the Grimm brothers, and she mentions the purchase of certain antiques. But it's the mention that Mandy had brought along one of her friends."

"Who?" Zoe asked.

"It doesn't say. But there was someone else with them who would know of those collectibles, someone we need to speak with if we can find out who it was."

"Tranter or Caulfield?" Zach said.

"I've viewed their social media posts of the time," Marcia said, "and there's no mention of a trip. And Mandy, as we've already learned, didn't do a lot of posting to sites."

"Zach and I can also start trawling through archives to see who else Mandy might've been close to," Zoe suggested. As she and Zach returned to their own PCs, Zoe said, "The good news is I've got a strong sense that we're closing in on everything we need to know about Mandy and Victoria Rutledge. The bad news, for you, is I'm not getting the same feeling about uncovering a link to an otherworldly realm."

"I've been thinking a bit about that lately," Zach said, "a weird thought. At least, I think it's weird."

"And what's that?"

"Maybe we're not meant, in the scheme of things, to find proof of the supernatural. Maybe there's a reason we need to always be searching."

Zoe didn't hide the intrigue in her voice. "Go on."

"Maybe it's by design. Perhaps having so many signs of the paranormal all around us but never definitively proving its existence, means that the human race keeps on striving to solve the mysteries of the universe. It means we go on exploring, considering alternatives, making other scientific discoveries along the way, but always pressing on, drawn by a need to explain the inexplicable."

Zoe regarded Zach. "If we knew all the answers, we'd stop being so inquisitive. Eventually, there'd be a kind of decline into entropy."

Zach shrugged. "Something like that, yeah."

Zoe mulled the thought over. There was a logic to it, a rather beautiful symmetry that suggested a balance to all things. She cast a quizzical eye over the professor. "But you're not going to back away from trying to find that proof, are you?"

He flashed his cheekiest of grins. "Not a chance."

They'd barely settled into their seats when Marcia's voice cut through the silence, calling them back over. "I've come across some more background on Victoria Rutledge," she said. "You need to see this."

Chapter Forty-Two

At the sound of the gunshot, Will's eyes locked onto mine, the urgency clear. The gunshot had been outside in the forest, its echo still ringing in my ears.

"Keep an eye on the hatch," Will said in a hushed tone. "I'll check the exterior for the shooter."

"Will, be careful," I urged.

He acknowledged the concern with a nod and then walked quickly back the way we'd come.

I steadied my breathing, my ears straining for any sign of movement from beneath the hatch.

Nothing.

My thoughts swirled. This place was far from what we had expected. The old barracks. The dark hatch. The unnerving silence. And now gunfire somewhere out in the woods.

Every second seemed like a minute as I waited to hear something from Will and then, when my comms crackled into life, it was Zoe.

"Something weird, Ilona," she said. "The military base had an underground nuclear fallout and general storage shelter and it was purchased, get this, by a wealthy, eccentric doomsday prepper, one of the early ones – Hank Elderson."

"Elderson?"

"Yeah. Died years back, but the property's been in the family since then. And they own the neighboring property, a much smaller acreage, with an adjoining internal road between them at the rear. The real shock, that Marcia's just uncovered, is that it was Hank's son, Ward, that married Victoria Rutledge after her first marriage ended. She kept her last name to honor Mandy. They had two kids – Martin and June."

"Martin Elderson!" I said. "The deputy PA. And June?" I prompted, my mind still processing that Martin Elderson was the current owner.

"Already ran the check on that. She joined the police force, married another officer, named Tom Tranter, now divorced."

"Wait, what?" I breathed, my heart skipping a beat.

I moved away from the hatch, back to the doorway, to ensure I couldn't be heard in case someone was down there. "Martin Elderson and June Tranter are siblings and Mandy Rutledge was their half-sister?"

"Yes." Zoe's voice was breaking up again. "Raised together."

As Zoe's words sunk in, the pieces clicked with a cold finality. This had something to do with the Eldersons. Martin and June – their connection to Mandy. Her boyfriend, Rob Caulfield. June and Mandy in their witchy outfits. Not just friends but half-sisters.

What is down in that hatch, now, all these years later?

"Stay on the line, Zoe," I instructed, as I headed back through the smaller room to the front doorway. "I need to find out why Will hasn't been back in touch."

I peered out into the twilight. No sign of Will and then, another gunshot echoed through the forest.

"What's that?" Zoe said, her voice breaking up even more than before.

"A gunshot," I said but even as I did, there was a shot of static and then silence. "Zoe?" My heart pounded as I realized the line was dead.

Steeling myself, I moved outside, scanning the undergrowth and the tangled web of forest. The shadows deepened in the fast-fading dusk. "Will?" I whispered into the darkness.

Every step I took was calculated, my pistol aimed and ready, as I strained to hear any sign of life.

"Will?" I tried again, slightly louder this time.

Still there was nothing – no answering call, no rustling of leaves, not even the distant sounds of footsteps tramping the brush. It was as though he'd simply vanished into the night, and the sound of the gunshot had come from nowhere.

Had he been hit? Panic clawed at my chest, every nerve end sparking on an even higher alert as my eyes adjusted to the semi-darkness. The dying light struggled to pierce the dense, gnarled branches, creating distorted shapes that loomed over me, surreal in appearance.

I didn't want to stray too far into the dark but at the same time, if Will was lying somewhere near, hurt, or…

There was a sudden rustle of movement and I spun around but too late. A split second of massive pain exploded through my body, blinding me with its intensity. My legs buckled and I crumpled to the ground, barely registering the impact as I hit the cold earth.

Everything went black.

Chapter Forty-Three

My head throbbed with a sharp, pulsating pain as I opened my eyes. It was pitch black, an all-encompassing darkness that was both claustrophobic and suffocating. My throat was sandpaper dry, desperate for water, my grogginess weighing me down. My gun, phone, and radio earpiece had been taken, and despite my clothing being intact, I felt naked.

Panic rose but I fought it down, reaching out, seeking something – anything – in the void that surrounded me. My hands cut through the inky blackness, finding nothing but cold air.

No sound and not even a sliver of light. It was as though I was… nowhere.

"Hello?" My voice came out weak, more a croak than a call. It felt dead in the heavy silence. I wanted to push myself to my feet but instead, my head lowered back to the cold ground. I drifted in and out of consciousness, shaken by a sense that endless time was slipping by, that everything I had ever known and taken for granted was slowly, maliciously being erased…

* * *

I woke again, unable to tell whether minutes or hours had passed. My head pounded, a little less sharply now, and I rubbed the sorest spot at the back of my skull, my fingers coming away wet and sticky.

As I always did, as I was trained to do, I coached my mind to focus, and to formulate a plan. I steadied my breathing and pushed myself to my feet, my legs wobbly. I inched forward, my arms reaching out but still finding nothing. Edging further, I poked the air to the left and the right. I had the overwhelming sense that the space I was in was infinite, the darkness impenetrable.

Nothingness.

I kept going, taking it slowly, resisting the urge to plunge ahead. I didn't know what might be right in front of me. I didn't even know if the ground would give way to a hole like the one beneath the hatch in the old barracks.

I paused, to give the returning strength in my legs a chance to stabilize. I sat. I kept my breathing even and forced myself to focus on the here and now, not the past that this darkness dredged up – memories of my teenage kidnapping, waking in a box, at the base of a deep shaft.

The panic, the frightening climb, the escape. It had shaped me but had never defined me.

I'd been gathering my resolve for just a minute when the silence was suddenly broken by a cold, disembodied voice with a mechanical tone that echoed around me.

"We had long since set up false trails to lead investigators away from us," the voice lamented. "Rodwell, that poor soul who imagines himself some sort of fairy-tale king and the PTSD-addled Judge Conrad. Ideal diversions. But you got involved, Agent Farris, and your resourcefulness has somehow brought you here."

I responded to the voice without letting my surprise show. "We gave John Raye a panic button. He must have dropped it outside so that you wouldn't find it on him when you… what? Put him in a space like this one?"

"Regardless, this creates an impossible situation for us, and for you and your colleague."

"Where is Agent McCord?" My demand was much stronger than my voice sounded.

The voice didn't respond to that and Will's face flashed in my mind, his earnest gaze, the furrow of concern that marked his brow when the answers on a case proved elusive. I swallowed hard against the fear of what had happened to him. "What have you done?"

"This goes far deeper than you or your team could ever possibly imagine, and it must be safeguarded." The voice was like ice, devoid of emotion.

"So, Agent McCord and I are collateral damage?"

"Every war has unfortunate casualties."

"This isn't a war. You're making people disappear and then executing and dumping them, but we've already traced the ownership of this property. We know that Victoria Rutledge is your mother and that Mandy was yours and June's half-sister. I know who you are, *Martin*."

Not what this disembodied voice wanted to hear. No response. There had to be a speaker, or maybe speakers, embedded in walls somewhere, creating a sense of omnipotence. But now the silence stretched out and it seemed I'd been left alone again.

I recalled the visit to Victoria in the nursing home when she'd mistaken me for someone close to Mandy, and she'd said, "Never tell…" Who was the person close to Mandy she'd mistaken me for?

Back on my feet, I swept my arms around once more, with more vigor this time, stepping forward with a confidence I didn't feel. What did I expect to find? A wall? A door? Then what? My brain was on fire, fearing what Elderson was planning next.

Chapter Forty-Four

I wasn't sure how many minutes passed and then, without warning, the black void shattered as blinding light seared through the space around me, and my eyes strained to adjust. Blinking away spots, I caught sight of a vast, high-ceilinged concrete chamber. I'd been placed in the dead center, far away from the walls. I spotted one of the tiny speakers, high on a wall. And then my gaze shifted to the steel bars behind an open door at the far end. The figure of Martin Elderson loomed behind the bars.

"You didn't like what I had to say before," I said defiantly. I didn't shout, I figured there were also tiny mics hidden, maybe in the floor, by which I could be heard earlier when I was communicating with the disembodied voice. I marched toward the door, determined not to betray any sign of vulnerability.

"Because of your incursion here, I've had to radically alter my plans," he said quietly. "As a result, mercifully, for you, you've only been subjected to an hour of isolation and darkness, whereas the others spend a week in here, the beginning of their penance, deprived of all light, sound, food, and with only minimal water. A dehumanizing process because, after all, these people are barely human. They've killed and they've been fortunate enough to walk away scot-free, to live the lives their victims never can, all because of technicalities, whether it's missing evidence or missing witnesses."

"Those aren't technicalities. They're essential components of the law you're meant to uphold."

"And I'm upholding justice, in ways our broken system never can. These people don't look back, they don't confess. They carry on and they *prosper*, Agent Farris, they commit the worst of crimes and they *prosper*. Well, no more, not these people, and in time, hopefully, despite all these setbacks, this enterprise will restart, and we'll set up in even more locations." He waved to unseen areas behind him. "After their week of isolation, we move our prisoners to one of eight small cells, where they serve their sentence until the time of their execution when we need the cells for newcomers."

I glared at him. "What gives you, and June and Rob Caulfield, the right to play God?"

"June and Rob? They wouldn't have the stomach for what goes on here. They don't know anything about this place, nor will they ever. They never got over Mandy's death but they've dealt with it in their own ways, becoming cops. We've kept in touch with Rob, his work with Missing Persons gives him a sense of purpose although I've never been certain his heart's fully in it. June is a relentless, by-the-book officer, determined to get justice for victims, that's the best role for her, but I've seen her distress whenever perps manage to elude justice. As for me, this isn't about playing God, this is about justice for Mandy." At the mention of his half-sister, a softer shadow crossed his face. "She was brilliant, funny, passionate about morality, and the rule of law, and yet she was taken from us so brutally and far too soon."

"I know Mandy was murdered by a mugger who walked free."

"The system failed her." Elderson's jaw tightened. "I couldn't just sit back and let him roam free. I tracked him down, intending him to suffer injuries for what he'd done but my helper pushed it too far, accidentally killing him."

"Vengeance isn't justice," I said. I had always been repulsed by the idea of people taking the law into their own hands.

"It wasn't vengeance, it was deserved penance for the murder of Mandy, just not the retribution we hoped. We felt her killer should have endured years of pain, or years in prison before meeting his end. We disposed of the body and we made a bond, to honor Mandy by ensuring others like her killer got the punishment they deserved. And this place presented us with the perfect opportunity." He made a sweeping gesture. "It was once a military radar station. Just one of dozens across the country selected for radar surveillance, to track and identify any suspected enemy aircraft in surrounding air space, with just a small crew of twenty or so officers. It was used early on during the Cold War but by the late 1960s, there was little use for it and the deactivated base was put on the commercial market."

Elderson's relaxed manner belied the circumstances, his speech easing back as though he was telling a familiar family story to young children. "It was bought by my grandfather, a wealthy defense contractor who was also one of the early doomsday preppers. A nutter, in my opinion, who was convinced nuclear war was inevitable. He had the old barracks and outbuildings demolished, apart from the one that covers the hatch, and as you saw, the forest has long since reclaimed the land above us. What was of interest to my grandfather, was this underground bunker, an unpublicized part of the base, intended to withstand a nuclear blast but ultimately just used for artillery storage."

It was starting to make sense. "Which explains the hatch."

"Thousands of square feet, with several rooms. And this massive chamber."

My chest tightened as I imagined the horror of being incarcerated here, with little or no human contact, not for weeks or months, but years. I could barely believe Elderson's cruelty and arrogance, all made possible by family wealth.

"Maintaining this must take a chunk out of the family fortune."

"Nowhere near what you might imagine," he said. "The original ventilation system provides the fresh air needed. A manual well gives us fresh water. We installed a generator to provide the electricity, of which we use very little. There's minimal lighting. Cooling or heating is only utilized if and when temperatures might cause death to our inmates. Every three or four days, either myself or my friend comes back here to check on them. It's not a luxury hotel, Farris."

"It's not even a *humane* prison." I forced myself to remain calm, to keep my responses as quiet and measured as those of Elderson. I was damned if I would let him see the panic and the anger I felt raging inside. "And this sniper who kills for you — and I gather for your mother — is just as sickeningly cold-hearted."

His eyes narrowed and a shadow crossed his face at my mention of Victoria Rutledge. "My mother was devastated by Mandy's death, but she would never have set up anything like this. Yes, she was an activist for improving the justice system, but behind the scenes, she was sweetness and light. After my father died and my mother got sick, I told them I would look after the properties and they were assigned to me."

"But she guessed what you were doing."

"Perhaps, but she never spoke of it."

"It's a sick delusion and you of all people, a man of the law, should be able to recognize that," I said.

Elderson didn't appear to be listening, he was lost in his own narrative. "Out there in the woods is my friend, equally as devastated by Mandy's death, who has become fixated with the stories of the Grimms that Mandy researched so thoroughly – an obsession that has ultimately proved to be of great benefit. The sniper believes that our prisoners still get off too lightly. And so, when our prisoner's time is up, I release them into the forest, letting them think they have a chance at freedom. The shooter deliberately misses them with the first few shots, and lets them run around in circles for a couple of hours, terrorized, before firing the fatal shot. Every shot a salute to poor Mandy. Each victim is then adorned with red herrings as clues and returned to where they were taken from – no evidence leading back here. It paints a picture for the police, a serial killer with a penchant for fairy tales. We grouped the first three for discovery over a short period, to help police see the links, although, as it turned out, that didn't happen until now."

"That's why you grouped the first lot in Tacoma. You were already keeping tabs on Rodwell."

"We knew when and where he'd scheduled his school performances."

I changed the focus. "Sam Reiberger is innocent. New evidence has come to light."

He was silent for a beat and his eyes darkened. "It's too late for Sam."

"Where is she?"

"She's been out there in the woods for a while, I'd say she's dead now. To assist with today's releases, I used my underworld contacts to hire a couple of heavies. And after they brought you down here, those two men have gone to prepare the same fate for John Raye. We've had to enact a last-minute change and fast-track him so that this place is clear of any evidence when your people finally come looking."

"Underworld contacts? The Warburtons?"

"They don't know what goes on here but from time to time they've loaned me some of their underlings for special assignments."

"And in return, a blind eye is turned to their operations."

He didn't respond but his stony look spoke volumes.

"You rant on about justice and law but at the same time you're prepared to call on a criminal like Monty Warburton to lend you his cronies when you need them. You're nothing but another warped hypocrite."

His stare never wavered. "A necessary evil but only a small one at that and rarely used. I can hardly call on law-abiding citizens to assist. But I planned that, in time, Monty would get his comeuppance via planted evidence to some crime or other, with no one knowing where it had come from. After which, I'd simply do business with his son. Oliver, not many realize, is champing at the bit to take over the family business from his father."

"Backup's already on its way, Martin. This is over."

"Actually, that's what I went to deal with before. I've sent a text from your phone to your other team members, telling them to hold fire as you and Agent McCord have everything under control, the shots heard were local hunters, and you are heading back in. It will buy us enough time. When they do get suspicious and come snooping, the last prisoner will be gone and there won't be a shred of evidence of anything that's transpired here."

"You'd already begun a process of clearing house, before this, with these last three victims. Why? You mentioned setbacks before."

Elderson glanced at his watch. "I suppose I can spare you another minute, it's the least I can do for a truly outstanding federal agent. I would've asked you to join us, Farris, but of course, you never would, even if you pretended to. In that way you're like June, earnest and traditional." He regarded me coolly, his face impassive. "Unfortunately, during my grandfather's day, this place was listed on old government records, as a survivalist bunker. The government is undertaking an audit of all known bunkers and fallout shelters, some damn nonsense about complying with environmental concerns. Ours was due in a couple of months."

"Which you were only aware of because you're a DA. That's why you suddenly stepped up murdering your inmates and having their bodies removed. There's no honor in this. Mandy would be disgusted by you and by your mother's silent suspicion of what you've been doing."

I saw his fists clench and his voice boomed. "Don't you dare—"

"She would've been disgusted by Stan Avery's murder. How do you explain that?"

"I asked my shooter to keep an eye on Jill Reiberger and the PI she'd hired," he shot back. "We needed to know if Avery turned anything up that implicated us. A day before Stan Avery followed that white hatchback, the shooter had already observed the hatchback following Avery at differing times. We had followed it ourselves, before Avery did, to the Leavenworth property and we discovered it belonged to the Warburtons." His voice calmed. "I didn't know why the Warburtons were following Avery and Jill, but then the Warburtons have got all sorts of things to hide, haven't they? But it presented me with a problem. Avery followed the hatchback and saw it on a property belonging to the Warburtons. I couldn't allow even the ghost of a chance that Avery's discovery might lead him to their connection with me. By having Avery shot, sniper-style, I knew it would be connected to the folklore murders and the various red herrings put in place leading down false trails."

"How might Avery have connected the Warburtons to you or to this place?"

Elderson shrugged. "The driver of the hatchback was one of the goons Warburton had loaned me from time to time. If Avery questioned that driver and he cracked and inadvertently let something slip... As I said, I could not allow even the ghost of a chance that our work here might be compromised." Elderson allowed an uncharacteristic glow of self-righteous pride but I wasn't finished with him.

"Mandy Rutledge is turning in her grave," I said with a calmness to match his, "her murder made into a monstrous mockery. You've become the very thing you despise."

But Elderson's façade didn't waver this time. "We will spare you the indignity of running for your life in the dark woods. My sniper will be back in here soon, at which time you will have to be dealt with."

"Will they, though? Agent McCord is out there, he's armed, and he knows what he's doing."

I could see it in his eyes – the unshakeable belief that he was on the side of right, that he was untouchable. "McCord is no match for my sniper," he said, with a dismissive wave of his hand, as if swatting away my words like flies, "and I gather he's already been shot dead." The creases around Elderson's eyes deepened as he stared at me with a cold certitude and then he turned and walked away, disappearing from view.

Chapter Forty-Five

The sniper

At first, they have no idea I am on their trail. They believe they can find a way through this. And then, once they come within a hair's breadth of death, when they realize that they can't outrun their past, panic sets in. I see it in the whites of their eyes. I could see my prey but they couldn't see me and that has always been part of the thrill.

I was trained to take in every minute detail of a scene: the patterns in every move made by my target, the lay of the land, the drift of the breeze, and the density of the light.

A person running and zig-zagging is governed by all of those things. An elite sniper matches those elements with the split-second timing of the shot. And in that moment, I see the wheels turn and the gears of justice locking into place.

A flicker of movement caught my attention and there she was, darting between the shadows, ghost-like amidst the towering trees. I'd followed Sam Reiberger as I had all the others, and whenever she slowed or stopped to catch her breath, I'd quickly take up a position, breathing calmly, my eyes registering every detail. I aimed my lightweight semi-automatic rifle, fitted with day and night vision scope that ensured targets were visible even in the lowest of light conditions, and my adrenaline hummed like my own internal soundtrack. With every one of these hunts, my mind brought forth my life as a US Marine, the precision and patience drilled into me with every mission. It was a solemn education borne of necessity, a transformation from citizen to soldier after Mandy's murder. My enlistment was an escape, a means to channel roaring grief into a sharp point of focus, and with each pull of the trigger, I sought to honor her memory. Even now, after all this time, I felt the heavy burden of the promise I made to myself at her funeral.

I was her best friend and I love her as much now as I did then, when I'd dreamed that one day she might turn from Rob Caulfield to me instead.

For years after she was lost, I'd consumed every word and image from her research and her thesis on the world of Jacob and Wilhelm Grimm, the folktales they collected reflecting a moral belief that fate would always intervene to bring retribution to evildoers, tales embedded with a code that was the same as that of the criminal justice system: to find the truth and deliver punishment to the guilty.

The images swirled through my mind. The hunter killing the wolf and saving the little girl and her grandmother; Gretel pushing the old witch into the oven and saving her brother; pigeons pecking out the eyes of the evil stepsisters; the silver button in the king's brother's gun bringing down the witch in the forest.

The stillness before my shot was sacred time stretched thin by anticipation. The distance was crucial so that, combined with the weight and speed of the bullet, it could pierce the skull and exit the other side.

I loved my time in the Marines and the training in sniping, ballistics, and stalking. But I had taken all of that to a whole new level, creating something in these woods more intricate and dynamic than any sniper would have ever seen. And it worked brilliantly, out here, for these criminals.

This was for all the murder victims. But most of all, it was for Mandy.

* * *

Sam Reiberger was covered in sweat, her stringy, long hair hanging limp down the sides of her face. It wasn't sweat from physical exhaustion as it wasn't long since she'd been set free and started heading through the dense woods with the sun low on the horizon, twilight spreading deep shadows across the conifers and the pine needles that littered the forest floor. The first shot had come just minutes ago, followed by another, with a bullet thudding into the bark of a tree just inches from her head. It was sweat from pure fear, palpable and intense, igniting every nerve end throughout her body, inflaming the blood that coursed through her veins, pounding in her temples, stealing away every second breath.

She ran, sidestepping around the gnarled trunks of the trees. Her eyes darted about, searching for the simplest movement, the slightest sign of her pursuer.

Silence. Not a sound other than for her thundering heartbeat, like a relentless drumming in her ears, and the crash of her footfalls through the undergrowth. Not even the twitter of the birds; it was as though they too had fled, their senses always heightened against unseen, unheard dangers.

Stillness. No other movement except for the light wisps of breeze which seemed to be conspiring with her pursuer so that the only prominent movement, the only sound, would be hers. An unmissable target.

The stillness and the silence reminded her of the first time she'd woken in this fractured reality, believing she was in limbo.

Nowhere.

How long had it been since then? Months, years? Time had no meaning here. Until now. Until these deep woods and this desperate run to… where?

She'd been taken from her cell, forced to dress in her old clothes, taken outside, and told she was being given a chance for freedom.

She did not want to think about the folktale but the full rhyme had been an unwanted mantra forced into her head, often playing over and over, words she thought she must have heard from the disembodied voice when she was half-asleep in her cell.

> *Turn back, turn back, thou pretty bride,*
> *within this house thou must not bide,*
> *for here do evil things betide.*

Those words sent a shiver slicing through her spine. She now realized she'd also heard her manic kidnapper reciting the verse through her drug-induced state when she was first transported to this place. She tripped, her hands flailing out in front of her as she sprawled across the rough ground of stony patches and scattered grass. As she pushed herself to her knees, in the dark recess of a massive tree stump right in front of her, she caught sight of a pair of eyes, glaring at her. She reared back and froze, the hairs shooting up on the nape of her neck, and her breath caught in her throat.

The creature in the blackened alcove shifted, a sliver of faded light illuminating its head and its eyes blazed with anger. An owl. So she and her pursuer weren't the only living things in this strange, unforgiving landscape. The owl hooted, the sound deafening; it was as though the creature was trumpeting her position.

God no…

She was about to spring to her feet when the owl darted out and in that same instant, Sam's ears were deafened by the thunderous crack of a gunshot. In the split second that followed, she felt the impact.

Chapter Forty-Six

Left alone in the chamber, the light from the open doorway enabled me to scan the vast, barren expanse, becoming acutely aware again of the drumbeat in my head and the chill of the air. The ceiling looked to be around eighteen feet, a haunting reminder of this chamber's time as an artillery storage hub. The walls were exposed brick that bore the scars of time – tiny cracks webbed across their surface like veins, particularly higher up. The urban climbing side of my brain kicked in. I imagined leaping, clinging to those cracks, and clambering up to the ventilation panel in the ceiling.

I took a deep breath and tried to calm the pounding in my chest. My mind flashed back to my teenage kidnap, and I could almost smell the dank, musty air of the shaft I had escaped from so long ago. The memory should have been paralyzing, but instead, it fueled my determination, reminding me of how I'd fought back and survived.

I could do this, and it wasn't as though I had any other options. I had to give it all I had. I flexed my fingers, feeling the familiar itch that came before a leap.

I kicked off my shoes so that I could use my toes as well as my fingers to wedge as deeply as I could into the tiniest of cracks. I took advantage of the large space, giving myself plenty of run-up. I crouched in a runner's starter position and then I sprang forward, sprinting across the expanse, aiming for a section where there was one of the larger gaps. I leaped, and smashed myself against the wall, clawing at the deep crack there. For a sickening moment, I slipped, scraping against the brick. Then my fingers latched onto another crack, and I clung there, feet scrabbling for a foothold.

There was a taste of dust and sweat on my lips and the brick bit into my fingers. Every muscle screamed in protest and my breath came out in ragged gasps but I could not, *would not*, let this chamber beat me. It was, after all, just eighteen feet, a far cry from the towering, multi-level structures I climbed whenever I had the chance to indulge in my secret and dangerous obsession but, of course, it lacked the ledges, ridges, windowsills, and pipes.

I reached back up to that larger gap and grunted as I heaved myself higher, my toes pressing into every recess and fissure they could find, however slight. I had to take it very slowly to ensure I didn't slip again as I fought off rising panic. I pushed everything else from my mind, and as I did, the chamber seemed to shrink away around me. It was just me and this rough patchwork of brick wall. One more pull, one more push. One more pull...

I felt relief surge through me as I reached the ceiling and I clung to the top of the wall, gasping for air. There was a narrow recess here along the line where the wall and the ceiling joined, and I dug my bloodied fingers in deep.

The first in a series of ventilation panels was positioned with its closest edge just several inches in from the wall. I reached across, and stuck my fingers into the grille, feeling it rattle beneath my grip. More relief when it came away more easily than I'd expected, but I couldn't do anything about the grille falling to the ground with a loud clang, the sound echoing, and wherever Elderson was in the greater compound, if he was close enough, there was a good chance he'd hear it.

Gathering whatever reserves of strength I had, I reached out and grabbed hold of the vent's opening. I swung my legs to create momentum, ignoring the pain that shot through me as I hauled myself up. My elbows found purchase in the ventilation tunnel and I thrust my head up and through, biting back a cry as my nerve ends screamed.

With more of my upper body in the tunnel for leverage, I managed to pull my lower half through.

It was the shortest and shallowest climb I'd ever done, but without doubt one of the most excruciating.

Kept in total darkness, the prisoners here before me would have never seen that rough wall, and even if they had, they wouldn't have been able to climb it. There was no way Elderson would ever have imagined it possible. I imagined Elderson's shock when he returned to find me gone. The thought brought a flicker of satisfaction but I quickly suppressed it – right now my only focus was on getting free and finding out what had happened to Will and Sam.

I began to crawl, the cold metal of the tunnel pressing against my palms and my breath echoed in the confined space, the metallic whine of the vent humming in my ears. There would be a point where this horizontal tunnel linked with a vertical shaft, where the air was being drawn from above ground. My only hope was to find it before my escape was discovered because, once Elderson and the assassin knew I was in this tunnel, I'd be a sitting duck.

The minutes dragged and the tunnel seemed to stretch endlessly, the darkness broken only by the occasional sliver of light that peeked through the grilles below. I'd passed a few of these smaller grilles, and as I inched over another one, I glanced down into what appeared to be one of the tiny cells. Visions of the prisoners who once inhabited these stark boxes of solitude flooded my mind. Emily Yarros, Jack Corris, and the others. I heard their anguished cries, begging for release. Despair, isolation – a fate worse than death for some. Some of them had been imprisoned here for years. I shook off the sense of dread and kept worming my way through the narrow passage.

My limbs ached from the effort, and with every inch forward, I felt as though the claustrophobic tunnel was closing in, ready to crush me into oblivion.

And then, another surge of relief washed over me. Just ahead, I saw the horizontal passage finally give way to a vertical air shaft. Reaching the juncture, there was enough room for me to stand, and looking up, my eyes were drawn immediately to a metal ladder embedded in the side of the shaft. A dim light filtered down. I grasped the cold rungs and my muscles strained as I began to climb, each step fueled by sheer determination.

The ladder creaked under my weight, a protest to years of neglect, and despite the urgency screaming at me, I took it slowly, cautiously, ready to react if there was a loose rung. The structure held and minutes later, I reached the grille that covered the shaft's opening. Beneath it and to the side, nestled like a secret, was a step leading to an alcove that harbored a hatch door. A portal once accessed by the military maintenance workers of yesteryear. I pushed it open and shouldered through into the night, the hatch opening onto the edge of a clearing. I was greeted by the last strains of twilight bathing the ground in an ethereal glow, casting long shadows among the Douglas fir trees that circled the space. The tranquil beauty of this scene was not lost on me, a stark contrast to the ugliness far beneath, but almost immediately, that peacefulness was shattered as movement caught my eye – the blur of a figure glimpsed briefly at the far edge of the clearing, moving quickly but dragging one leg, then just as quickly swallowed up by the darkness and the foliage.

I took a moment to catch my breath and gather my strength. And then the boom of a gunshot from somewhere in the forest on the other side, an unnatural, alien sound in this most natural of landscapes.

I sprang to my feet and sprinted across the clearing.

Chapter Forty-Seven

I plunged into the undergrowth on the other side, keeping low in the long grass. The damp earth clung to my hands as I crawled forward, using the tree trunks to shield me as much as possible. With the long grass brushing against me, I moved ahead furtively, searching for the figure I'd seen running here, and for the source of the gunshots.

"Sam? Will?" I whispered under my breath, in the vain hope that they were close by, but the silence was damning.

And then all of a sudden there was a burst of activity, the sound of someone trampling through the undergrowth. I veered toward the sound, and moved faster toward it. I knew that Will would move with much more stealth if he was trying to avoid a shooter. But what chance did Sam have, out here in the dark, frail and disorientated after months of imprisonment?

Another gunshot. It echoed through the night like a thunderclap and I froze, my heart hammering in my chest. The crushing silence that followed gave me the distinct impression that there'd been a hit.

I surged forward, navigating the forest with desperation. Every shadow seemed to lunge at me, and then I stumbled upon a body lying in the brush. I felt an icy grip tighten around my chest as I reached down with shaky hands, turning the head of the lifeless figure.

John Raye.

Elderson's hired underlings had already deposited him in these woods, leaving him as prey. I had to hope they had returned to the bunker, unaware of my escape. But before long they would return to move the body.

Before I could make a move, there was a rustle that seemed to come from everywhere. I pressed myself hard against the earth and began to slither away, toward another broad, gnarled trunk, but another gunshot pierced the night, the bullet thudding into the ground mere inches from my head. Cold sweat dripped from my forehead and stung my eyes as I rolled to the side.

I rolled twice more, navigating around the edges of the nearest tree trunk. I pulled myself up and pressed my back against the bark as though it could offer some kind of protection. *Focus.* I thought back over every survival tactic that had been drilled into me since I joined the FBI. *Identify the position of the enemy.* I peered around the tree, my gaze slicing through the foliage like a blade, searching for the slightest sign of movement.

That's when it struck me. I'd been pressed against the earth when the bullet thumped into the ground right in front of me. The angle from which the bullet had to have come was not from ground level, it was from somewhere above me. My eyes snapped upward and I realized, with horror, that I was in the crosshairs of a shooter who had the high ground, from up there in the trees.

Chapter Forty-Eight

My gaze swept the treetops, and I wondered how the killer had moved away so quickly. I caught a glimpse of something hanging down through the foliage, a flicker of light touching its braided surface. Rope? I focused on the light-tinged patch. It was a rope but it wasn't the only one.

If my head was still aching I didn't know it. Adrenaline coursed through my veins like a wild river. Moving as stealthily as I could, I inched forward, eyes still on the canopy overhead, and I made out similar shapes. How many more I couldn't say, but if there were hundreds of these ropes spread out over the near vicinity, then together with the intricate web of branches, it meant the shooter could utilize the air, as much or even more so than the ground, to swing through these woods, unseen, but with their eyes constantly keeping sight of their prey.

I'd seen a network of ropes like this before. FBI trainees were sent across an obstacle course that contained ropes as well as walls, trails, and tunnels. Climbing a twenty-foot rope was just one of the challenging physical requirements, and there were times when there was a whole array of these, hung from scaffolding, with trainees scaling up them simultaneously. Similar setups weren't uncommon in various survival training programs. Military training, where recruits climbed, and swung while eluding the enemy and discharging weapons. *Elite* soldier training.

It made sense. The folklore murders were the result of a single bullet to the head, fired from a distance. It took the military-grade precision of an armed forces sniper to achieve that, time after time. Particularly in a scenario like this one. Elderson's words came back to haunt me. "…McCord is no match…"

What Elderson didn't know was that climbing and traversing steep heights was right in my wheelhouse.

Was the sniper watching me now? Staging these executions preceded by mock escapes in the twilight and early evening, when visibility was at its worst, gave the shooter yet another advantage. I did not doubt that they would be equipped with infrared night goggles.

I launched myself away from the tree and ran while zigzagging so that I wouldn't present an easy target. I reached the spot above which the rope hung. It stopped about twenty or so feet off the ground, so I took a run-up to the nearest tree, leaped, grabbed hold of a notch between the trunk and the first branch, and pulled myself up. Compared to what I'd just been through, climbing this tree was a walk in the park. I shimmied a little higher, reached up, and grabbed the next branch, once again pulling myself onto it, every muscle straining, my heart doing its own leaps and bounds.

I climbed higher, past the bottom end of the rope. I'd need plenty of the rope beneath me if I was going to effectively wrap my body around it to assist in climbing and swinging.

I reached the next branch. Crawling out across this one wouldn't get me quite close enough to the rope, but the next branch above me would. That was when a bullet whizzed past me, mere inches from my head; a whisker closer and it would have grazed me. For a marksman this precise, that miss was deliberate. They were playing their game with me, the same sick game they played for hours on their intended prey before they fired the final, fatal shot.

But I knew the killer didn't intend to draw this out. Not for long, anyway. They needed to finish this, dispose of the bodies and the evidence, and vanish. I posed an unexpected threat that needed to be eliminated, fast, with little to no time for the game.

I was exposed where I was, out of reach of the rope, and crawling out on this branch would make me an even easier target. *Damn.* My best option was to jump down to the ground, more than twenty feet below, and try to land without breaking anything.

My eyes roamed the darkness. I couldn't see where the shooter was. But then, a voice came from the distance. "I didn't think you'd see the ropes, not in this light. But, of course, once you had, you'd climb, wouldn't you, Ilona?"

I recognized the sound, the same muffled voice I'd heard from a distance in the alley, the person who'd watched me urban climbing and then used it as a threat to warn me off. But Elderson hadn't mentioned my climbing and I sensed this shooter hadn't revealed my secret. "You didn't tell the others?" I called out, at the same time reanalyzing my surroundings for any option other than to jump. This killer was unpredictable, and the fatal shot could be fired at any moment.

"I thought I'd keep your little secret up my sleeve; leverage, in case it came in handy. I liked you, maybe thought you could be persuaded to join us if a situation like this came about, but Martin made it clear you could never be trusted."

Liked me?

There was something about the voice that was familiar, and not just from that brief encounter in the alley. I needed to get this phantom to say more.

I glanced up at the fractured fading shards of light filtering through the canopy, and down at the forest floor, with its gnarled tree trunks and blades of grass and pockets of brush. The eerie silence and darkness were like something out of the Grimm tales, like the deep woods in *Hansel and Gretel,* but something else about the time and place made even more sense.

"What is all this?" I shouted into the void. "A natural shrine to Mandy because it evokes the tales she loved?"

"Everything about this place, and what we do here, is in memory of her," came the response. I'd struck a nerve. The reply had been shouted back, less guarded, and the voice I could now tell was female.

"You and Mandy were good friends," I called back. "But she was more to you than that, wasn't she? Even though she had a boyfriend, you hoped that maybe, one day, she'd like you *more*. But Mandy would've despised what you're doing here."

"You don't know what you're talking about." Another shot, fired in anger, shattered the night air, whizzing past my head.

My hands were shaking, my heart pounding, my nerves tightening so hard it felt like my skin was being stretched. I chanted inwardly to myself to remain calm. Breathe. In. Out.

Anger was loss of control, exactly what I wanted to invoke in this shooter. Not something this elite markswoman would ever normally allow. Except she'd never had words like that, about Mandy, thrown at her while she was engaged in a kill.

"What happened after Mandy's murder?" I yelled. "Let me guess. You joined the army, took on the most punishing training regimen, became a sniper, using your missions to vent your angst over her death, but it simply became an addiction, because hostility isn't how you help grief. You just crave more, and you left the army and became part of this… abomination." I very slowly shifted my position, hoping I'd distracted the shooter enough so as not to notice that I was priming myself…

"For justice," called the sniper.

"Mandy would never have condoned this…" I'd tucked my leg behind me, stretching it back, and in the split second before the killer could reply, I pushed myself off the branch, grabbing hold of it and swinging out, and then letting fly, aiming for the rope, stretching my arms out as far as I could to reach and grasp it. One chance. A long shot. If I was a hair's breadth short, I'd fall, but it was my best – my *only* – option.

I missed.

My head was a whirl of thoughts as I plunged down but instinct kicked in. Like a parachutist in freefall, I spun my body and aimed myself at the rope, just in time to grab hold of the bottom end. It wasn't enough by which to haul myself up, but I did manage to swing.

I dropped onto a branch of the tree alongside, just as another shot rang out and the bullet thudded into the bark of the trunk just inches from my head.

I slithered down the trunk to the next branch below and jumped to the ground from there.

No more shots were fired. I glanced up but I still couldn't see my adversary, nor hear the rustle of movement. She was too good for that. She'd be repositioning, biding time, watching me, lining up for the kill. Every one of these moments out here, every one of these kills, satisfying an obsession, an urge for an imaginary revenge. An inner turmoil that life as an army sniper hadn't been able to quell.

I kept low and darted through the undergrowth toward a wide clearing that was ringed by the forest. I needed to get to the other side. The killer couldn't swing across it but at the same time, I couldn't run through it, out in the open and exposed to the infrared rifle scope. I had to skirt around the edge of the clearing to a spot where there was only a short gap in the open to cross.

Once I'd got to the next grove of trees, across the clearing, I'd climb to give myself both the advantage of height and the chance to then… what? I was unarmed, with only the fast-fading twilight for visibility, and being hunted by a zealot who was not only an elite sniper with night vision, but who had mastered the use of these ropes in the forest. It wouldn't take her long to sprint across the same clearing and be back in the trees.

Who was she?

It was someone close enough to Elderson and Mandy to have become a part of this. Someone who knew me, they'd known my name when they confronted me in that alley. Someone who *liked me*. I cast my mind back to my first meeting with Martin Elderson. He'd walked in with his very savvy assistant. Later, she'd approached me, giving me the false trail that led to Judge Conrad. She'd shown an interest in me that had been less than subtle. Her limp, she'd said, was the result of an old sporting injury. But what if that injury had been suffered on an army mission, leading to her being discharged? The figure I'd seen earlier could have been this killer, dragging their leg as they pursued John Raye.

I replayed her voice in my mind. Even from a distance, with the voice raised to a shout, I now recognized the timbre.

All those years ago, when Mandy's suspected murderer was killed, the person responsible, standing alongside Elderson, was a close friend of Mandy's who'd had strong feelings for her. Someone who was now also in a position where they knew people in law enforcement and could gain access to items such as speed spikes.

Steph Allsworth completed the picture.

Chapter Forty-Nine

She'd always been in control. As an army sniper, zeroing in on her target. As the shooter who was the real folklore killer, her identity unknown, up above her prey, with infrared-vision goggles that her victims didn't have.

Our check on courthouse staff with military service hadn't thrown up her name. I had no doubt she and Elderson had taken steps to cloud her background. Maybe they'd simply altered her social security records at the courthouse.

Steph Allsworth was used to having the upper hand and the advantage of surprise.

She didn't have either now, nor did she have as much time as she normally would, and that was what gave me the opportunity I needed. I could climb, and I could swing through these trees, matching her in her domain. More importantly, I knew who she was, and her connection to Mandy. I could taunt her with that, distract and destabilize her, as I had when I invoked the anger that saw her lose her laser-like focus by firing before she was ready.

One major problem, however. She had a weapon and I didn't.

Or did I?

I was perched on a branch, thirty feet up, and my eyes fixed on my hands, encircling and gripping a hanging rope.

There appeared to be hundreds of these ropes, and they were as much mine now as they were hers. My survival training kicked in deeper. *Utilize whatever's within reach. Formulate a plan.*

I had my mind, my body, the ropes, and I had the trees.

Trying to taunt and distract Allsworth wasn't going to be enough. She would bounce back from that. She was a hardheaded professional, relentless, driven, and skilled to the max.

I had to go higher than she normally needed to go and I needed to outswing her. With a swift push, I launched myself and swung between the trees. I focused on the thick, wide branch I was aiming for and landed it. Strands of hair clung to my face, damp from sweat.

This branch was intermingled with several other limbs, forming a ladder-like structure that enabled me to climb higher. My muscles burned with fatigue but I couldn't allow that, or anything else, to slow me down now. I needed to reach the perfect vantage point if I had any hope of stopping Steph Allsworth.

As I reached a height of about forty feet, I paused to catch my breath. Leaning against the trunk, I surveyed my surroundings. The dim light provided just enough visibility for me to discern the maze of ropes crisscrossing between the trees. It was clear most of them had been attached at this height, providing Allsworth with plenty of leverage as she hunted her human prey.

I scanned the shadows below for any sign of her. I was certain she would have followed my trail across that clearing and into this thicket of trees, her rifle at the ready. After just a few minutes, a rustle caught my attention and I caught a brief glimpse of her, an apparition, swinging through the deepening darkness, twenty feet below.

I grabbed hold of the nearest rope, and swinging with precision, I lowered myself down and soared toward the spot where I had seen her. I landed on a branch, crouching low.

"I know who you are, Steph," I called out. "You think Mandy would approve of this? She'd be turning in her grave." I injected as much venom as I could into my words.

No response and the forest was still, but I knew she'd heard me. I could feel her eyes, searching, calculating.

The sudden crack of a gunshot pierced the night air. The shot missed but it gave me an idea of where she was now. I scrambled higher on the tree, seeking a better outlook. Another shot rang out, splintering the bark beneath my feet. I had anticipated it, but my breath still caught in my throat at the near miss. My tactic had worked, she was off balance, taking shots without having a clear enough line to me, but she was getting closer.

Gritting my teeth, I swung on the next rope, arching my body to gain height. As I soared, I spotted another rope just within reach. My fingers closed around it, and for a moment I was weightless, free of gravity, my senses lifting with the exhilaration I felt when I urban climbed. I caught sight of Allsworth below me, her figure illuminated through the gloaming. I leaped across and grabbed hold of a thick, sturdy branch.

"You're out of time," I yelled, my voice fierce and determined. "It's over, Steph."

She'd disappeared again, and the forest was still. Her silence confirmed what I already knew, that surrendering wasn't in her nature. I climbed higher.

Another shot thundered in my ears, the bullet lodging in the tree just inches from my face, splintering the bark and sending tiny shards billowing, stinging my eyes. Even though she wasn't used to her target being up here, swinging through the trees, she wasn't far off the mark, and she wouldn't miss too many more times.

The time for drastic action was now.

My eyes peeled across the dark, shifting shroud of foliage, the first shards of moonlight casting silvery threads.

Movement. Flashes of Allsworth swinging onto a branch, and perching, taking aim. In that split second, I felt the weight of this deathly dance weighing down on me. I grabbed hold of the rope, and slid down it, my fingers burning, as I swung, hurtling toward her, a totally crazy act that would be the last thing she'd have anticipated. We collided, and the impact sent her rifle flying from her grasp, but to my horror, it remained tethered to her body by a strap.

Allsworth's eyes widened in surprise as she toppled backward, but her grip on her rope was vice-like, and she recovered quickly, swinging away in a wide arc. She looped back with lightning speed and slammed into me with her feet, catching me off guard and the blow sent me reeling.

I plummeted, panic spiking as I desperately flung my hands out for anything to stop my descent. Miraculously, my hands found the rope again, the rough fibers biting into my skin as my body jerked to a stop. I quickly swung away before another shot could be fired, clambering onto another branch, my muscles burning. But in my haste, I came down onto the branch with too much weight. This one wasn't as sturdy as the others. It cracked, and once again, I toppled.

I was close enough to the sides of the tree and there was a smattering of branches beneath that broke my fall as I clutched at them. I pressed the full length of my body against the bark. My hands and feet were a spiderweb of deep, bloodied cuts and scratches, my blouse and pants torn, my skin enveloped in sweat, my throat so dry it was an effort to swallow, every muscle and nerve end a mass of pain. Despite all that, I had to find the strength. I had to keep moving so that I wasn't a clear target, and I had to climb. Down on the ground, I would be like all the others who'd met their end there, standing no chance against the predator above.

I climbed, staying with the same tree because I was going to need the rope that dangled alongside it, and because I needed to keep Allsworth within this proximity, and lure her after me. A plan was taking shape in my mind, inspired by the extreme sport of rope swing jumping I'd been watching on videos. It was incredibly dangerous but if I could manage it, my best hope was to break Allsworth's grip on her rope and send her plummeting to the earth.

There were enough branches to help me scale this tree rapidly, and at around thirty-five feet, I settled myself in the fork of a branch. I reached across to the rope, pulled it toward me, and began drawing up the length of the rope beneath me. Hand over hand, I spooled the rope as I pulled it up and onto the branch, keeping an eye out for any activity from the area below where I'd last glimpsed Allsworth, aware that she'd be lining up for another shot once she'd zeroed in on my current position.

Once I'd drawn up the full extent of the rope, I took the end of it and looped it around my waist and under my legs. I secured it back to the rope around my waist, tying a figure eight to create a makeshift harness, a trick sometimes employed by rope swing jumpers. The remaining thirty-five or so feet of the rope hung slack, allowing me to swing and drop as needed.

I waited and watched. Then, movement below caught my eye, a rustle rippling through the leaves, evidence of Allsworth swinging, higher now, seeking a better position to sight me and take her shot. I caught just a flash of her rope, hanging from above where she must have been, caught in a tinge of light. And then, through the lattice of leaves, there was Allsworth, on another branch.

Taking a deep breath, I leaped, aiming my body like a bungee jumper, and I hurtled toward her, the air whooshing past my ears. Grappling her rifle into place before aiming, Allsworth glanced upward, barely having time to register my body rocketing down before I rammed into her, knocking her clear of her spot. I fell several more feet before my harness snapped taut, jerking me to a stop and breaking my fall.

Suspended between the trees, I glanced down, low enough now to see the forest floor, where Allsworth's body lay crumpled.

She would have fallen a little over twenty-five feet, with a thick mosaic of branches breaking her fall along the way, so while she'd be injured, I hoped she'd survived.

I freed myself from the harness and slithered down the nearest trunk, but approaching Allsworth, I could tell from her inert form, and the angle of her head, that she was gone. I crouched down alongside her, my breath ragged and my heart still pummeling my chest, and I wished there had been another way.

That was when I heard the sounds of feet trampling the shrubs, heading rapidly toward me, and not from one direction, but two.

Chapter Fifty

The last thing Will recalled before he lost consciousness was an excruciating pain in the side of the head. He'd crashed to the ground and in the seconds before blacking out, he'd heard the voice of one of the two men looming over him.

"Tie him to the tree. We'll come back, but first we've got to deal with Farris."

Will didn't think he'd been out too long but when he woke, the last vestiges of twilight were sinking.

He was in a sitting position. His hands had been tied behind his back by a length of cord which was then looped around the trunk of a pine. His gun, phone, and comms were gone. The rough bark of the tree pressed against his back as he pulled against his restraints but this only caused the cord to dig deeper into the flesh of his wrists.

His mind raced. As his eyes adjusted to the dim light, he glanced around for something, anything, that could aid an escape. He hadn't moved too far from the barracks and his chest tightened at the thought that his assailants had gone there to catch Ilona unawares. The same blow he'd received to the side of the head would leave Ilona with a blinding headache, as it had him, but he knew that it could also prove fatal. His heart beat faster at the thought. He forced himself to steady his breathing. First, he had to find a way to get free. The forest floor was littered with fallen leaves, twisted roots, and bracken. But there were also a few fallen branches. His eyes landed on one of these, just a few feet away. Short and thin but with a jagged end that looked as though it could be sharp enough to cut through the cord binding him.

His assailants had made the mistake of leaving his feet unbound. That had been their first mistake. Or, at least, Will hoped it was.

He stretched out his right foot but the branch was just beyond reach. He cursed under his breath. So close...

There was another broken piece of branch not far to his side, and he found he could angle his leg just enough to shift this one with his foot. This one had no sharp edge, but it was long enough that he could push its point against the sharp-edged branch, and then slide the sharp branch closer to him. He squirmed as much as he could, using his heel now so that he could maneuver the sharp branch, still being pushed by the other one, alongside him and within reach of his hands.

There was just enough give so that he could slide his tethered hands down lower to the base of the trunk, low enough for his fingers to pinch the branch and manipulate it into his palm, ignoring the pain of the rough bark against his skin and the bite of the cord as it sliced into his wrist.

He began to saw into the cord at its edge, working blind, unavoidably cutting into himself as well, but he winced and kept sawing, determined. Time seemed to slow down and he could not see behind him to know if he was making any progress, and could not feel any change in the tension of the cord.

This isn't working.

He pushed away the sense of hopelessness, gritted his teeth, and strained harder, his fingertips stinging, his hands bleeding from the rough bark, but he willed himself to keep trying — carving and slashing at the cord. Every second felt as though it stretched into infinity. He felt a tear in the cord, and he worked away at it. Even if he couldn't hack all the way through, it might be possible to weaken or loosen it enough to rip the remaining shreds with the grip of his fingers.

Sweat dripped from his forehead despite the cooler night air, and his hands shook. On a couple of occasions, he almost lost his hold on the branch and he had to carefully manipulate it fully back into his grasp.

How long had it been? A lot longer than it would have taken his assailants to trek across to the barracks and surprise Ilona.

I can't dwell on that. Focus… on this…

He felt more give and he kept pushing the sharp point of the branch, slicing further, but his hands trembled and he felt any remaining strength rapidly draining out of them.

A shot rang out in the distance. And then another one. Will's heart skipped a beat, his breath catching in his throat.

All of a sudden, the cord snapped and his right hand was free. He reached across his body and untied the other hand, and then gasped in relief as he rubbed his bloodied wrists.

He stood upright and felt the cold night air rush over him. He'd become disorientated, he needed to get his bearings. His adrenaline surged and he set off, determined to find his way back through the dense surroundings, terrified that Ilona had been shot. But after a few minutes, it seemed he'd headed in the wrong direction. And then, as he pushed his way through the foliage, he heard a low groan nearby.

Ilona? No…

He moved faster and just ahead of him, in a less dense area, he saw a figure lying still on the ground. Running forward, he saw that it was a young woman, but not Ilona. Sam Reiberger? Beside the woman, lay the bloodied, inert body of an owl.

At the sound of his approach, the woman's head raised, eyes wide with fright.

"It's okay," Will said, crouching beside her. "I'm Special Agent Will McCord. Are you Sam?"

The woman nodded nervously, raising herself to a sitting position, eyeing Will with uncertainty.

Will gestured to the dead bird. "What happened here, Sam?"

"Someone's… hunting me…" Her frail voice cracked, and her eyes watered, any sobbing held back by her state of shock. "The owl flew out, right over me, got hit, fell against me…" Sam's eyes tilted upward. "The shooter must not have seen it… from up there. Maybe they thought they'd got me because I… I… couldn't move. Frozen. Just lying here. Heard shots but, from somewhere else…"

Will extended his hand. "Let's get you out of here, Sam."

Chapter Fifty-One

I moved away from Allsworth's body and pressed deeper into the tangle of forest. The direction of the approaching footfalls seemed to shift with the rustling of the leaves. I came across an area where the trees were sparser, and I skirted its edges, but then a figure materialized out of the dark just ahead of me. A tall man, athletic build, his pistol aimed directly at me. I raised the rifle but as I did, the man called out in a deep voice.

"You can fire at one of us, but the other one will take you down."

He glanced to his left and I followed his gaze. Another man, shorter, stockier, stood primed at right angles to me, his gun also trained on me.

"Drop the rifle," the tall man ordered.

"Elderson's sniper is dead," I called back. "This is over."

"Drop the rifle and maybe we can come to some sort of agreement."

Yeah, right.

At that moment I heard my name called. Unmistakably Will's voice. He rocketed out of the undergrowth, tackling the stocky man to the ground. I reacted, dropping to my knees as the tall man's shot rang out. From a crouching position, I fired back, hitting him in the shoulder. His pistol flew from his hand as the force of the shot flung him backward.

I marched forward, the rifle leveled at him. I saw that there was a spool of cord in a utility pouch around his waist. The two men had come prepared for every eventuality.

I placed the barrel of the rifle against his temple. "Roll over on your stomach."

His nostrils flared at me but then he did as I'd instructed. I took the cord and bound his hands and feet. He'd keep.

I headed across to where Will restrained Short and Stocky. I threw him the remaining piece of cord.

"I get to return the favor," Will snarled in the man's ear.

Further back, watching from the scrub, I saw Sam Reiberger and an overwhelming sense of relief coursed through me.

"Sam, not sure if you remember me. I'm a friend of your sister's. We're going to get you home."

Turning back to Will, I saw that, like me, he was without his comms. "Our comms will be in the compound beneath the hatch," I said. "You stay and keep watch on these two and I'll go call in the cavalry."

"Who's down there?"

"Martin Elderson."

"Ilona—"

"I can deal with Elderson, Will. He'll be watching the entry hatch for these two to return. He won't see me coming."

Will flashed a quizzical look. "Why not?"

"Because he won't expect me to be coming back, and he won't expect it to be via the way I left."

* * *

With the rifle slung over my shoulder, and the tall man's pistol stuffed into my waistband, I descended the vertical shaft. Once in the horizontal tunnel, I slid the rifle along beside me. The first grille I came to was over a corridor. I removed the grid, pushed it to the side, and squeezed through, pulling the rifle behind me. The drop here was a normal ceiling depth and I landed easily, despite the pain that seared through my feet as they touched the hard floor.

Brandishing the weapon, I crept forward. The small cells were on either side of the corridor. I glanced into one of them. An aged mattress was on the floor, pushed against the wall. Against the opposite wall, a toilet, and a washbasin. Nothing else. I thought again of Jack Corris, Emily Yarros, and the others, locked in one of these, in some cases for years. Had they managed to keep their sanity? An ice-cold shiver rippled through me.

I crept on along the corridor, unsure whether what lay ahead was the massive isolation chamber where I'd been, or whether it was an area closer to the hatch that led up to the barracks.

It didn't take long to find out. I rounded a curve that revealed an area with seats, and a bench, and past those, a ladder embedded in the wall, leading to the hatch high above. Seated at the bench was Elderson, and seeing me, startled, he jumped to his feet, grabbed a pistol, and aimed it.

"We have your two thugs, and Steph Allsworth is dead," I said coldly, matter-of-factly. "Time to give it up, Martin."

"Neither of us will miss at this close distance," he said. "We both fire, we're both dead." He jerked his head toward the ladder. "The alternative is you let me go. Give me the chance to run, as we gave our inmates here. I'll drop the pistol when I get up to the hatch. If you catch me, so be it, but it's a huge stretch of land out there, and I know it like the back of my hand, so maybe I'll have a chance before your backup sweeps in. Either way, we both live, Ilona."

"I'm a crack shot and a fast mover," I said. "So, I like my chances. But I won't kill you, Martin. I'll wound you, and you'll live to spend the rest of your life in prison, where I'm certain the other inmates there will find your profession, and what you've done here, of great interest."

"You think what you've done here, Farris, destroying our work, is justice? You're simply defending a system that's mired in its own corruption, bureaucracy, and political expediency, bowing to do-gooders."

"You'll get to tell it to a judge, something that your victims here, guilty or not, never had the chance to do."

"Or maybe not." He raised his pistol a fraction higher, tightening his aim, and my pulse quickened as I prepared to return fire, but then, in just a split second, Elderson pivoted his gun and shot himself through the side of the head.

Chapter Fifty-Two

Aftermath

I'd spent the morning and the night before in the hospital, having medical treatment for the extensive bruising and cuts all over my body, and in particular, my fingers and toes. Will insisted that the two of us take a couple of days to relax and refresh before tackling the paperwork that a case like this left in its wake. I didn't argue. I was tired and sore and I wouldn't even be able to release any tension with an urban climb, not in this condition.

The moment Brooke Goodman had seen the police dispatches, she'd been on the phone to me and then to both Will and Detective Radner. This was a story that would stun the city for a long while to come, the suicide of a state prosecutor, the death of his legal assistant, but most damning of all, their part in the murders of more than a half dozen people.

The rain drizzled softly against the window of my apartment when my phone buzzed on the coffee table and I picked it up to see Jill Reiberger's name on the screen.

"Now that I know Sam is safe," Jill said when I answered, "I know that it's time." Her voice was laced with a resolve that I knew belied the angst she must have been feeling. "I'm staying here in Seattle, with Sam, and I'm turning myself in to the police here."

"Your previous good character will stand you in good stead," I said, trying to sound more optimistic for her than I felt.

"Sam will come in with me but I wanted to ask if you'd come with me as well, for support. You've done so much already that I hate to ask, and I understand if you don't want to be there. But..." There was a crack in her voice. "It would mean a lot."

I hesitated for a moment, but there was really no question in my mind. "Of course, I'll go with you."

"I just wish there was a way I could make up for what I did in DC." Her voice wavered.

"The important thing is you're doing the right thing now. You just have to take it one step at a time. I'll see you soon, okay?"

"Okay."

As I ended the call, I couldn't help but feel a sense of relief wash over me. I was glad Jill had decided to hand herself in sooner rather than later because the alternative would have been far worse. If I had to arrest her, knowing the heavy weight of regret she felt and everything we'd been through together in the search for Sam, it would have been a devastating blow for me as much as for her.

As I drove across town, the streets slick with water after a rainy afternoon, it occurred to me that Jill's confession about the bribe she'd taken from the Warburtons would add another link in the chain of evidence that was toppling their criminal enterprises. Hopefully, that was something that would work in Jill's favor when she faced the courts.

The flickering neon vacancy sign was a familiar sight as I pulled up outside the motel. Jill opened the door and ushered me in, her eyes heavy with unspoken words. In her tailored suit, she looked every inch the defense attorney she'd been and I wondered if this was too much of a cruel reminder of the world she was about to leave behind. It was a fall from grace that pained me to even contemplate. But this decision, her decision, was the first step towards redemption.

"So glad you're here." Her voice was barely a whisper.

"Of course," I said, stepping into the room.

Sam sat on the edge of the bed, her expression hollow. Her long, dark hair was combed neatly, but it couldn't hide the gaunt face beneath. She'd been through hell at the hands of Elderson's vigilante imprisonment and the damage to her psyche would take time to heal, if it ever fully did.

"They let you out of the hospital already," I remarked.

"I'd had enough of confined spaces," she said, her voice low, "and after this, Jill is helping me find somewhere with a bit of extra room and a nice yard."

Her casual clothing hung off her frame, the fabric loose over a body that had seen no sun and scarce nourishment. Yet, underneath, I sensed a resilience, the old, feisty Sam, and I expected that side to her would slowly but surely make its way to the surface in the months ahead.

I took a seat. "We can go now, or whenever you feel ready," I said.

Jill nodded, steeling herself. "I'm as ready as I'm ever likely to be."

Sam reached out and squeezed her shoulder.

"I've told Detective Radner to expect us," I said, "although, until you give him your statement, he doesn't know what exactly we're coming in for."

I pulled my phone from my pocket and sent a text to let him know we were on our way. I couldn't think of a better person to handle Jill's confession with professionalism and empathy.

The drive to the Seattle Police Department was silent, each of us lost in our thoughts. The rain had stopped when we arrived, and the sun peeked through scattered trails of clouds. As we stepped from the car and approached the entrance, Jill's hand found mine, her fingers gripping tight as though she was hanging on for dear life. I squeezed back, and then she, Sam, and I walked into the building.

Chapter Fifty-Three

With a heavy heart, I returned home as the last rays of sunlight faded from the city skyline, painting it in deep shades of purple and orange. I made my way to the balcony, seeking solace and a moment to switch off. As I gazed out at the twinkling lights that made up the familiar cityscape, I let my thoughts drift back to the night I had taken Will for a drink, trying to distract him from his grief over the tragic loss of his friend. We'd reminisced about old times and shared our experiences, both good and bad, serious and fun. Despite the somber circumstances, it had been a memorable and comforting night.

A buzzing sound from my front-door intercom interrupted my quiet evening. I walked over and pressed the button to answer. "Who is it?"

"It's me," came the reply.

Without hesitation, I released the building's first-floor entry lock. "Come on up."

A minute had passed when Will arrived at my front door, holding a bottle of sauvignon blanc. "On the spur of the moment, I thought we both deserved a glass of the good stuff, but maybe I shouldn't have come without asking first—"

"You can come over whenever you want, you know that," I reassured him. "And if there's wine involved, even better."

He grinned and I beckoned for him to come in. I took the bottle from him and he was about to say something when his attention was drawn to the TV which I had on mute. "Our old friend."

Brooke Goodman was broadcasting from the front of what appeared to be the care facility where we'd visited Victoria Rutledge. I unmuted the sound.

> *Tributes are flooding in today for a prominent advocate of justice reform, who passed away this afternoon at the care facility where she had been living. Victoria Rutledge, who had been battling dementia for several years, was known for speaking out against flaws in the legal system after her daughter Mandy's murder twenty years ago. Her efforts shed light on the injustice of murderers walking free due to loopholes in the process.*

I poured the wine and handed Will a glass, and we exchanged knowing glances as we stood and watched the remainder of Brooke's report.

Sadly, Ms. Rutledge's passing came less than twenty-four hours after her son, deputy state prosecutor Martin Elderson, reportedly committed suicide, and his legal assistant and former US Marine, Steph Allsworth, died in a confrontation with a federal agent. Elderson's sister, SPD Detective June Tranter, has issued a statement requesting her family's privacy be respected during this time of extraordinary shock and grief. The emerging details of Martin Elderson's involvement in a string of murders have raised questions about Ms. Rutledge's potential knowledge of this, before her illness, as co-owner of the property where the crimes occurred.

The news of Elderson and Allsworth's twisted form of vigilante justice would rock the world of law enforcement and be the subject of analysis for a long time to come.

I switched off the TV and Will and I talked for hours, not about work, but about old times, good memories, and our families. And then, in what seemed to be a moment that arrived all of a sudden, I looked at my watch and it was 3 a.m.

"I've got an idea," I said, getting up from my chair. "Grab your coat."

Will glanced at his watch. "You've got an idea? Now?"

I gave him a spontaneous peck on the cheek. "Come on."

The sudden closeness was unexpectedly magnetic, neither of us moving out of the personal orbit of the other. Our eyes connected. And then Will placed his arms around me, and I leaned in and his lips touched mine. I returned the kiss, the years melting away, all the doubts, regrets, and second thoughts fading ghost-like into the past.

"Lead the way," he said, smiling and taking my hand, his touch electric.

Warmth flooded through me and we went out to my car.

I'd only had a couple of wines earlier so I was good for the half-hour drive north.

The beach at Golden Gardens Park stretched out before us, the sand bathed in the moon's silvery light. I parked the car, angled so that we were facing the Sound. In the distance, the water glistened, reflecting the stars. The forested slopes that rose behind us created a sense of intimacy.

"You want to tell me what this idea of yours is—" He paused and I saw the realization dawning in his eyes, his mind throwing back to our earlier conversation, days before, when he'd opened up about how he was always looking for the light. He faced me, a wide grin lifting his tired eyes.

"We'll build a little fire on the beach," I said, "and then we're going to sit and watch the sunrise."

THE END

If you enjoyed this book, please let others know by leaving
a quick review on Amazon. Also, if you spot anything
untoward in the paperback, get in touch. We strive for the
best quality and appreciate reader feedback.

editor@thebookfolks.com

www.thebookfolks.com

Also in this series

THE PIPER'S CHILDREN (Book 1)

A boy is found wandering in the woods, dressed in medieval clothes and speaking a strange language. When another child turns up, it doesn't shed any more light on the mystery for FBI agent Ilona Farris. Only by digging into her own past will she begin to work out what is going on, and who these children are, seemingly lost in time.

THE WHISTLER'S OMEN (Book 2)

Special FBI agent Ilona Farris faces a problem when a man is murdered in Seattle: the victim was meant to have died in a plane crash twenty years previously. Worse, spotted by the scene is a man dressed in a straw hat and long coat who rumor claims is the legendary El Silbón, a lost soul who stalks the living. Finding out the truth will be tough and perilous.

THE STORM KILLINGS (Book 3)

As tornado season gets under way, the FBI's advanced computer system highlights an anomaly in the casualties. It looks like someone is using the chaos caused by the weather as cover to kill unsuspecting women in their homes. Special Agent Ilona Farris heads into the eye of the storm to catch them in the act.

THE DEVIL'S ARTIST (Book 4)

When a massive wreck on the interstate kills several people, a mural in Seattle that seems to glorify the disaster creates outcry. However, upon discovering that the painting was created days before the event, criminal investigators are baffled. Are they dealing with a psychic artist, or someone who played a role in the incident? Soon other murals appear, and the race is on to stop further tragedy.

FREE with Kindle Unlimited and available in paperback!

More fiction by Iain Henn

DEAD SET ON MURDER

Eighteen years after disappearing without a trace, Jennifer's husband's body turns up, yards from her home. Apparently without aging one bit. She knows something is seriously amiss. Fortunately homicide detective Neil Lachlan shares her concerns. But when the case overlaps with a manhunt for a serial killer, it will put Jennifer's life on the line.

THE GREATEST BETRAYAL

Liz Carter is the proud owner of a successful advertising business when she begins a whirlwind romance with handsome airline pilot Callan McKenzie. Yet after his estranged ex contacts him, he disappears without a trace. Liz resolves to move on with her life, but a chain of events has been set in motion that threatens all she holds dear.

FREE with Kindle Unlimited and available in paperback!

Other titles of interest

THAT CARE FORGOT
by James Warren

Junior attorney Rebecca Holt isn't too happy when given the pro bono case of a convicted murderer. Yet Nick Malone isn't really interested in his parole hearing, rather he is obsessed with a serial killer who terrorized New Orleans in the 1990s. When Malone reveals his secrets, Rebecca is faced with a life-changing decision.

FREE with Kindle Unlimited and available in paperback!

A MURDER IN PEMBROKESHIRE
by Nicola Clifford

When a woman is found dead in her car in a remote part of Britain, the likely explanation is suicide. The pathologist's verdict of carbon monoxide poisoning will confirm it. But Sergeant Vicki Blunt, recently demoted to uniform after clashing with her boss, has a hunch something more sinister has happened. Can she further risk her career by investigating?

FREE with Kindle Unlimited and available in paperback!

Sign up to our mailing list to find out about new releases and special offers!

www.thebookfolks.com